Opposing Cells

by

Scott Weberg

*To Uncle Ken:
Enjoy the story!
Scott Weberg*

ISBN 978-1-4303-1321-2

Copyright © 2007 by Scott Weberg. All rights reserved.

Scripture taken from *THE MESSAGE*. Copyright © 1993, 1994, 1995, 1996, 2000. Used by permission of NavPress Publishing Group.

Cover portraits by Anna Alger.

Edited by Amy Gingerich.

*To my wife, Amy,
who supports me in so many ways;
thank you for allowing me to write,
and for being my best proof-reader.
I love you.*

Acknowledgements

In addition to Amy, my wife, I would like to thank my children – Nathan, Andrew and Ariana – for putting up with all my writing time on the computer.

Thanks to all the friends and family members who read versions of this manuscript and offered their feedback. And a special thanks to my writer friend, Rachel, who contributed detailed critiques of some of my chapters. Anna, thanks for the great portraits on the cover.

I must also acknowledge the American Christian Fiction Writers organization, for providing me opportunities to learn the craft. Many of you have encouraged me along the way.

To Jesus – Author of my life – thank you for inspiring me.

Prologue

Marseille, France. Fifteen years ago.

Ibrahim sucked cold air into his lungs and ran. Sirens screamed in the night a block behind. Not loud enough to drown out the sound of shoes hitting the pavement, or heartbeats pounding in his ears.

"Ibrahim!" Paolo shouted his name again.

He veered into a narrow alley and urged more speed into his long legs. The darkness prevented him from seeing the ground but he dared not slow down.

Footfalls echoed in the alley behind him. Paolo was older, faster, and gaining.

"Ibrahim, wait!"

He thought about slowing for his friend. Adrenaline wouldn't allow it. Besides, Paolo had meticulously planned the entire evening. He could take care of himself. *Is this what it's supposed to be like, Paolo? Running in the dark, lungs burning, expecting a bullet to end my fifteen years in an alley? Why did you talk me into this?*

Rain drops hit his face, and Ibrahim remembered his mother's funeral, a vivid and cruel picture that tortured his mind. It had rained that day too, like a gray backdrop to the blackness that now suffocated his soul. Even two years later, he missed her. She would definitely not approve of his actions tonight.

His mind snapped back to the present, and Ibrahim wondered if the timer would work. *It has to work! How many minutes has it been?*

He skidded to a stop at the end of the alley. Seeing that the street beyond was void of traffic, he launched himself forward again, but a new sound stopped him short. A low *whump* rocked the ground beneath his feet. Ibrahim dropped to his knees and whirled toward the sound. Three blocks away an orange glow illuminated buildings, then faded. Paolo scrambled to his side and gripped his shoulder as a few pieces of debris clattered to the street with the rain.

"Ibrahim!"

He now looked at the older boy. There was a tremor in Paolo's voice. "Did you hear it? That was *our* doing, Ibrahim!" Paolo clapped him on the shoulder and a street light reflected in his wild eyes. "We did it! Allah will smile on us now, little brother!"

Ibrahim looked back up the street and shivered. Was Allah smiling? He glanced upward and saw only darkness and rain.

Then he and Paolo ran.

Chapter 1

Louisville, Kentucky. Present day.

Terrence Whitman checked his watch for the third time in five minutes. *Come on, people. This is worse than I expected.* He stood in the checkout line at the city's largest toy store on the day after Thanksgiving. In front of him, a roundish woman used both hands to transport a mountain of toys from her cart to the moving checkout counter. The sounds of cash registers filled the air, as throngs of people waited to exchange their hard-earned money for Christmas goods.

Terrence looked down at the two items he held in his hands. They were the latest craze in action figure toys, and he had managed to grab them before the shelf was bare. At first he felt like a conquering hero as he imagined the faces of his sons, Nicholas and Anthony, on Christmas morning. But now, after spending nearly thirty minutes in the checkout line watching materialism at work, he wondered if this worst-shopping-day-of-the-year shopping trip was worth it.

As he stepped forward and placed his items on the counter, another check of the watch revealed only forty-five minutes to get home and change before the babysitter arrived. He couldn't remember the last time he and Angela had gone out without the kids, and Terrence cringed at the thought of her reaction should he arrive home late again. Not that he would blame her. Career demands had kept him from his family of late, something he had once vowed would never happen. Fortunately, the point-of-sale project was back on schedule now, which would allow him to make things right again at home.

Outside, he pulled his coat closer against the bitter wind. Suddenly his foot was sliding. *Ice.* He stumbled forward, crashing with some force into the shoulder of a man who quickly approached the toy store.

"Oops! Sorry about that!" Terrence apologized as he caught his footing. He turned to look at the man, and briefly took in the short black hair and dark complexion. The man wore a black winter coat, with his hands thrust deep into the pockets. A black duffle bag hung on his shoulder.

Terrence meant to reiterate his apology, but the words halted when he looked into the other man's face. The eyes smoldered like dark flames; the expression cold, hard as stone, something beyond anger. Terrence took a step backwards.

Abruptly, the stranger turned and rushed into the store. Terrence felt a chill when he saw the familiar image of a white bird in flight – and the letters *KCG* – on the man's retreating duffle bag.

"I don't remember seeing him bef–"

At that very instant, an explosion ripped through the front of the toy store. Windowpanes transformed into millions of shards of glass, hurled like shrapnel across the parking lot. A pickup truck swerved wildly as the blast threw Terrence directly into its path.

♦

Angela walked to the top of the stairs, hands clenched. She closed her eyes and took a breath. "Boys! If you don't stop fighting, you'll both find yourselves on your bed."

From somewhere in the basement came two answers in unison, "Yes, Mommy."

She walked back through the kitchen, stooping to pick up little three-year-old Briana on the way. Angela was dressed for dinner in dark slacks and a deep red sweater. She wore the diamond and sapphire heart necklace that her husband had given her for Christmas last year.

She frowned at the clock on the living room mantle. A few minutes past six. Both Terry and the babysitter were late. In the case of the babysitter, who was practically a member of the family, tardiness was unusual. Terry, on the other hand, had acquired a habit of losing track of time.

"Now where do you suppose your Daddy is, Briana?" Angela switched on the TV to the local news, mumbling to herself. "I should have known. It's far too much to expect a full evening alone with my husband."

The scene on the television arrested her attention and her thoughts went silent. The sight was chaotic: sirens blaring and police vehicles flashing, with civilians and rescue workers rushing here and there. In the background, a storefront had been devastated by some kind of explosion. Fire burned through the gaping front wall, and black smoke billowed into the darkening evening sky. Several cars in the parking lot were damaged, and a white pickup truck had smashed into a light pole in front of the store.

Angela gasped. *That's Berrenger's Toys! Terry is there... was there.* Her heart began to race, and she leaned toward the television as if the reporter at the scene was speaking directly to her.

"...no information yet as to the cause of the explosion. Eyewitnesses claim that the explosion came from the checkout area at the front of the store, where checkout lines were filled with Christmas shoppers. There is wide speculation here that this is the work of terrorists, but local authorities are saying nothing at this time."

"Is there any indication of the number of casualties?" asked Robert Schultz, the anchorman at the WLKT studio.

"No official reports at this time, Robert, but rescue workers have already indicated at least eleven dead, and possibly dozens more injured."

"Okay, Tim. We'll come back to you as soon as we hear anything new."

As the view on the television switched to the grim face of the anchorman, Angela put Briana down and firmly told her, "Briana, go play with your dollies in your room."

"Yes, Mommy."

Angela thanked God that the little girl obeyed, and turned back to the television, where the anchorman was offering a recap.

"For those of you who joined in the middle of that report, we want to quickly summarize this late-breaking story. About forty-five minutes ago there was an explosion at the Berrenger's Toys and Hobbies store on Hurstbourne Lane. Authorities are offering no speculation as to the cause at this time, though from all appearances this would seem to be a terrorist bombing, which would make it the second such attack in just three weeks. Rescue workers at the scene are indicating at least eleven deaths, with possibly dozens more injured. We will keep you updated with any new information as we receive it here. But for a moment, let's turn to the other headlines for the day…"

Angela's heart pounded like a drum in her chest. She ran to the kitchen and snatched up the phone, dialing her husband's cell phone number.

"Please, Terry," she pleaded, "answer your phone." One ring. Two rings. Three. She choked back a cry as the answering service picked up. She put down the phone as her hands began to shake, and she felt her knees going weak. Her mind raced, unable to focus. *Oh God, what do I do? Terry, where are you?*

Just then the front door burst open and Angela heard a familiar voice. "I'm here! I'm so sorry I'm late!"

◆

Ned Parker stared blankly through the large windows that comprised one wall of his seventeenth floor corporate office. Below him several hotels stretched out along the famed sugar-white beaches of

Florida's gulf coast. It was easy to see why Kellor Computing Group had chosen Panama City, Florida to be the sight of its worldwide corporate headquarters.

Ned turned from the tranquil scene before him and sat down at his desk, where papers were loosely arranged in piles. His eyes fell on a picture frame, where his two daughters smiled back at him from their apartment at UCLA. When had he seen them last? He doubted he could remember that far back. Not that they would *want* to see him. The smiles in the picture were for the camera, not him.

The phone rang, startling Ned out of his pondering thoughts. He knew it would be the call he was waiting for. *There truly is no rest for the weary.*

He picked up the receiver. "This is Ned."

"Mr. Parker. It's James. I got your message to call." The accent was always hard to figure: definitely foreign, but difficult to place.

"Yes, James. I need a status on when we can expect the next order to be placed. We filled the last shipment almost five weeks ago, and delivered everything that was agreed upon."

"Mr. Parker, there is no need to worry." James sounded overly calm, almost patronizing, as he continued. "This client cannot be rushed. It takes some time to process a shipment of this size."

Ned found a pen at his fingertips, and began to tap it on the desk. "James, you assured me that they already had the infrastructure to handle this deal. Has that changed in the past five weeks? Is there something else I should know?"

"No, of course not. But there are multiple warehouses located in different places, which requires a certain amount of coordination and planning." Here James paused before offering the more accurate reason for the delay. "Not to mention that our client is evaluating all angles of this endeavor. As you are aware, there are other objectives."

Ned closed his eyes and grimaced. He didn't want to know about the other objectives.

"We can't let this drag on forever, James. If we don't get these sales this quarter, none of this may matter."

"Don't worry, Mr. Parker. Everything is under control. I'll call you as soon as I know something."

Ned hung up the phone and his gaze returned to the picture. He had sacrificed much to become CFO of the world's third largest technology company. Now the company's financial fate very possibly rested on the abilities of a brilliant young VP on the other side of the planet. *We can't lose this deal, James.*

♦

Roger and his wife Pam cleaned the supper dishes while Jacob and Matthew played in the back yard. The ringing of the phone interrupted their casual conversation.

"Hello," Pam spoke into the receiver. Her gaze met Roger's and a shadow crossed the smooth lines of her face.

Roger's stomach knotted. "What is it?"

Pam's face went from concern to disbelief, as her mouth dropped open.

"Oh, Angela! Maybe he's on his way home and just has the cell phone turned off." Her voice was calm, but her expression began to be fearful as she heard the response. Then she looked at Roger, unable to find words to say.

"What is it?" Roger said, his tone harsher than he wanted.

Pam covered the mouthpiece with her hand. "Terry hasn't come home, and he's not answering his phone even though it was on earlier!"

Roger tried to grasp what Pam was saying, but could not understand why it seemed so critical that Terry was late. "I don't …"

His confused query was interrupted as Pam spoke back into the phone.

"No! Angela, don't leave your house yet. You don't have any idea where to go. Just a minute." Now she turned to Roger again.

"There's been an explosion in the store where Terry was supposed to be. Turn on the local TV, and see if they say which hospital they are taking people to."

Roger hurried to the other room and scooped up the TV remote. His heart began to beat faster as he took in the video footage before him. From the charred black storefront came billows of dark smoke. Fire and rescue vehicles flashed red and blue lights. Many people rushed around, calling for their loved-ones, while others simply sat on the pavement staring with wide eyes and pale, ghost-like expressions.

Pam continued the phone conversation. "Angela, you should start calling the hospitals in town to see if Terry's been admitted. Call us back to let us know what you find out."

Roger remained glued to the television for several minutes, yet hearing nothing regarding victims and hospitals. Suddenly he got an idea.

"I'm going to call 911!"

The dispatcher informed Roger that he did not have any information on individuals, but that some ambulances had initially been dispatched from Northpark City Hospital.

A few minutes later Angela called, and Roger answered the phone. Her voice was controlled, though the fear and dismay were obvious.

"I didn't find out anything. His name is not in anyone's computer system yet. But I *know* that Terry would have called by now, Roger."

"I called 911," Roger responded, "and found out that at least some ambulances were dispatched from Northpark. I'm pretty sure that it's the closest hospital to the store. Do you want me to meet you there, and we'll see if Terry is there?"

"Yes! I'm going now. The babysitter can watch the kids."

"Okay, I'll see you in a bit."

Roger hung up the phone and hurried to get his jacket and car keys. Pam handed him the cell phone at the door.

"Please call me as soon as you know anything," she said, and kissed him goodbye.

As Roger exited the freeway onto city streets, nearing the hospital, he thought of his long-time friend. They had met as co-workers over ten years ago. It had always seemed an unlikely friendship. Roger was the stuff athletes are made of: tall, lean and broad shouldered with a mess of black hair. Terry was shorter, with thinning brown hair and average looks and build. Roger was quiet and reserved, while Terry possessed a natural ability to communicate.

Aside from the obvious differences, both men were intelligent and each possessed strong commonalities of character. They shared a steadfast belief in the reality of God, and the ability to relate to him. A quiet, humble life was preferred over fame, fortune or power. It was these shared qualities that became the foundation for their friendship, and even though they now worked for different companies, their families had remained close over the years.

Roger said a prayer as he turned into the hospital parking lot, "God, please take care of my friend."

That simple request, spoken out of a deep trust in God's goodness, brought a feeling of calm within his being.

Chapter 2

Marseille, France. Fifteen years ago.

Ibrahim fit his key into the lock and entered the two-bedroom apartment he shared with Paolo. He let his backpack of school books fall to the floor, and two faces looked up from the old green couch.

"How was school, little brother?" Paolo chuckled. "How many tests did you pass today?" Ibrahim didn't answer. He was used to the ribbing from his friend, and the way Paolo referred to him as "little brother" when they truthfully weren't brothers at all. Paolo turned to the other man, grinning. "Ibrahim is the smartest kid in school. A real brain."

The stranger's face was serious as he stood and offered a handshake. "People call me Griz." Short and stocky, and a little older than Paolo, Griz possessed such a dark piercing gaze that Ibrahim felt compelled to look away. Ibrahim shook his hand, surprised by the unusually strong grip.

Paolo was still grinning in an over-enthusiastic way. "As in 'grizzly' – the fiercest bear in the world. Griz has a reputation for being formidable."

Griz sat down and motioned to the empty chair. "I've heard a lot about you, Ibrahim."

Taking his place in the chair, Ibrahim now felt more uncomfortable than ever, pinned down by those dark eyes. He sent a questioning glance Paolo's way, but said nothing. Paolo continued his excited chatter.

"I never had much use for school. I prefer to learn practical stuff. Like how to make a timed explosive. But I have to give the credit to Ibrahim on that one. He helped me make it work in the end. Like I said, a real brain."

Griz leaned forward, continuing to probe Ibrahim with his penetrating stare. "Paolo has been telling me about you. Your demonstration the other night was most impressive. I was wondering if you and Paolo would be interested in helping us out on a regular basis."

"'Course we would!" Paolo's eyes had that wild look that had recently become common.

So this was it. The moment Ibrahim knew was coming. Griz was the one Paolo had been talking about, the one who had set him on the path of following Allah's ways. According to Paolo, Griz had shown him his destiny.

Ibrahim didn't quite believe in destiny. Life was just – life. His mother had always said there was no use trying to find meaning behind everything. He could still hear her voice in his head. *Do your best to live right, and leave it at that.* She didn't believe in God. She had learned too much, seen too much to believe in an all-powerful God. And she had navigated life well, before she died.

"Good then. I'm glad to hear it." Griz finally turned back to Paolo. "Tonight there is a group of us that are meeting to discuss Allah's ways and direction for this city. You are both welcome to attend. We must prepare for the coming war."

Ibrahim's chair creaked as he shifted positions. "War?"

Griz smiled and he leaned forward again as he answered. "Yes, Ibrahim. The war with Allah's enemies."

Chapter 3

Louisville, Kentucky. Present day.

Colors swirled. Movement was constant, now light, now darker, ever changing. The sound of many voices murmured imperceptibly, coming and going, never quite in focus. The intricate dance of hue and noise continued for several moments. Or was it several hours?

Eventually the blur began to take shape. Colors separated, and sounds unjumbled. Coherent thought took form. There were trees and green grass, the fragrance of flowers, the sound of birds on the wind, the brightness of sunshine and the perception of summer heat. Terry was standing on a hill, looking down a winding paved road. The outline of a small building became apparent, and once again there were voices. Whose house was this? No. Not a house. A church. A very small church.

Suddenly the image became clear, and the doors to the church swung open. About twenty people of all ages streamed out into the sunlight. They were smiling and talking happily about all the trivial things that folks talk about after church.

Finally, a middle-aged man and an older man came out of the church, followed by a boy of not more than six years.

The middle-aged man shook the hand of the older man. "Mr.

Wendover, thanks again for blessing us with another insightful message this month. I know that you drive nearly two hours to get here."

The gray-haired man smiled warmly, and there was a sparkle in his eye. "The blessing is mine, my friend." He put his arm around the boy and continued, "To preach God's Word is a blessing that cannot be easily matched in this world."

"Well, I know that it is an equal blessing to the people here. We've been without a pastor in these parts for over a year now. It's hard to find someone that can re-locate to such a rural area and pastor a church. Finding lay preachers to come from time to time has really kept us going."

Terry smiled at the scene before him. He knew the old man well, and the child too. *Grandpa. Always bringing me along when you preached.*

As six-year-old Terry walked with his grandfather across the dirt parking area to the car, he asked, "Grandpa?"

"Yes, Terry?"

The boy paused, not wanting to be disrespectful. "Why did you ask me to say the prayer at the end of church?"

The old man turned and gave his grandson a look of genuine surprise.

"I have *no idea*! I was going to ask someone to close the service with a prayer, and your name just sort of came out. I immediately thought to myself, 'Why did you ask that poor little boy to pray in front of the whole church?'"

"I know!" little Terry responded. "I was surprised too!"

The grandfather opened the car door for his grandson, and then stooped down to look him lovingly in the eye.

"Terry, I think that you said the most beautiful prayer I've ever heard. Your mom and dad will be very proud when they hear about it."

The boy smiled in embarrassment. "Grandpa?"

"Yes, Terry?"

"Do you think God will let me teach people about him when I grow up?"

Grandpa Wendover beamed, and his eyes danced with the youthful energy of one who is long accustomed to enjoying life. "I think God has a wonderful purpose for your life, Terry. As long as you follow him, you won't miss it." He ruffled the boy's hair. "Now, let's go fishin'!"

♦

Angela sat next to the hospital bed, looking intently upon her husband. Terry's head was bandaged, and the left side of his face was bruised and swollen. There was a thick bandage on his left elbow, and his forearm was scraped badly. The sight was one of pain, and yet Terry's breathing was deep, slow and peaceful. It was Saturday evening, and she remembered the words of the doctor after she and Roger had arrived at the hospital.

"Your husband is a very lucky man, Mrs. Whitman. The worst of it is that he has a mild concussion. We'll watch that for the time being, to look for any swelling in the brain. Beyond that it's cuts, bruises, and a broken rib. There were some shards of glass embedded pretty deeply in the back of his head and neck, but they didn't do any serious damage. Things could have been a lot worse."

"When do you think he'll regain consciousness?" Angela asked.

"It's hard to tell right now. It could be within the hour." The doctor walked over to the bed and looked again at Terry's chart. "Or it could be sometime tomorrow. I don't expect there to be much swelling from the concussion, but we'll have to wait and see."

Roger cleared his throat, and asked softly, "He's not in any immediate danger, though, right?"

"That's absolutely correct," the doctor smiled. "If things continue on this course, he'll likely be home in two or three days."

Angela gently caressed Terry's hand and sighed. It was now a long twenty-four hours later, and he remained unaware of the world around him. He continued to lie on his back, motionless except for the slow rhythm of breath. The sound of the heart monitor was constant in the background, like a metronome keeping time for an unhurried tune.

Presently, there was a soft knock at the door, and Angela turned to see her best friend, the familiar smiling face framed by short brown hair.

"Pam!" Angela stood to meet her friend with a long hug. "Thank you so much for coming!"

"You know I had to come."

Angela sat on the edge of the bed, and Pam sat in the chair.

"How are the children?" Angela asked.

"Oh, they're fine! Roger had them all playing hockey in the hallway again this afternoon, and now they're playing video games, of course."

"Of course!" Angela chuckled, and then continued in a serious tone. "Did the boys seem scared at all?"

"I think they're okay right now. Of course we prayed at dinner time, that Terry would get better soon. Nicholas commented that the doctors said his daddy would wake up at any time, and then he could come home. They both seemed all right. And of course Briana proudly announced, 'Daddy is sick and has to stay at the doctor's house until he feels better!'" Pam laughed. Her laugh had always been full of life, and could bring light to a dark place. "She doesn't know any better than that."

Angela smiled. "That's good."

Pam turned her gaze to the heart monitor above Terry's bed, and after a moment asked, "Has there been any change?"

"No." Angela looked at the floor. "The doctor was in again today. He doesn't know why Terry's not waking up. There's still not any significant swelling in the brain, and his heart is beating strong." Her voice broke. "He's just not waking up."

Pam took her hand. "I'm sure that he'll wake up soon, Angela. We're all praying, and I have a strong sense of peace in my spirit. God is taking care of him."

"I know that he is." Angela looked at her friend through teary eyes, and managed a smile.

Just then there was another knock at the door, and the two women turned to see who it was. Angela recognized the visitors – one woman and two men – as three of Terry's co-workers.

"Please come in," she said, smiling.

The woman stepped forward first, and handed Angela a large bouquet of flowers and a card. She looked to be in her early thirties, medium height with light brown hair to her shoulders. She smiled at Angela, and her expression was one of genuine sweetness and concern. Angela gave her a hug.

"Thank you, Jennifer." Angela turned toward Pam to make introductions.

"Pam, this is Jennifer."

The two women shook hands and said hello.

"Jennifer is a manager at Kellor Computing," Angela continued, "who works with Terry's group on a regular basis."

Next Angela turned to the man who had entered behind Jennifer, tall and good-looking, though his blond hair was uncombed and out of place.

"This is Mitch, another manager who works with Terry quite often."

Mitch said hello to Angela and Pam, looking somewhat nervous about his current surroundings.

"Jennifer and Mitch have been dating for …" Angela paused and looked at Jennifer, "… is it almost a year now?"

"About ten months." Jennifer smiled and looked at Mitch as she took his hand.

Finally Angela directed Pam to the other man, who was younger and dressed casually in jeans, t-shirt and sneakers. "And this is Joel, a member of Terry's team."

Joel had a friendly easy-going look, and nodded his head with a smile.

"Thank you so much for coming," Angela said to the visitors.

"We couldn't believe it when we heard what happened," Jennifer said. "We decided to pitch in for the flowers."

"The whole team contributed," Joel offered. "They all send their best, along with several others in the department."

Mitch moved to Terry's bedside. "How's he doing?"

"Not much change yet." Angela ached inside when she looked at her husband, and she struggled against the fear that was growing in her heart. What would she do without him? She quickly pushed the question from her mind and continued.

"The doctors seem a little stumped. They don't seem to know why he hasn't regained consciousness yet. There is no indication of significant damage from the concussion. It's very frustrating!"

"Well don't you worry," said Mitch, smiling. "Terry has always moved at a little slower pace than most manager types in this world. He's rarely riled or in a rush." The others smiled knowingly.

"Yeah," added Joel, "he's just taking his own time, regardless of what these doctors think he should be doing!"

Angela laughed, and it did her good. The gnawing fear lost some of its hold on her in that moment. Inwardly, she thanked God for friendship in time of need, and she reaffirmed her faith in his goodness.

◆

James al-Masri climbed out of his rented black *350 Z* sports car and stepped out of the heat into the warehouse. Removing his dark sunglasses, he used a handkerchief to wipe perspiration from his forehead and let his eyes adjust to the dim light. He straightened his silk tie and smoothed the wrinkles from his shirt and black slacks. It most often paid to look sharp in his world.

Satisfied, he walked down the wide aisle toward the office near the loading docks at the back of the building. On either side of the aisle were pallets of boxes containing various computer equipment, stacked a full ten feet in the air. Halfway across the building, the stacks of pallets came to an end, and the cement floor was bare. James smiled as he surveyed the empty space. *A few more weeks and this place will be full.*

It was certainly no coincidence that he was the youngest vice president at Kellor Computing Group. Barely thirty years old, he had no doubt that he was one of the brightest businessmen in the world. He knew how to make things happen.

James opened the door to the small back office, which consisted of little more than a desk with a phone on it, two chairs, and a filing cabinet. He sat down and quickly skimmed over some packing slips that were on the desk. Finally he picked up the phone and dialed a number.

"Hello Mr. Ahman, this is James."

"Hello, James."

"I just wanted to let you know personally that the last shipment was unloaded this morning. Everything is here and accounted for. Kellor Computing is anxious to receive confirmation of the next order."

"All in good time. Did you tell Parker that he has no reason to worry?"

James smiled. Ahman was powerful and in control, never in a rush. "Yes, I spoke with him yesterday. I told him that you were carefully evaluating the – shall we say – additional objectives of this business venture. However, he is concerned that the sales need to be booked this quarter in order to have the desired impact. I assured him that it wouldn't be a problem."

"We should be able to move forward soon, as long as things go as planned over the weekend."

James leaned back in the chair and propped his feet on the old wooden desk. "I understand. I have confidence that early next week we'll be able to finalize your next order."

"Until next week then. As always, it is a pleasure to do business with you, James."

"Thank you, Mr. Ahman, the pleasure has been all mine."

Chapter 4

The man walked with purpose across the parking lot, navigating with the throngs of people. The brisk November air did not keep the regular crowd away from New Heights Christian Center. People by the thousands converged on the Chicago mega-church for the eleven o'clock Sunday morning service. The sun was bright and the atmosphere surrounding the church was filled with energy. Local police were on site as usual, directing long lines of slow moving traffic at each of the intersections leading into the church complex. Volunteer workers wearing bright orange vests were directing vehicles through the parking lots to ensure optimum flow of traffic both in and out of the area. He avoided the eyes of the churchgoers that made their way with him into the entrance of the main building.

Inside, the spacious church lobby rivaled the very finest of city convention centers. It was complete with multiple information booths, smartly dressed staff prepared to answer any question, and escalators leading to the upper levels of the main sanctuary. An impressive array of artwork adorned every wall, and a huge sculpture of Jesus washing the feet of his disciples served as the focal point of the main entryway.

It was this sculpture that caught the man's attention, and his pace slowed, then stopped. He thrust his hands into the pockets of his dark overcoat, and turned his face upward to look at the sculpted face of Jesus. In the moment that he paused no one noticed him. It was already 11:05, and dozens of people hurried past him toward the sanctuary, eager to find their seats. He finally turned and continued on his way with the rest of the crowd.

The main floor of the ten-thousand-seat sanctuary was mostly full, and the music had already begun. While the crowd continued on past the doors leading to the center aisle of the sanctuary, the man walked directly through. A thin, elderly gentleman in a suit immediately approached him, wearing a badge marked *Usher*.

"Sir, there are no open seats in this section," said the man with a warm smile. "Your best bet now is to head up to the side sections of the second level."

"I have a seat near the front that my friend is saving for me."

The usher looked at him skeptically. Agitated, he quickly embellished the lie. "Don't you remember me from ten minutes ago? I only went to the restroom!"

The usher paused for a moment as if trying to remember, and then he relented. The man quickly walked past, moving toward the front of the church.

On the platform the band was playing an upbeat song. Everyone was standing and singing along with the words, which were displayed on a huge screen overhead. Many people on the ends of the rows actually stood in the aisle, lifting their hands toward heaven as they worshiped. He weaved his way slowly around them, still choosing not to look at their faces. His heart was beating faster now, and he set his jaw like steel. It was time. Could he go through with it? Would the others go through with it? Yes, he knew they would.

He stopped, and in his left pocket he felt for the small detonator button. Finding it, he took one last deep breath of air, and pressed it.

♦

Angela sat on the edge of Terry's hospital bed, and smiled at the children sitting on the floor. Nicholas and Anthony were nine and eight years old, and their little sister Briana sat between them. Six-year-old Jacob Givens and four-year-old Matthew Givens were also there.

They were singing. The two families had decided to have a Sunday church service right in the hospital room. Pam led them with her lovely soprano voice, and the melody was enough to drown out the constant sound of the heart monitor, if only for a few minutes. Angela's heart was lifted as she held her husband's motionless hand and joined in the song.

After the singing, Roger read some verses from the Bible. Angela was encouraged by a verse in the book of First Peter: *God's eyes are watching over us, and he hears our prayers.* She knew that God was listening to her prayers for Terry.

When they had finished discussing the verses, Roger closed his Bible and looked at the children. "Since we know that God listens to our prayers, let's pray for Terry right now, that God will help him to wake up real soon. Do you want to do that?"

"Yes!" said Briana. "Yes, yes!" exclaimed the other children. They gathered around the hospital bed – three adults and five trusting children – and began to pray.

◆

The colors swirled again, this time darker than before. It was cold, and the world refused to take shape. As logical thought struggled into existence, fear was the dominant emotion. A presence was near, an unseen evil. Terry peered into the growing darkness, desperate to locate the menacing persona.

Slowly, a shape began to form. Terry realized it was a large rock standing before him. Its outline was made known only by a dim orange flicker of light coming from behind. He reached out and placed his hand on the rough stone and felt its coldness.

Suddenly he remembered the eyes — like dark flame, smoldering behind cold stone. The face of the suicide bomber loomed before him and Terry shrank back, raising his arms in a vain attempt to shield himself from the fearful vision.

At that moment the scene faded, and Terry was alone. Then a voice spoke. It was the whisper that he had heard before in his heart; a whisper that he now could recognize. The voice of God didn't come often, but when it did it was something that Terry never forgot.

"I will require that you walk in what you know, and set people free with what you have."

With that whisper, Terry finally opened his eyes again to the conscious world.

Briana was holding his hand as they prayed for him, and he gave her hand a gentle squeeze. She looked up into his face, and was delighted to see him looking back at her. He winked at her and smiled.

"Daddy!"

Anthony had been in mid-sentence in his prayer. "Wha-? Daddy's awake!" he shouted, jumping up and down.

The emotion that followed was indescribable. There was joyous laughter and shouting, as well as hugs and kisses and tears.

Angela looked overwhelmed with relief. "You're finally back," she said to him through her tears.

Terry smiled as he looked into her eyes. "I'm not ready to be apart from you quite yet." "And God wasn't ready for me to come home either," he added, looking into the faces of his family and friends.

◆

The next few days were a blur for Terry. The doctors immediately began a fresh battery of tests and x-rays. They watched him closely over the next forty-eight hours. His condition was very good, all things considered. Because of the concussion, Terry was not to participate in any strenuous physical activity for six weeks. His broken rib caused him some discomfort, and prevented him from taking a deep breath. The cuts and bruises were also a painful annoyance, and kept him from sleeping well at night. But overall Terry was alright, and would be able to return to work after a week of rest.

On his last day in the hospital, the local police, the FBI, and agents from the CIA interviewed Terry. They took great interest in the fact that he had actually seen the terrorist face to face as he entered the toy store. The cold, hard face and dark eyes had been clearly etched into Terry's mind, and with the help of an artist, the likeness was soon sketched on paper as well. It turned out that the security tape did not show a clear view of the man's face, so the eyewitness sketch proved to be useful.

Terry also told them about the black duffle bag with the Kellor Computing logo on it.

"Who can get their hands on a duffle bag like that?" one of the agents asked during Terry's final interrogation. He was an enormous man, well over six feet tall, clean-cut, and looking like a middle linebacker in a suit. His quiet demeanor, however, kept Terry from being altogether intimidated.

"Well, there is a company store in every regional office building, as well as the company merchandise catalog that everyone gets each year. Pretty much any employee during the last several years could have ordered that bag for themselves or a family member."

"Or as a gift for a friend or acquaintance," the agent added. "Do you know how many people work for Kellor Computing here in town?"

"The regional office here employs over twelve hundred people, and there are also a handful of field and consulting offices. I think it's nearly two thousand, altogether."

The agent looked glum as he jotted his notes.

"Including the warehouses and distribution centers," Terry continued, "we employ over twenty-two thousand people in the United States, and another seven thousand internationally."

"How long have you worked for Kellor here, Mr. Whitman?"

"A little over five years."

A second agent – much more average looking than the first – leaned forward in his chair. "And you had never seen this man around the office before?"

"No."

The second agent continued to press the question. "Ever seen him at other work functions, like company parties, picnics, training conferences?"

"No, sir."

Both agents looked perplexed.

"Please think very carefully, Mr. Whitman," said the first agent. "Are you *sure* that you never saw this man before?"

Terry closed his eyes and pictured the face one more time. He thought hard, searching his memory, as he had several times in the past twenty-four hours. Finally he opened his eyes.

"No, I don't recall ever seeing him before."

The agent looked at Terry for a moment, his great hand holding pen to paper, as if contemplating another question. The lines of his face seemed hard, yet his eyes were relaxed and sincere. Terry wondered at the peaceful air of a man whose very occupation was to battle against evil in the world. Finally, he sighed and closed his notebook. Reaching to an inside pocket of his jacket, he pulled out a business card, which he handed to Terry with a genial smile.

"Take my card, Mr. Whitman. If you remember anything at all please give my office a call. If I am not there, they will know how to get in touch with me at all times."

"Okay, thanks." Terry looked at the card as the two men left the room. "Agent Josh Kepler, Federal Bureau of Investigations," he muttered to himself. He had received two such cards already today, but something about this man conveyed integrity and sincerity beyond the others. Terry decided that this would be the man he called, should the need arise.

Chapter 5

Marseille, France. Fifteen years ago.

"I told you, I'm not going," Ibrahim repeated. Paolo's eyes flashed with anger.

"You *will* come with me, little brother!"

He made his voice firm. "No."

"What's wrong with you? Haven't you learned *anything* over the last few weeks? This is important, this is destiny!"

"Maybe my destiny isn't the same as yours."

"Course it is! Why do you think you came to live here, Ibrahim?"

Ibrahim lowered his eyes to the floor. "To get away from my father, nothing more."

"Because he drinks too much."

"Yes."

"Because he hit you."

"Yeah, so?"

"So why did your father start drinking?"

"It doesn't matter now." Ibrahim turned to walk away, but Paolo caught him by the arm.

"Your father couldn't cope with your mother's death, Ibrahim. Neither of them believed in Allah. They had no destiny in life! Now one is dead and the other is a hollow shell. *That* is what brought you here, little brother."

Ibrahim felt heat on the back of his neck, and his voice rose to a shout. "Are you saying my mother deserved to die? Are you saying Allah killed her to get at me?"

Paolo's face softened. "Griz says that even the Christians' Jesus taught that anyone who wasn't willing to leave their father and mother to follow him was unworthy. The way I see it, Allah wanted to make it easier for you to find him. Look at what your father has become without a destiny. You have to choose to be better than him."

Ibrahim shoved Paolo away with both hands. "I *am* better than him! And don't you *ever* suggest that my mother had no purpose in life!" He grabbed his book bag and stormed to the door. "Allah knows that I helped you make the devices. That should be enough for him to not consider me his enemy. Take the explosives, Paolo, and go make your destiny."

He was through the door before Paolo could answer, slamming it hard enough to shake the walls.

Chapter 6

Panama City, Florida. Present day.

Ned Parker leaned back in his office chair and allowed a rare smile to spread across the hard lines of his face. He felt the weight of the corporate world lift from his shoulders.

"James, you've outdone yourself this time!" he exclaimed into the phone. Then he repeated what he had just heard. "A twenty-six million dollar purchase order. That is better than I had even hoped for!"

"Yes, I am very pleased as well, Mr. Parker. This might get us a full nickel on our earnings-per-share this quarter, plus another two cents for the first order."

"It might be just enough to save our skin. I'm assuming that this is for a variety of products, like last time?"

"That's correct. A wider variety than last time, but very similar."

"Excellent. Fax a copy over here right away, so we can get cracking. Al-Masri, you just made a significant leap towards that Senior VP position."

"Thank you, sir," James said, then hesitated. "There is just one thing."

Ned felt a pang of nervousness in his stomach. "What is it?"

"They want you to make one-point-five disappear this time."

The weight of Ned's world fell once again upon him. He leaned forward, propping his elbows on the desk and holding his head in his hand. James waited silently on the other end of the line.

Finally Ned answered. "No. They can't bring this up right at the end of the deal, James. It was one million for each order. You tell them-"

"Mr. Parker," James interrupted, "I assure you that I already tried. I pushed them hard, to the point of jeopardizing the whole deal. In the end I got them to pay us two-to-one for the increase, and they added a million to the order. I promise you, Mr. Parker, that no one else in this company could have done better."

James paused, waiting for an answer.

Ned's mind raced with questions. "Who's pockets, exactly, am I lining, James?"

"You know that I don't know that." James sounded calm and in control, as always. "We agreed from the beginning that we didn't want to know any details, right?"

Ned cursed under his breath, but didn't say more.

"They won't sign the order until you agree to the new amount. And they won't release payment until it's delivered, just like last time."

James was pressing him for a decision. And what choice did he have, really? He had already walked too far down this path to turn back.

"Okay, fine." The answer seemed to drain much of the remaining energy from his body.

"Don't worry, Mr. Parker," James offered. "You are making the right decision. You are doing what you have to do. It's just a business deal like any other, and the benefit to Kellor Computing is immense."

"Okay, thanks. I'll see you on Monday."

On the other side of the world, James smiled as he made a second phone call from the warehouse office.

"Mr. Ahman, I have splendid news for you. I was able to get one-point-five this time."

He listened to the response.

"Yes, I thought you would be pleased. I'll wait here for your fax of the signed order, and will stop by to pick up the original tomorrow."

◆

As distressed as Terry had been by his brush with terror, he was even more so by the coordinated attacks that had been carried out on Sunday. Along with the rest of the nation, he watched hours of live news coverage on television for several days as events unfolded. There had been three suicide-bombing attacks on three different churches in different cities, coordinated to occur within minutes of each other. By Friday afternoon, with no one claiming responsibility for the attacks, news commentators had far more questions than answers.

"People want to know," stated one co-host of a daily news program, "how something like this is even possible in our country. Fifty-one killed last Sunday and over three hundred wounded in three churches in Chicago, Dallas, and Denver. Coordinated to occur within 18 minutes of each other, and timed to inflict maximum casualties in those churches. It must have taken months, or more likely years to plan."

"I agree with you, George," responded the second co-host. "And no one is forgetting the toy store in Louisville last Friday, and the shopping mall in Minneapolis three weeks ago. The war on terror is no longer the far-off war. It has finally arrived on our own shores."

"And we are supposed to have the best military and the smartest intelligence gathering agencies in the world, Steve. So everyone wants to know – how can this happen? Where were our civil protectors three weeks ago in Minneapolis? Where were they last Friday? And where were they on Sunday morning? Why wasn't this violence prevented?"

Good question, Terry thought as he tried to get comfortable in his favorite chair. His broken rib continued to give him pain in most positions.

"Well let's talk for a minute, George, about the ongoing success – if you can call it that – of the war on terror. There has been a growing sense of fear among people in this country that we may not be able to win this war."

"There should be no reason that we can't win this war, Steve. We have the most powerful military in the history of the world."

"But look at the events of the past several years. Immediately after September eleventh, 2001, the United States launched this all-out war on terror, and the results have been mixed, even from the beginning. The war in Afghanistan was successful in destroying the infamous Al-Qaeda terrorist training camps, but Osama bin Laden remained at large and the group continued operations around the world."

"That's true."

"Within two years," Steve continued, "the war on terror had successfully stopped much of the cash flow that had been supporting terrorism. Governments were pressured to freeze certain bank accounts and shut down organizations that were suspected of supporting terrorism. Saudi Arabia reigned in several major 'charities,' closing their foreign offices and confining their activities to their own nation."

"I remember that well," George interjected. "We had a spokesman for one of them on our show."

"And we still continued to see well-coordinated terrorist attacks the world over. They even began to target Saudi Arabia. Riyadh has been hit especially hard."

"But what about the war with Iraq? We were successful in ridding the world of a very visible regime that was highly sympathetic to terrorism around the world. That is a clear example of our ability to win this war."

"No, that's wrong, George. Let me explain to you what the war with Iraq should tell us. It only took our military forty-three days to win that war, from the time the bombs began to fall in Baghdad until President Bush declared the end of major hostilities. Forty-three days! That is what our military is capable of doing very well – winning conventional wars. But how long after that did it take to actually find Saddam and his sons?"

"Quite a bit longer."

"Nearly three months to find and kill Uday and Qusay. That's about twice as long as it took to defeat the army of the entire nation – to find two men that are hiding right under your nose! It was still months later before they got Saddam himself, and then al-Zarqawi took up residence in Iraq and the terrorist activity continued for years."

"Okay, we've got only a minute before the break," George cut in. "So tell us your point in less than a minute."

Steve took a breath. "The point is that a war against terror is very different than a conventional war. Having the best military in the world does not in and of itself guarantee victory in a global war against terror. Finding and eliminating individual terrorist leaders is a very tricky business. Iraq was an illustration of this in a relatively confined area."

George raised a hand to interrupt his co-host, but Steve continued.

"More importantly, terrorist activity has continued around the world during this entire time. Terrorist groups have obviously expanded their operations to include well-organized attacks right here within our own back yard. This is a clear indication that we've lost some ground in this war."

"Okay, Steve, time to go to our break." George looked into the camera. "When we come back, we'll be joined by Senator Tucker Cranston of Missouri, who heads up the Senate Committee on Governmental Affairs. We'll get his opinions on what the government's role should be in battling the new terrorist threat here at home. And we'll ask him if we should feel safe going to church this Sunday. Stay with us."

Just then the phone rang and Angela answered it. A moment later she brought the receiver to Terry.

"It's Mitch, from work," Angela said. Terry lowered the volume of the television and took the phone, hoping that nothing had gone wrong at work.

"Hi Mitch! What's up, man?"

"Hey! How are you feeling, now that you're finally home?"

"Oh, not too bad. I still have a minor headache from time to time, but my ribs are starting to feel better." Terry decided not to mention the nightmares. They had only interrupted his sleep three of the last five nights. He was sure they would soon pass.

"That's great, Terry. You just take it easy and get lots of rest."

Terry chuckled. "That won't be a problem with Angela by my side every day."

Mitch laughed too. "So when are you able to come back to work?"

Terry saw through the question. "What's happened, Mitch? I suppose Ops is wanting to redefine the scope of our POS project again?" *Anything to make life difficult.*

"Well, not so much the scope as the time line. And it appears that this is coming from *way* up on high this time. The international business guys apparently made a deal with some foreign company, and they need to ship two hundred POS systems very soon."

Terry sat forward in his chair, and pressed his free hand against his temple, where a minor headache was lurking. "How soon?"

"Half of them before January first."

The date seemed to fall with a thud in Terry's brain. "*What?* That can't be! The software's not even through QA yet. There are still several priority one bugs throughout the system!"

"I know, I know. Now don't get all upset, Terry. I've been dealing with this for you over the past two days, so let me finish the story."

"Go ahead." *This is all I need. Just when I was getting caught up.*

"My hardware implementation guys are already putting the order together, all the monitors, printers, PC's and such."

Terry had to interrupt to ask, "One hundred full systems?"

"Yes. One hundred complete systems, worth over thirty grand each."

"That's unbelievable." Terry felt like shouting. "Someone really doesn't know what the heck they are doing up there."

"Well," Mitch sighed, "that's what your guys thought when

Marketing told them about it."

"Oh, no." Terry could guess what had happened.

"Joel basically reacted the way you just did. He told them they were crazy, and could wait until the software was certified like the rest of the world. It didn't go over too well."

Terry tried to ignore the pain that was growing in his skull. "What happened?"

"Well the next day Fritz got a call from none other than the CFO, Ned Parker."

Terry responded in slow drawn-out syllables, "Ho-ly buckets! Fritz is going to fire me."

Mitch laughed wryly. "He asked me to look into the matter and offer some direction to your guys on this. So I talked with them and got the scoop on the state of your product. Then I went back to Fritz and told him that it didn't look like we could deliver a certified system in that time frame."

"I appreciate that."

"Well don't thank me, because they didn't accept that answer. This must be a very big deal, Terry."

"A big deal? Are they prepared to deliver a system that crashes every single day? How would that make them look?"

Mitch didn't respond.

"This doesn't even make any sense." Terry got up from his chair and began to pace. "What company would need that many POS systems at the same time? You couldn't possibly install and configure that much hardware in a hundred locations all at one time. I'm sure there has to be some sort of a rollout schedule that would give us more time. Did anyone ask them about that?"

"No, but you can ask them yourself in a few days." Mitch paused, then quickly added, "That is, if your doctors will allow it."

"What do you mean? Who can I ask?" He didn't really want the answer.

"Ned Parker."

Another thud in Terry's brain. His head was now beginning to throb in sync with every beat of his heart. He tried to focus on Mitch's voice.

"Fritz already had a meeting scheduled with Parker next week in Panama City, and now your presence has been requested too. Parker wants to get together and agree upon an appropriate solution. Fritz has to be there on Monday, but your meeting is scheduled for Tuesday morning at eleven."

Mitch paused for a second and then offered, "Fritz said that I could go in your place if you are not able to travel. I think that would be best, right? I'm sure your family would rather have you at home after what's hap-"

"No," Terry interrupted. "The doctors say that I should be able to return to work on Monday, as long as I don't strain myself physically. You don't know our application, and it's my responsibility."

"Are you sure? I just thought-"

"I'll be fine. I have to make sure my team's image isn't tarnished with Parker, and then see if I can get him to listen to reason."

"Okay, but at least wait until Monday to make a final decision, and make sure you're feeling up to it, alright? I can go ahead and make travel arrangements for you to fly down and back on Tuesday. But if you can't go, I'll take your place."

"Alright, that sounds good." Terry was about to say goodbye, and then thought of one more question.

"Is the meeting just the three of us? Fritz, Parker, and me?"

"No, there is some international VP that will be there. He had some Arab-sounding name, like al-Rabin or something."

"Al-Rabin?"

"No, wait," Mitch said suddenly. "I remember. It was al-Masri. I think he's the VP in charge of sales in Europe."

Terry was certain that he had not heard the name al-Masri before. Upon hearing it for the first time, however, there was a twinge somewhere deep inside, almost imperceptible, like a little yellow warning light flashing on a forgotten panel. Terry quickly disregarded the feeling as he hung up the phone and went in search of an aspirin.

Chapter 7

FBI Agent Josh Kepler rubbed his eyes and leaned his head on the headrest behind him. His limbs were stiff and he was beginning to notice a dull ache in his back. The clock in the dashboard read 10:33 a.m. He had been here for more than six hours.

Josh refocused his eyes and scanned the empty parking lot around him. The elementary school provided a perfect place to sit unnoticed on a Sunday morning. A handful of vehicles had departed from houses along the other side of the street, presumably to carry their occupants off to church services, but no one took notice of the lone white sedan parked near the far end of the lot.

From his vantage point, Josh looked down a short side street to the third house on the left. He sighed and tried to stretch his legs. There had been nothing whatsoever of interest to see. The house, like the others in this lower middle class neighborhood, was fairly unremarkable, with a one-car garage and a small, adequately kept front lawn.

"Come on, Ismail," Josh muttered to himself, "where have you got to in that SUV of yours?" He thought of the events of the last few days that had led him to this dull neighborhood in Birmingham, Alabama.

The suicide bombing in Louisville had set matters in motion.

The subsequent sketch of the terrorist had been faxed to all agencies, and by Tuesday afternoon there was a potential match. Three months earlier a Saudi man by the name of Ali Kabeer Aljabari had entered the country from Canada on a temporary work visa. He had flown into Chicago, accompanied by two companions: another Saudi named Ismail Faraj and a Canadian named David al-Haji. The three men had promptly dropped out of sight.

Josh had been certain that Aljabari had indeed carried out the bombing in Louisville, so he flew to Chicago to take up the investigation there. The names and photographs of the three men were faxed to law enforcement agencies across the country, and local authorities began to search for their whereabouts in Chicago. Josh arranged to visit several witnesses from the scene of the New Heights Christian Center church bombing. To each witness, he showed the pictures of the suspects, and asked if any of them resembled the man who had attacked the church. The first half dozen witnesses were unable to positively identify the attacker as one of the pictured men, and by the end of the day on Wednesday no new information had been uncovered.

On Thursday, however, Josh's suspicions began to be confirmed. It was still morning when the Chicago Police Department ascertained that David al-Haji had been working the past two months as a mechanic in a local garage. Later that afternoon Josh visited another witness from the church, an elderly usher named Thomas Blanchard.

"Mr. Blanchard," Josh began, after sitting down at the kitchen table, "I've been told that you may actually be the best chance for an identification of the terrorist who entered your church last Sunday. Can you tell me exactly what you saw?"

Mr. Blanchard, a frail-looking man with nearly white hair, nodded his head. "Yes, sir, I sure can. He walked in late for the service, almost right up to me. I stopped him and told him that there were no more seats in the middle sections."

At this point the old man stopped, looked down at the table, and slowly shook his head. Josh waited for him to continue. When he did, his voice was soft.

"He insisted that a friend was saving him a seat down front. I shouldn't have let...." Mr. Blanchard's voice wavered as the words stuck in his throat, and he bit his lower lip hard.

Josh leaned forward, his hands folded on the table, and for a moment he studied the grieving man in front of him.

Then he said in a calm and reassuring tone, "Mr. Blanchard, you and I are not responsible for the evil that roams this world, seeking whom it may devour. We will not be judged for evil's terrible acts. We will be judged according to our own hearts, and whether we inwardly sought that which is right."

The aged and misty eyes rose slowly to meet his own, and Josh noticed the look of surprise there.

"God will take care of *your* heart, Mr. Blanchard," Josh smiled. "You can be sure of that."

The man looked fragile and tired, but suddenly the smallest of lights came back into his eyes. He smiled ever so slightly, and nodded his head in agreement.

Josh stooped to retrieve his briefcase from the floor next to his chair and placed it on the table.

"Now perhaps," Josh said in a business-like tone as he removed the photographs from the briefcase, "you will be able to assist me in my attempts to track down the source of this evil." He slid the three photographs across the table. Mr. Blanchard looked down at the faces and his reaction was immediate. He jumped up with such force that his chair clattered to the floor.

"That's him!" His face went pale, and his thin index finger slammed down onto the photograph of al-Haji. "Dear God! That's him!"

After taking his leave from Mr. Blanchard, Josh had immediately flown to the National Counterterrorism Center in Virginia to direct an all-out man hunt for the third suspect, Ismail Faraj. The effort to trace his whereabouts was fiercest in Dallas and Denver, where the other church bombings had occurred. Josh at first expected that Ismail was already dead, a victim of his own terrorist act. If he were found alive, however, he could likely provide vital information on terrorist activities within the

United States.

Thursday evening passed into Friday morning with no sleep and no further discoveries. Friday then wore on into Saturday, and still nothing. Josh had slept fitfully for a few hours on Saturday morning.

Finally the hours of investigation paid off. Ismail Faraj was discovered to be living in Birmingham, Alabama, and had in fact been at work all week long. By Saturday evening a Birmingham detective was watching Ismail's residence, and police were on the lookout for his dark blue SUV. Josh arrived a few hours later and took up the watch at the house.

Now he was becoming agitated. The clock showed 10:40 a.m. and still there had been no sign of life from within the house.

"Where could he be," Josh mumbled to himself, and he thought of the many church services that were about to begin all over the city. "God, please don't let the killings continue today."

As if in answer, the radio burst to life, causing Josh to jump in his seat.

"Suspect spotted in blue SUV! Repeat: suspect spotted!"

Josh slammed the key into the ignition, as the voice on the radio continued.

"Pursuing onto I20 West, heading toward I65."

The white sedan roared to life, and Josh spoke into the radio, "Heading your way, Detective Watts. Don't let him make you out." Josh sped out of the parking lot and accelerated down the quiet street. His heart and mind were both racing, and his chest felt tight with apprehension. "Please, God," he pleaded, "don't let it happen again!"

◆

Terry sat in his living room in a folding chair, strumming his guitar and singing. On the floor around his feet, the five children played along with various toy instruments, including bongos, bells, and plastic egg-shakers. Angela sat in a rocking chair, while Roger and Pam sat on the sofa. The families had decided to have church at home since services had been temporarily canceled at their church after the previous Sunday's events. Their voices rose together as one on the final refrain.

> *You sent Your son from heaven*
> *Love's greatest sacrifice*
> *For all to see*
> *My Love came down from heaven*
> *And paid the dearest price*
> *Just to be with me*

The song ended and Angela gathered the instruments from the children, as Terry placed his guitar back in its case. Then he picked up a Bible and began to teach the children about God's love, and how his only son, Jesus, came to the earth to offer new life to the world. At this point little Matthew raised his hand.

"Yes, Matthew?" Terry asked.

"What about the terrorists? Does God love them too?"

Terry's mind flashed back to the moment he collided with the suicide bomber at the toy store. "Yes," he answered quietly, "God loves the terrorists too."

"Do *you* love the terrorists?" Matthew looked up at him with wide-eyed innocence, unaware of the sudden knot in the pit of Terry's stomach. After a few seconds of silence, he heard Angela shift in her chair and clear her throat to speak.

"I think God wants us to love everyone, Matthew."

It was a good answer. The right answer. Terry shook off whatever it was that had paralyzed his mind and opened his Bible to a familiar verse. He read out loud. "To you who are ready for the truth, I say this: Love your enemies."

Terry read the last three words emphatically. He smiled at the children. "Yes, God loves everyone, even his enemies, and we should love them too. Love always triumphs over hatred. Do you all understand that?"

The children nodded, and as they bowed their heads to pray,

Terry wondered if any of them really did understand.

◆

Josh spoke into the radio microphone, "After this next exit I'll take up position in front."

"*Roger,*" came the reply, and then, "*Too late. Suspect is taking this exit. Exit 115. All units be advised.*"

Josh maneuvered his vehicle into the exit lane. The blue SUV was two cars ahead, with Detective Watts' unmarked car in between. He hoped that there would be other patrol vehicles nearby.

Before Josh had time to think about how to bring Ismail to a halt, the SUV unexpectedly accelerated toward the intersection ahead. The two pursuing vehicles did the same, now with lights flashing.

"*Suspect fleeing, heading south on Fairfield Boulevard!*"

All three vehicles hurtled through the intersection, which fortunately was void of traffic, and raced dangerously down the street. Josh watched the SUV as it approached the next intersection. The stoplight was red, and a large brown pick-up truck was crossing from the left. The SUV turned sharply to the right, skidding around the corner just in front of the truck. Detective Watts also tried to make the turn in front of the pick-up, but now there was no room. His vehicle slid sideways and impacted the other with a sickening smash.

Josh braked hard and swerved left to avoid the accident. As he skidded into the intersection he braced himself for the impact of the next vehicle that might be coming through.

The impact never came.

Stomping the gas pedal, he continued the chase. The SUV was now a block ahead, and a little ways beyond it Josh took in a sight that made his heart jump fully into his throat. A large brick church building loomed on the right side of the street.

The scene in front of him seemed to slow down, and Josh noted every detail as it unfolded. He saw well-dressed people getting out of their vehicles in the church parking lot as the SUV swerved past. A father walking in a cross-walk just managed to scoop his daughter out of the way of the speeding blue vehicle, and Josh glimpsed the wide-eyed look on the man's face. Trying desperately to steer through the crowded parking lot, he watched as the SUV now bounced up a curb and came to a halt upon a spacious green lawn. The door flew open, and Ismail stumbled out into the sunlight, arms flailing. Josh noted the blue jeans and brown jacket, the jet black hair and the white sneakers. There was no more than fifty yards distance between the terrorist and the glass-paned doors of the church, which were being held open to allow patrons to enter.

And then they were running. Ismail across the green lawn, and Josh across the remainder of the parking lot with weapon in hand.

"GET DOWN ON THE GROUND!!" Josh screamed. He knew he could not close the distance in time. He would have to kill Ismail. But even as church-goers ducked and screamed, there were yet innocent bodies in the way. Still running and shouting "GET DOWN!", Josh raised his gun and tried to aim. Ismail was sprinting full out, and almost to the open glass doors when his backside finally came into clear view.

There was no time for careful aim. Josh slowed his pace only slightly and pulled the trigger three times. The first bullet missed its target and hit the glass pane to the right of the open doors. The next two slammed into Ismail's right shoulder and back, lifting him from his feet and sending him sideways into the glass window. The combination of the first bullet and the full grown man caused the window to shatter, and hundreds of pieces of glass fell like rain as Ismail crumpled to the church floor. Dozens of bystanders screamed and ran in different directions.

Josh was twenty yards from the shattered window, still running. He saw no sign of movement from the body in the brown jacket. No indication that Ismail was still aware of his surroundings. Until a sudden deafening explosion rocked the church lawn, and thousands of shards of glass fell like rain around him.

Chapter 8

Marseille, France. Fifteen years ago.

Ibrahim hesitated a moment in front of the familiar door, then knocked. *Please let him be sober.* The door opened, and his hopes fled as the smell of liquor hit his nostrils. His father surveyed him through glassy blood-shot eyes. Ibrahim had always been amazed at the contrast between his father and mother. His mother had been a petite and fair-skinned American business woman. His father was a large man of dark native African complexion, working in local law enforcement. In his current state he was a man to be feared.

"What do you want, boy?" It was more of a slurred snarl than a question.

"I thought ... uh ... I thought I might see how you were doing, that's all."

His father looked confused, as if his brain was working in slow motion. "You can't have any money, if that's what you want!"

"No, no. That's not what ... I only thought..." *Should I ask him now?* "Uh... I was wondering if I could come visit for a few days." There. He had asked. Nothing registered on his father's face, so he added, "Whenever it's convenient for you, of course."

Slowly an emotion made its way into the dark facial features, a mocking sneer. Ibrahim's nerves tensed.

"You think you can just show up here now, boy? Huh! After six months of nothing? After telling your old man that you never want to see him again?" He laughed, a raspy, grating laugh.

Ibrahim lowered his head. "I guess I shouldn't have said never."

Suddenly his world was spinning, and the ground came up hard. His jaw smarted and he smelled dirt against his face. *He hit me!* He scrambled to clear his head and get his feet under him, as his father yelled.

"But you *did* say never! And I've decided I like it that way, having my life to myself again! So go back to your own useless life, boy!"

Ibrahim backed away from the house, rubbing his jaw as his father turned to go back inside. There was still another question he had to ask.

"Do you believe in God, Father?"

His father paused in the doorway, without looking back.

"Not any more."

The door closed, leaving Ibrahim standing in front of the house alone, blinking back tears. He stared at the door for a full minute, as if his brain had stalled. *Alone!* The thought hit him like a tidal wave. No brothers or sisters, grandparents dead, never knew any aunts or uncles. The universe suddenly seemed immense, and Ibrahim was alone in it, without a place, without purpose.

Picking up his book bag, he began the long walk back to Paolo's apartment. He thought about what Paolo had said earlier. Had Allah really intended him to live with Paolo? Was there really a larger purpose unfolding in his life? He looked up at the stars, wanting to believe. One thing was certain, Paolo was now all he had in the world. His only friend. His big brother.

Paolo! He had gone with Griz tonight to.... Ibrahim started to jog. *Allah, don't let him die. Not yet. Not tonight.*

Chapter 9

Louisville, Kentucky. Present day.

The aroma of baked ham and homemade bread filled the Whitmans' kitchen. Angela's memory returned to her own mother's kitchen and weekly after-church dinners with her family. She smiled at the sound of the children playing and laughing in the basement, and thought of her brother and two sisters, who now had families of their own. Hers had been a good childhood, characterized by love and faith, and sheltered from the harsher realities of an increasingly violent world.

Angela sighed as she removed the ham from the oven. Pam looked up from where she was assembling the ingredients for a garden salad.

"What are you thinking about?"

Angela hesitated before answering. "Oh, I don't know. It just seems like our children are going to have a lot more to worry about than I ever did when I was young. I remember being taught in Sunday school to love our enemies, but the only enemies I had were the girls that picked on me at school."

"I know. Those verses take on a whole new meaning. Think of the Church at the time of the New Testament – they were often persecuted or murdered for having a relationship with Jesus. And yet he taught them to love their enemies."

Angela slowly began to slice the ham. "Showing love often demands sacrifice, doesn't it?"

Pam stopped mixing the salad and looked up. "Yes, it does, but not so great as the sacrifice Jesus made for us all."

Angela smiled. "That's true."

"Are you worried about Terry going on this trip?"

Angela was unprepared for the question. Pam knew her well. She resumed slicing the ham, as if the task demanded her complete attention. "It's silly. I shouldn't worry."

"It's perfectly understandable, Angela, after what happened to Terry."

"It's not just that." *Should I say what I am really feeling?*

"What, then? Tell me what's on your mind."

She continued to work the knife through the ham. "Terry has been working so many hours lately that we don't get to spend much time with him. I asked him not to go on this trip, Pam. I wanted him to take more time to rest at home. But he wouldn't hear of it."

"Did his manager say he has to go?"

"Terry didn't even ask. He just agreed to go." Angela fought against unwanted tears. "He says it's really important." The knife sliced through the ham and smacked against the cutting board. "It's always important."

Pam sighed. "I'm sorry, Angela. Hopefully Terry will get..." her sentence was interrupted from the living room.

"You ladies might want to come see this." Roger's voice was filled with urgency, and the two women immediately put down the kitchen utensils and walked to the other room.

Terry and Roger were sitting on the couch, staring wide-eyed at the television. The scene appeared to be captured from the side of a two-lane highway, and the camera was focused across a field towards a rather small-looking church building. The myriad of red and blue flashing lights from the church parking lot suggested the worst. The red-colored banner across the bottom of the screen left no doubt:

"TERROR ALERT – MORE SUICIDE BOMBINGS."

The reporter on the scene was recapping the facts. "... agents arrived about fifteen minutes ago, and reporters are not being allowed into the area, so the information we have at this time is very limited. Local authorities have confirmed that this was in fact a suicide bombing. The explosive was detonated inside the church building as much as forty minutes ago, which would have been just as members were gathering for Sunday school."

The camera panned from the church building back to the reporter as he concluded his summary. "One thing is certain. This is definitely a different situation than the attacks of last Sunday, which were carried out against very large metropolitan churches. This church in Sioux Falls, South Dakota, is a relatively small congregation of no more than two hundred people. The injury toll will likely turn out to be far less in a church of this size. The fear that this will cause, however, may actually be greater for the millions of Americans who attend churches of more average size. Back to you, Robert."

The scene switched to the anchorman in the studio.

"Thank you, Trent. And now we are going to take you quickly back to Birmingham, Alabama, where we have an update on the earlier attack at the Fairfield United Methodist Church there. Julie Stevens is our correspondent in Birmingham. Julie?"

The woman who appeared on the screen was dressed as if she had been ready to attend church herself earlier in the morning. Her face showed an earnest expression. In one hand she held a microphone, while her other hand clutched a small notepad.

"Well, Robert, we do have some new facts to report here in Birmingham. The information now coming back from the medical and rescue units puts the number of deaths at four – which includes the bomber himself – and at least twenty-three have been taken to area hospitals for varying degrees of injuries.

"And if you will remember, Robert, the earliest reports from the scene were that a plain-clothed police officer was actually in pursuit of the terrorist, and that several gun shots were fired just before the explosion."

"Yes," the anchorman answered, "what is the word on that story?"

"I spoke to eyewitnesses," the reporter glanced down at her notepad, "who say that a man dressed in blue jeans and a gray sweatshirt chased the terrorist on foot across the lawn towards the front of the church. He was shouting repeatedly for people to 'get down'. We now know that the man was in fact an FBI agent. One of the witnesses that I spoke with said that he saw this agent shoot the terrorist in the back as he reached the doors, and seconds later the explosion occurred. We do not yet know the agent's identity, but…"

"So it's reasonable to believe," the anchorman interrupted, "that if this FBI agent had not been there, things could have gone much worse."

"That certainly seems to be the case, Robert. Obviously the terrorist would have intended to go all the way into the crowded sanctuary, but was prevented from doing so. However – and this is very interesting – I spoke on the phone just a few minutes ago with an official from the Department of Homeland Security. He is the one who confirmed that the agent was one of several in the FBI who were in pursuit of the man who carried out this terrorist attack. But this Homeland Security official indicated that there will likely be an internal investigation into why the FBI was unable to prevent this attack altogether. So there may not be agreement yet on whether the FBI saved lives here today, or actually cost them. Back to you, Robert."

"Thank you, Julie." The anchorman looked back into the camera. "We have to take a short break for station identification, but we'll be right back with continuing live coverage on these stories. Stay with us."

Terry lowered the volume of the television, but Angela could not take her eyes from the screen. There were no words to express the horror, sorrow and disbelief she felt inside.

♦

Josh absent-mindedly allowed the interstate signs to direct him toward Birmingham International Airport. His thoughts spun in his head, desperately searching for a logical path to follow.

"This is ridiculous," he said out loud. "They can't force me to leave now!"

Josh pulled the white sedan onto the shoulder of the freeway and slowed to a stop. There he sat, hands on the steering wheel, barely conscious of the traffic racing by. In his mind he found himself suddenly reliving the moments of terror: the feel of his gun recoiling, the sight of the crumpled body, the sound of the explosion. He leaned forward and rested his forehead on the steering wheel.

Several minutes passed as Josh replayed in his mind the events of the last hour. Almost immediately after the explosion, agents from the Department of Homeland Security had descended upon the scene. One of them had ensured that Josh was not injured, and then handed him a plain white envelope.

"Agent Kepler, I need to inform you that Homeland Security is taking over from here. By order of the Attorney General, all agents within the Bureau's Counterterrorism Division are to return to their field offices immediately, where you will assemble and turn over all information related to your current investigations. The order is in the envelope."

Now Josh snatched the order off the front seat next to him, and looked at it again. He had protested, of course, and had even called his boss right then and there. He knew, however, that the order was legitimate. He had in fact been expecting something like this for a long time, ever since the DHS had begun to deploy field agents of its own. Josh wadded up the sheet of paper and threw it over his shoulder into the back seat. Then he let out a long sigh and resignedly put the car back in gear.

"I guess some things are inevitable," he murmured.

♦

It had been a subdued lunch for Terry, Roger and their families. The adults had turned off the television and prayed together before calling the children up for the meal. After sitting down at the table Terry informed the little ones that there had been more attacks on churches that morning. This resulted in a barrage of questions, which Roger and Terry answered with the few facts that they knew.

After lunch, Angela and Pam began to clean up the kitchen and the children returned to the basement to play. Terry and Roger settled themselves in the living room to check the news channels for an update.

In addition to the churches in South Dakota and Alabama, a third church had been struck in San Diego, California. This final attack of the day, however, had resulted in only two deaths and eight injured. The pastor – having heard about the first two bombings – had canceled services for the day, and very few of the congregation were actually present when the terrorist walked into the church.

No known terrorist group had claimed responsibility for the wave of suicide bombings, though many pointed to a statement by a captured al-Qaeda terrorist that had gained attention a year earlier. While the prisoner had not offered much in the way of useful information, he stated emphatically that "al-Qaeda is evolving, growing, and becoming more than the al-Qaeda of the past. New faces will soon appear, the new faces of Allah's servants. All enemies will be brought to their knees." The news media was now reporting that new terrorist cells were likely started years earlier throughout the Western Hemisphere. There was a growing speculation that these cells operated independently of any direct oversight from known terrorist groups in other parts of the world, and probably used the Internet to coordinate activities on a wide scale.

In addition to the attacks themselves, a statement from the White House was now getting equal attention from the news media. It had been announced that due to the alarming increase of suicide bombings on United States soil, the President had sent a proposal to Congress requesting that all federal law enforcement agencies be placed under the direct supervision of the Department of Homeland Security. The proposal outlined a six month plan for merging a dozen various agencies into a mere handful of divisions with "the ability to respond quickly and effectively to any security threat." Apparently this change had been in the works for several months, and was now being accelerated in an effort to deal more successfully with the current situation.

The White House also announced that all U.S. airports, borders, and ports of entry would be shut down for forty-eight hours to allow a comprehensive review and tightening of security procedures.

The official statement contained an appalling lack of detail, and the press was scrambling. Reporters found any person who might possibly be a source of information, and asked the questions that were begging to be answered. Would this merger of agencies result in a disruption of current investigations and other law enforcement activity? Would any active agents lose their jobs? Would the details of the plan be made public? Could this bold restructuring possibly be accomplished in six months? Why exactly had it been necessary to close the nation's airports?

No one from the Department of Homeland Security was available for comment so reporters and their sources could do little more than speculate. Terry wondered if the whole of the U.S. Government was experiencing as much chaos as the news media.

It was nearly two o'clock when the phone rang and Terry picked up the cordless receiver.

"Hello?"

"Terry, this is Fritz." Terry noticed at once that his boss sounded a bit ill tempered. He suddenly remembered that they were supposed to be flying to Panama City this week, which would now be impossible.

"Hi, Fritz."

"Well, I suppose you've been watching the news today."

"Yes, it's awful."

"Yeah." Fritz barely paused before continuing. "Well, I called Ned's office this morning to see about the meetings this week since our flights have been canceled. I just got a call back, and he still wants us there." Terry's heart sank. He had not slept well all week, and his ribs and head still ached from time to time. At the moment he did not relish the thought of spending almost twelve hours behind the wheel of a car.

"Certainly we could talk about the POS project on a conference call," Terry said, now sounding rather irritated himself.

"This meeting is important, Terry. Your team was pretty adamant that you couldn't deliver your software for this project."

Terry's jaw clenched at the accusation. *Like all this is my fault!* He said nothing, and Fritz continued.

"Ned wants to make sure that we are all on the same page, and understand what's driving this. He also wants us to meet this European marketing VP while he's here. He is supposed to be a very sharp guy, the youngest VP in the company."

Terry sighed. "I thought he was supposed to fly in today. Wasn't his flight canceled too?"

"No, he flew in yesterday."

"How convenient. So, are you getting a car?"

"Yeah, I'm leaving in a few minutes, so that I can be there for the meetings tomorrow. You can drive down tomorrow. Our meeting with Ned is on Tuesday morning at eleven. We'll get some lunch, and you can drive back Tuesday afternoon or Wednesday morning if you want. I won't be coming back until Thursday. Hopefully I can get a one-way flight back by then."

"All right." Terry was miserable. But what could he do? "I'll make car and hotel reservations today."

"Good. I'll see you at the office on Tuesday morning then."

Fritz was in a hurry to get off the phone and begin his trip, so Terry decided not to ask for details about the sudden purchase order that was causing so much stress for his team. "Okay, see you then."

As Terry hung up the phone and reached for the yellow pages to look up a car rental location, the phone rang again.

"Hello?" Terry said into the receiver.

"Hey Terry, what's up?" It was Mitch.

"Hey dude," Terry sighed as he flipped the pages of the phone book. "Well, I just found out that I have to *drive* to Panama City tomorrow."

"No way!" Mitch sounded astonished.

"Yeah, to meet with Parker about this POS order. He must have been pretty ticked off that some no-name on my team tried to tell him 'no'. I guess this is my punishment."

"Man! Sorry about that. How are you feeling?"

"Oh…" Terry decided to be honest. "Not a hundred percent yet. My ribs still hurt a little, and I'm not sure that driving for twelve hours will help. I'll be alright though."

"Hmmm." Mitch was pondering something.

"What?" Terry asked.

"Why don't I come with you? I could drive."

"No, you have work to do here."

"I only have one meeting tomorrow, and I can get someone to sit in on it for me. I'll catch up on email from the hotel when we get there, and I can work from the office there on Tuesday."

"No! That would be stupid. You'd miss at least a day and a half of work."

"It's not stupid!" Mitch raised his voice to surpass Terry's volume. "It won't cost the company any money if I share your room, and I've worked more than enough hours to make up for a little lost work time." Terry knew that to be true. "Besides," Mitch continued, "you shouldn't be traveling yet anyway. It would be better if you'd just let me go instead."

"Well, *that's* not happening."

"Then I'm driving, and you need to just get over it!"

Terry laughed. "All right, all right." Inside he felt relieved at the thought of having some company on the road. "When do we leave, boss?"

◆

Late that night, long after packing and long after watching another hour of sketchy news analysis of the day's events, Terry lay wide awake in bed. He rolled over and looked at the digital clock on the nightstand. It showed 1:08 a.m. *God, please help me get some rest.*

Angela slid over next to him in the bed. "What's wrong?"

Terry didn't want to answer. He remained quiet. Angela stirred and raised herself up on her elbow, peering at him in the dark. Her hand found his under the covers.

"What's wrong?"

Terry sighed heavily. "I watched those video clips all day, showing the result of those church bombings." He paused, thinking about how to express his emotions. Angela waited silently. "It took me right back to the toy store, Angela. Right back there, like I'd never left it. I could hear the explosion again. Feel it hit me, the pieces of glass in my skin, throwing me to the ground." He steadied his voice. "I knew that pickup was going to hit me, I could see it coming, and...." Terry bit his tongue and willed the image from his mind. He didn't want to talk about that moment of fear and helplessness, and how it still gripped him.

Angela gently squeezed his hand. "Do you want me to pray for you?"

"Yes, please pray for me."

Chapter 10

Terry and Mitch left the office for Florida just before 10:00 on Monday morning. Terry was pleased to be out and about after being cooped up inside for a week, and Mitch was eager for three days out of his office and away from the daily grind. In the car their conversation first focused on the most common non-work-related topics, such as sports, music, and politics. Eventually the dialog returned to work.

"So, tell me," Terry began. "What do you know about this order for two hundred new POS systems? Who exactly is this for?"

Mitch shrugged. "I don't know for sure. I got the feeling it was a big European company, since this European Marketing VP is involved. But then I heard something about the Middle East, so who knows?"

"The Middle East? What are the big markets for us over there? Israel and Saudi Arabia?"

"Yeah, probably. I think we do some business in Egypt, if that counts as the Middle East. Maybe it's a market where we've never done business before, and that's why it's such a big deal."

"Maybe." Terry was unconvinced. "So they never said anything about a rollout schedule? Or what kind of stores these systems are for?"

"No, I was never in on the conversations at that level of detail."

Terry sighed. It was bad enough having to meet with the CFO

over a disputed project deadline. Going into that meeting without any of the relevant details made it much worse. He leaned his head back on the headrest. "The User's Guide is not even finished in draft form yet. If we ship this out, and they plan on actually using the system, it will be a disaster."

"Evidently they have accelerated all that. The Training Department is already working from the functional specifications to come up with a User's Guide."

Terry shook his head. "It won't be right. We've made some changes since those functional specs were last updated."

Mitch didn't respond. Terry felt the familiar ache beginning in his temple once again. *This is insane.* "Let's change the subject, I'm getting a headache."

Mitch reached for the radio controls. "You rest a little while. I'll look for some good music."

◆

Josh literally jumped out of the chair in which he had been sitting and raised himself up to his full height of six feet three inches. He slammed one huge hand down on the desk in front of him, and with the other pointed directly across at his unit chief.

"This isn't right, Joseph, and you know it!" His face felt hot and his voice boomed loudly in the enclosed office.

The unit chief, Joseph Seeley, was known for being cold, calm and ruthless. His eyes widened ever so slightly at the sudden uncharacteristic outburst of anger, but he remained seated behind his desk, motionless. Josh's partner, who had been managing the research work from their Indianapolis office, looked up at him in astonishment, his mouth gaping. *You ain't seen nothing yet, Dickerson.*

Josh continued the tirade. "To suspend us! And after we were only a few steps behind those sons-of-...." Josh pressed his lips tightly together and the last word stuck in his mouth. His thoughts raced. He could feel the blood pulsing in his head, and his jaw was clenched with rage. In his mind he could see Ismail's body crashing through the window, feel the explosion, hear the screams. He had been so close to preventing it, and now he was going to lose his ability to make it right.

His hand was now shaking, and Josh promptly slammed it down on the desk next to the other one and in fury shouted the only thing he could think of. "HOW CAN THEY DO THIS?"

The unit chief looked steadily back into his eyes, and remained silent for a moment. When he finally responded, his voice was low and firm.

"Are you finished, Kepler?"

The raging wind suddenly left his sails. *You're wasting your breath, Josh.* He slumped back into the chair next to his partner, and said nothing. The chief relaxed slightly.

"The DHS will have access to all our information," offered Seeley. "They will be able to continue the case right where you left off." He looked away from the two agents, and his jaw tightened visibly. "They also want to review our procedures to determine if we could have been more..." he paused, searching for the appropriate word, "...successful."

Dickerson swore loudly. "DHS – the *Debacle* of Homeland Security! How many years have those idiots been around? Let's turn on the news to see how successful *they've* been in securing the homeland! I gotta agree with you there, boss – these DHS guys are real pros!"

"That's *enough*, Dickerson!" Now it was Seeley who raised his voice. His eyes bore into the two agents before him, and his sentences tumbled out in rapid succession. "There will be no more discussion! My hands are tied, and you two are suspended while they review your procedures and conduct on this case. Gather your personal belongings and check your badges and guns at the desk on your way out."

Dickerson immediately rose from his chair and stormed out of the office. Josh watched him go, and then turned back to his boss. He wanted to say something, to argue, to bargain, to beg if need be. But as he looked into Seeley's eyes, he realized the conversation was in fact over. He slowly stood up and turned to leave.

"Kepler." Seeley's voice was suddenly softer than normal, almost hinting at empathy. Josh stopped at the door, but didn't turn.

"Use your time wisely, Kepler." The unusual tone persisted. "You've been through it the last couple of days. If you need help, get it."

"Thanks," Josh mumbled. He wouldn't admit to himself that the suggestion might be worthy of consideration.

"And Kepler."

This time Josh turned to look at his boss. Their eyes met, and he noticed the look of gravity there.

"You might want to pray to that God of yours," Seeley said softly, "and ask him to make sure this doesn't get worse than a simple suspension."

Josh nodded slightly and offered a faint smile as he closed the door behind him.

◆

Terry finished the last of his French fries and drank another swallow of his soda. He stared out the window at the passing billboards along the freeway. Having at least nine hours yet to drive, they had stopped at the fast food restaurant only long enough to use the restroom and get lunch to go. The food had for the moment forced Terry's headache away. He tried to think of a topic of conversation that he and Mitch had not yet covered.

"So, how are things going with Jennifer?"

"Oh, pretty good." Mitch smiled as he changed lanes to pass a semi truck. "Really good, actually."

"Oh? Things getting a little more serious?"

"Yeah, I guess. We've been spending a lot more time together the last couple months. It seems like work has slowed down a little for us, so that has helped."

"That's cool." Terry looked at Mitch and smiled broadly. "So have you persuaded her to venture out on the white water rapids yet, or climb up a two hundred foot cliff?"

"No," Mitch chuckled. "Not yet. She's not quite as much of an adventurer as I am. But she likes to watch sci-fi movies, and she's a great cook."

"Well, what more is there?" Terry decided to make a statement that was really a question. "Sounds like she would make a good wife."

Mitch hesitated. "Well, that's the one thing that worries me." He ran a hand through his ruffled blond hair. "I think that Jen's starting to think like that, actually."

"And that's a bad thing? You two have been dating for almost a year. Don't you ever think about marrying her?"

"I know about marriage from my parents, and that just doesn't work for me."

Terry raised his eyebrows. "Oh, really?"

"Yeah, like you said, I'm about climbing mountains. And I don't want kids and the whole family thing."

"Does Jennifer want kids?"

"Yeah, at some point anyway."

"And you don't *ever* want to have kids?"

"I guess *never* is a long time, but not right now. I want to be able to do what I want, when I want, and a family wouldn't allow me to live life that way. If I had my own kids, I wouldn't be like my parents and basically ignore them. I'd spend the time with them that they deserve."

"Hey, it sounds like you would make a good family man then."

"Yeah, but I don't know if I'd like it!" Mitch laughed. "I'd be dreaming about climbing a mountain somewhere."

"You might be right," Terry chuckled. "But if you really love someone the new reality will become better than the good old days. God made us to need close relationships, you know."

"Oh," Mitch rolled his eyes, "right, whatever." Terry knew that Mitch did not exactly believe in God. He had acknowledged before that there *might* be a God, but did not seem open to discussing it. Out of respect for their friendship, therefore, Terry did not often press the subject. This time he decided to press just a little more.

"I'm telling you, man," Terry smiled and attempted a not-too-serious tone, "you should give God a chance. He's the author of love, and joy, and peace – you know, all those positive things. He could help you figure out the best course for your life!" He hoped Mitch wouldn't be offended, and was relieved to hear him chuckle.

"All right," Mitch reached for the radio controls, "maybe I'll think about it." He rolled his eyes again as he tuned in to a country music station and started to sing along.

Terry grinned. He doubted that Mitch would give God any serious thought today. But he also accepted that it was not his place to convince or persuade another to believe. His place was simply to let God work things out, and be available to participate whenever God started to do something obvious. For now, he was content to sing along with his friend and the radio, making the best of the long drive ahead.

Chapter 11

Marseille, France. Fifteen years ago.

Ibrahim turned the key and shoved the door. "Paolo?"

He exhaled in relief as he saw Paolo ... and Griz, looking up at him from the couch. What was Griz doing here at this time of night? "How did it go tonight?"

Paolo stood and began to pace. "It didn't, Ibrahim. We've been here all evening."

"What? Why?"

"Waiting for you!" Paolo's eyes flashed, but then he looked away.

Griz sighed. "The plan for tonight included you, Ibrahim."

"But you could have easily brought someone else to take my place."

"No." Griz shook his head. "You and Paolo are new to the group. This was more for you than the rest of us. Allah wants you to understand your purpose in his plans, Ibrahim."

Paolo threw up his arms. "He's too concerned with school books and passing exams!" His tone was accusing. "He wants to go to college in the United States, of all places – the home of the enemy!"

Ibrahim felt a vat of emotions boiling inside. "My mother was born there! She went to school there! She wasn't my enemy, Paolo."

"No," Griz responded, "she wasn't our enemy. But she did leave the United States, didn't she, Ibrahim? Before you were even born?" Ibrahim responded with silence. "And she lived in various places over the years, eventually making her home here in France, a very different social and political environment than the United States."

"So?"

"So she must have realized somewhere inside that the United States was not right for her, not the ideal place to belong. Do you know how rare that is, Ibrahim? That a person born into the arrogance of the United States would willingly leave and find a home somewhere else? It just doesn't happen."

Ibrahim sat heavily in the chair and rubbed his head. He had never thought of it that way before. He had always wanted to study at Stanford someday, like his mother. And she had never discouraged him in that respect. But why had she left the United States? He realized that he didn't know. Why couldn't he have just another five minutes to talk to her again? He would give anything in the world for that.

Griz continued. "Paolo, I think its fine for Ibrahim to attend school in the United States someday." Ibrahim and Paolo both looked at him, prompting a hint of a smile. "It's good for Allah's servants to be familiar with the enemy's territory."

Ibrahim didn't know if he liked the prospect of going to the United States as a spy in a holy war.

"You may not want to think in those terms," Griz said, as if reading his mind. "But make no mistake, Ibrahim, you have enemies. And they will kill you if they can. There are those who would eliminate Allah's servants from the face of the earth. The Israelis, and all who support them. They would never admit it openly, but if they could kill you – and Paolo, and myself – and get away with it, they wouldn't hesitate to do so." Griz stood and moved toward the door. "They will never allow Islam to rule the earth as intended by Allah. That is why we must fight, to bring about Allah's will. It is our greatest purpose."

Ibrahim stood and watched Griz at the door. He thought of the rejection he had experienced on his father's doorstep only hours earlier. Could this man truly hold the key that would open the door to a new life? His soul ached to believe, but his mind and body were exhausted. He needed to sleep now, and weigh the course of his life in the morning.

Paolo followed Griz to the door. "Are you leaving already?"

"It's getting late, and Ibrahim looks like he needs a good rest."

Reading my mind again.

"When you are ready for the mission, Ibrahim, let me know. Your destiny is with Paolo, with us. We know that, and I think you are beginning to realize it too," he paused, then smiled and added, "little brother."

Chapter 12

Panama City, Florida. Present day.

Long after darkness had enveloped Panama City, Florida, a shadowy figure shuffled like a rat down a narrow street. Dark warehouses loomed on either side, and a cool night breeze whistled through power lines overhead. Presently the man reached an alleyway, where he stopped and quickly looked back up the street. For a moment he strained his eyes against the darkness, probing for any would-be followers. At this hour there was no one present to observe him on his errand.

Finally he turned and ducked silently into the alley. There, the darkness pressed closer, impeding his progress. He reached into a pocket, retrieved a very small flashlight, and flicked it on. The light was dim, illuminating only a few feet ahead. It was enough. He hurried on like a fleeting shadow and after a few paces came to a large dumpster. Again he turned abruptly and peered into the black veil behind him, straining his ears for the sound of footsteps.

None came, and the man breathed easier. He knelt down by the dumpster and directed his light into the narrow space between it and the warehouse. A sigh of relief escaped his lips. It was here! Right where he had been told. He thrust out his arm and snatched a dirty backpack from its hiding place. His hands trembled slightly as he unzipped the bag.

In the faint glow of the flashlight his eyes fell on stacks of bills; twenties, fifties, hundreds. There was no one within earshot to hear the eager reaction of a shadowy man in the alleyway.

"*This* will serve Allah well!"

◆

Terry sat bolt upright in his bed, heart pounding, beads of sweat on his forehead. He looked wildly about the dark room.

Where am I? His thoughts screamed in his head. *Is someone else here? God help me!!*

Terry's eyes finally came to rest on the digital clock next to the bed, which displayed 12:45 a.m. Suddenly he remembered that he was in a hotel room in Panama City. He had been dreaming again, reliving the moment before the explosion at the toy store.

He tried to remember the dream, even as it began to evade him. The terrorist's face was still clearly etched in his mind, but this dream had been different. The terrorist had interacted with him in some way. He closed his eyes and focused his thoughts.

He remembered. The terrorist had taken the duffle bag from his shoulder. Terry clearly recalled the black leather bag with the white Kellor Computing logo on it. In his dream, the dark complexioned man held out the bag with both hands, offering it to Terry. At the instant he had reached for it, the bag had exploded, ending his dream and shocking him back to consciousness. He put his head in his hands, still shaking.

"Dear God, please help me to be alright."

Chapter 13

Terry sat restlessly in the waiting area outside of Ned Parker's office, and tried to keep his heavy eyelids open. *I've got to get some sleep, just one night of peace.* He observed the administrative assistant as she worked. She looked to be in her fifties, with short salt-and-pepper hair and an energetic personality. She had introduced herself simply as "Mary Beth" and immediately offered to get him something to drink while he waited. Terry took another sip of the diet cola and inwardly asked God for wisdom and humility during this meeting. He then occupied his thoughts by rehearsing the answers to questions that might be put to him by the CFO.

At precisely 11:00 a.m. the office door opened and two men and one woman emerged. They were nicely dressed in business attire, and chatted in friendly tones as they passed. Terry stood, leaving his drink on the small table, and Mary Beth smiled and indicated that he could go in.

As Terry entered the luxurious office, three men turned from the window where they had been talking, and moved to greet him. He knew Fritz well enough to discern the tension in his smile as their eyes met. He recognized the CFO immediately, though he had never met him in person. Terry was impressed by the commanding appearance; tall and broad with steely, penetrating eyes. A smile broke the chiseled face as

Mr. Parker reached out a hand.

"You must be Terrence Whitman." His handshake was firm, and his tone was warm and relaxed.

"Yes, sir," Terry returned the smile.

"I appreciate you making the trip, Terrence, especially under all the recent circumstances." Mr. Parker looked Terry directly in the eye as he spoke, and Terry wondered what opinions of him were already being formed.

"It was not a problem, Mr. Parker."

"How are you recovering from your unfortunate experience the other week? Are you well?" Terry had not anticipated this concern for his well-being. He was surprised that the CFO was aware of his brush with terror. Inside, he felt his guard drop to some extent.

Terry smiled again. "Oh, things are getting back to normal, I suppose." Then he added, "God was obviously taking care of me that day."

At this comment Terry noticed a movement from the third man, standing to his left. He turned and observed a nearly imperceptible smile at the corner of the man's lips. A veiled sneer? Terry could not be sure.

"Terrence," Mr. Parker gestured toward the man, "I'd like you to meet James al-Masri, vice president of international sales for our European and Middle-East divisions."

Al-Masri smiled and nodded silently as he shook Terry's hand. He was almost as tall as Parker, but standing next to the CFO his slim frame made him seem much smaller. His dark eyes were set close together on the thin face, and it seemed to Terry that they were scrutinizing him with interest. He felt a sudden shudder inside, and turned away as they moved to sit in plush chairs around Parker's desk.

The CFO immediately got down to business. "Terrence," he began with another friendly smile, "Fritz has assured me that your boys will be able to come through for us with version one of the new POS software within two weeks."

Terry stifled the urge to protest, and simply nodded politely. The meeting was scheduled for thirty minutes, and there would be plenty of time to object without rudely barging into the conversation. Terry had learned in the past to always listen carefully and be slow to offer an opinion. *Doubly true when conversing with anyone who's job title is a mere three letters that begin with "C".*

Parker continued, nodding toward Fritz, "He didn't think it was necessary to bring you down here for further discussion, Terrence, and neither did al-Masri. But I thought it was important to give you a proper explanation." Now the CFO looked directly at Terry with an intensely serious expression on his face. He spoke slowly and clearly, as if to reinforce the importance of what he was saying. "I understand that what we are asking of your team – and other teams as well – is not within the normal bounds of what we ask of our employees. I know that to you and your programmers this probably looks like a hastily-made decision coming down from a senior management team that doesn't have a clue what we are doing. Am I right?"

Terry was taken aback. He didn't yet know where this conversation was going. How should he answer such a loaded question? He noticed Fritz look nervously down, while al-Masri's cold and persistent gaze remained on him. He shuffled in his seat and opened his mouth. "Well…" he faltered.

"Oh, come on, Mr. Whitman!" Parker laughed. "I respect people who tell it to me straight, so let's not B.S. around the bush!" Terry's eyes widened and he blinked back at the CFO, who now wore a cunning smile. "You probably think that whoever made the decision to sell one hundred point-of-sale systems before the close of this year is a dolt who doesn't deserve one-tenth of the salary that we're paying him!" Parker leaned forward. *"Am I right?"*

Now Terry couldn't help but grin. "Well, not me of course. But I'm sure that at least one or two of my programmers may have thought that, sir."

"Of course they have! And they might actually be *right*, don't you think, al-Masri?" At this, the CFO gave the marketing vice president a sideways look. Al-Masri stiffened slightly, but forced a smile across his lips. He said nothing, and Terry was suddenly aware that al-Masri had not stopped looking at him since they sat down.

Parker looked back to Terry. "You see, Terrence, al-Masri is not paid to know the technical details of software development. He's paid to be one of the best marketing and sales guys in this industry. And that he is." His tone turned serious again. "Now we all know that the economy has not done us any favors of late, and our financial numbers haven't been too good." Parker paused and sat back in his chair. His eyes narrowed as he looked at Terry, giving the impression that he was deciding how much to divulge.

"The truth," he finally continued, "is that our numbers are worse than anyone knows yet, Terrence. We were on the verge of missing our targets for this quarter, even with the lowered expectations we put out last month. If something didn't happen quickly, we were going to take a beating like we haven't seen in years." He paused again, and Terry sat quietly, waiting with interest for the rest of the explanation.

"And then, up to the plate steps James al-Masri." A smile broke across Parker's face, and he chuckled. "James had been working on a comprehensive package for our largest customer in Saudi Arabia, and now he really turned up the charm." The CFO turned back toward al-Masri. "Didn't you, James?"

"Well," al-Masri was nonchalant, "I *am* the best at what I do."

"I think you just might be." Parker looked back to Terry and continued. "As a last minute clincher to the deal, al-Masri threw in two hundred full-blown POS systems at a thirty percent discount. That's enough to take care of any store they open for the next year. They finally agreed to the deal, Terrence, and the profit from this one deal is enough to make up those pennies of earnings that will save our stock price."

Parker leaned back in his chair with a satisfied smile and looked across the desk at Terry. Was he waiting for a response?

"So," Terry began cautiously, "if two hundred systems is enough for every store they will open next year, why do they need one hundred of them right now?"

"That was *my* requirement, Whitman," al-Masri said coldly. He was clearly getting impatient with the conversation. Terry immediately felt a nervous tightening in his chest at the prospect of a conflict, and his emotions bristled with defensiveness. He knew he should not allow anger to dictate his next response, but the events of the last ten days had been exhausting, leaving him precious little restraint. There was also something about the marketing VP that put him on edge. As he turned to look at the man, Terry's heart was giving a clear warning; *don't trust him.*

"Perhaps," al-Masri's dark eyes flashed and his tone patronized, "you could simply do as you are told, without questioning the intricacies of international business deals that you don't understand."

"And *perhaps*," Terry felt his face grow hot, and he fought to restrain the volume of his response, "if *you* understood a little bit more about the product you're selling, you wouldn't make deals that are going to be an embarrassment to your company!"

Al-Masri leaned forward, his eyes now like black flames. Fritz's face turned ghost-like, and he shuffled noisily in his chair, but said nothing. Terry felt his heart suddenly pounding in his ears, and every muscle tensed as he forced himself to hold al-Masri's gaze. His stomach churned, and he inwardly rebuked himself for verbally sparring with a vice president. *Great career move, Terry.*

Al-Masri's face was like steel, and he opened his mouth to speak, but the CFO held up a hand.

"Terrence, let me explain." Parker's voice was still calm, much to Terry's relief. "It's not enough for us to simply make the sale. We also have to move the physical inventory. It all figures into the final numbers."

Terry decided to offer one more question. "Why not just ship all the computer hardware now, and install the software a few weeks later?"

"The contract has already been signed, Whitman," Al-Masri quickly responded. "We are to deliver one hundred fully configured systems. End of story."

Terry shook his head and chuckled. "That's great. Just great." He sat back in his chair and looked at Parker. "I'm telling you the truth when I say that the system will ship with at least twenty priority one bugs, and three times that many priority twos and threes. It's just not ready, sir. If they try to put this in a store, it will make us look like idiots."

"Just get it ready to ship, Terrence." Parker sounded sympathetic, but firm. Then he looked at al-Masri. "We'll tell them that this is still an alpha version and to expect some instability until we get them a patch. Let's say, by the end of January." Looking back at Terry, the CFO asked, "I trust that another four weeks will be enough to address the priority one issues?"

Terry understood that the question was not really a question. "I believe so, sir."

"Good." Parker stood up, and the others followed suit.

As Terry walked through the office door and back into the waiting room, he listened to Parker inform al-Masri of their lunch plans with a member of the board of directors. Terry expected that he and Fritz would find Mitch and have lunch on their own.

Suddenly Terry's thoughts froze, and so did his feet. Fritz, who was following behind, walked right into him before he could pull up short, exclaiming, "What the...?" Terry felt like the air had been sucked from his lungs, and his brain faltered as it tried to absorb the impact of the sight in front of him.

On the table in the waiting area – the very table on which Terry's drink had been sitting just moments before – there now sat a black duffle bag. It was *the* black duffle bag. The one that he had seen in his dream during the night. The one that was slung over the shoulder of the man that had nearly killed him. He wanted to run, but something kept his feet rooted to the floor and his breath held in his chest.

"Terrence?" It was Parker, sounding concerned. "Are you alright? Your face is white as a sheet! Do you need to sit down?" The three men looked at Terry in bewilderment.

Finally Terry spoke, nodding toward the bag. "That bag is the one he was carrying." His voice sounded small and hollow in his ears.

"What?" asked Fritz. "Who are you talking about, Terry?"

"The terrorist, of course. The suicide bomber. He had his bomb in that bag, with our logo on it."

There was a moment of silence, in which all four men gazed at the duffle bag now sitting in the CFO's waiting area. Parker broke the silence first, by clearing his throat, and speaking in an uncommonly hesitant manner. "Surely you don't... I mean ... not that *exact* bag, of course."

Al-Masri suddenly strode toward the little table. "Well of course not this *exact* bag!" Seizing the bag from the table, he ripped the zipper open. Terry jumped back with a gasp, every muscle in his body tensing uncontrollably. His knees went weak and he stumbled into a nearby chair.

Al-Masri turned toward him, holding the now open bag. His expression softened. "I apologize, Mr. Whitman. But it's alright. This duffle is empty. See?"

"Yes, I see." Terry felt dizzy, short of breath, and unbearably silly. "But it's exactly the same." He shook his head and chuckled. "I even told the FBI that anyone could get one of those from our company store, but actually seeing it put me right back in that moment." He took a deep breath and looked up. "I'm sorry for my reaction."

Al-Masri smiled, for the first time, in a friendly way. "No apologies necessary. It's completely understandable. You should get something to eat, and then go back to the hotel and rest. We'll check up on you this evening and you can make the trip back tomorrow."

Terry nodded. "That sounds good to me."

"Unfortunately," al-Masri offered, "Mr. Parker and I have an important lunch meeting to attend to, so we won't be able to join you."

"Right," Parker again cleared his throat in an awkward way. "We will check up on you later though, Terrence."

"Thanks." Terry stood slowly to his feet and turned to Fritz. "Let's see if Mitch is ready for lunch."

Chapter 14

Marseille, France. Fifteen years ago.

Ibrahim woke out of a deep sleep, falling.

He yelled and put out his hands in time to protect his face as he hit the floor with a grunt. The room was dark and something was terribly wrong. Suddenly Paolo screamed.

"Hey! Get off me!"

"Get them into the other room!" Ibrahim did not recognize the booming voice.

He sprung to his feet, but strong hands grabbed his shoulders, lifting him, throwing him through the doorway to the floor. He rolled to his feet again and swung his fists through the darkness at nothing. A hand gripped his neck from behind and pain exploded in his lower back. White light danced before his eyes, and he crumpled to his knees gasping for air.

Paolo's screams suddenly stopped, and the room was quiet. With a click the lights came on and Ibrahim squinted around the room. He was on his hands and knees near the door. The chair was overturned, and Paolo was sitting on the couch, staring wide-eyed into the barrel of a pistol. Four men occupied the crowded room with them, dressed in street clothes and eying them like captured prey. One of them stayed by the door away from the others.

The shortest of the four spoke first. "Hello, Paolo. Sorry to barge in on you like this, but we had an urgent need to talk to you."

"Who are you? I haven't done anything!"

"No? Why don't you tell me where you were on Thursday night."

Ibrahim tried to remember Thursday night. He had been studying for an exam, and Paolo had been somewhere with Griz. *Doing what?*

"I went out with some friends." Paolo sounded convincing.

"Where? And with who?"

"To a dance club. Who are you, and why are you here?"

"I am Lieutenant d'Artois with the National Police, and I will ask the questions. Who were you with on Thursday?"

Paolo looked forward and set his jaw. "I didn't do anything to be treated this way."

The lieutenant nodded to his men. One of them jerked Paolo off the couch and held his arms behind him. There was no point in resisting, with the other's gun in his face. The lieutenant stepped forward and struck Paolo several times in the face and stomach. The first officer then let him slump to the floor, blood running from his nose and lip. Ibrahim wanted to do something, but the man by the door stepped menacingly closer.

The lieutenant began to pace in front of the couch. "We know that you have had contact with a group of Islamic extremists, Paolo. We've linked recent terrorist activity to this group, and we happen to know at least a half dozen of the key members." He paused to gauge Paolo's reaction. "What do you say to that?"

Paolo remained expressionless. "I'd say that whatever is extremist to you may be considered worthy devotion to others."

The lieutenant looked at Ibrahim. "Maybe I'll ask the boy and see if I get a better answer. What is your name, boy?"

Ibrahim's stomach churned, and his head felt light. "Ibrahim, sir."

"He's my cousin," Paolo sounded unconcerned, "just visiting for a few days. He doesn't know my friends." Ibrahim was surprised at the ease and effectiveness with which Paolo lied.

The man near the door suddenly spoke – and Ibrahim was shocked when the words came out not in French, but in perfect English. Ibrahim had learned enough English from his parents to make out the meaning.

"You're wasting time. Ask him about Fabre."

An American agent! Ibrahim was certain of it. CIA? The lieutenant looked at the American with disdain, then turned back to Paolo and continued in French.

"We want to talk with a man called Griz. Where can I find him?"

"I don't know."

"You do know, Paolo. We all know that you do. Now you can tell me what I want to know, or you can go to prison forever, and I will ask the next person on my list. It's your choice."

Paolo looked up at the lieutenant with a sneer. "I think that every person on your list will tell you nothing that you want to know."

The American moved past Ibrahim. His gun was drawn and he pointed it at Paolo's forehead. There was a moment of deathly silence in which it seemed time stood perfectly still. Paolo looked at Ibrahim, his eyes for the first time showing fear.

The sudden gunshot made Ibrahim jump and he tore his gaze from the bloody scene, but not before it was mercilessly imprinted on his mind. His screams were silenced by a rough hand across his mouth, and the hot barrel of a gun against his cheek. The American spoke in broken French in his ear.

"If you want to live, you take a message to Griz, yes?"

Ibrahim couldn't stop his body from shaking. He glanced toward the floor where Paolo lay, twitching, in a growing pool of blood. He nodded in response.

"Tell Griz that we kill his followers until he surrenders. Yes?"

Ibrahim nodded, and fought the feeling of nausea in his gut. The American released him and shoved him toward the door. "Go!"

Ibrahim glanced at the lieutenant as he turned, and observed a satisfied smile at the corner of his mouth. Then he ran as far into the night as his legs would carry him.

Chapter 15

Panama City, Florida. Present day.

Al-Masri got off the elevator at the 17th floor and glanced at a clock on the wall. It was 7:30 in the evening, and the building was mostly devoid of activity for the day. He quickened his pace as he approached the corner office, and tried to anticipate the conversation he was about to have with the CFO.

Immediately after the morning meeting with Terry and Fritz, he and Parker had met the CEO and a member of the board of directors for lunch. The rest of the day had required them to attend separate meetings, and they did not get an opportunity to converse alone. Until now. Ned had called his cell phone between afternoon appointments, and curtly ordered him to be in his office at 7:30 p.m.

Al-Masri walked past the receptionist's desk, now vacant, and paused for a moment as he put his hand on the knob of the large wooden door. Then he went inside.

The CFO was standing at the large windows, staring silently out at the hotel lights on the beach below. Al-Masri closed the door and slowly crossed the floor to the great oak desk, where he waited.

Parker let out a heavy sigh. "How could you have been so

careless, al-Masri?" He continued to survey the scenery through the window.

Al-Masri chose not to respond. He would allow Parker to state his concerns, and then calmly reassure him to stay the course.

"Using that bag to deliver the money." Ned finally turned and gave him a penetrating look. "It was the bag I presented to you personally, wasn't it?"

Al-Masri offered a nonchalant smile. "It can't be proved, Mr. Parker."

"Come on, al-Masri!" Ned nearly shouted. "Don't add stupidity to your carelessness! You are better than that." The steely eyes now glinted with anger. "That bag can be traced back to me."

Al-Masri pretended not to notice the outburst. "That bag has been blown to shreds, it would seem. There is no evidence."

"Whitman *saw* it!" Ned's voice was rising in volume, and his face was flushed.

"He doesn't know what he saw. You heard him. He told the FBI that you could buy the bag anywhere."

Parker huffed angrily and turned back toward the window.

Al-Masri took a breath, and continued in his practiced serene tone. "You are overreacting, Mr. Parker. I was able to speak with Fritz again this afternoon, and commented on Terry's reaction to the bag." At this Ned turned and looked at him with eyebrows raised. Al-Masri shook his head, "Fritz doesn't know either."

"It would be too easy," Ned responded, "for Whitman to figure it out. Eventually he will." A look of fatigue suddenly swept over his face, and the broad shoulders sagged slightly. His voice softened. "It doesn't really matter, does it?"

"What do you mean?" Al-Masri studied the aging CFO.

Ned turned back to the ocean view once again. "It doesn't matter if they find us out, James. We have to turn ourselves in."

Al-Masri shook his head slowly. "Sir, you are still overreacting. You need to think clearly…"

"*Overreacting?*" Ned rounded on him. "Don't you get it? Do

you even have a clue to what is happening here?" His face wore a look of disbelief.

"Mr. Parker," al-Masri now strained to keep his voice calm, "you are not just talking about the end of our careers here. You're talking about prison."

"I'm talking about TERRORISM!!" Ned bellowed.

Al-Masri narrowed his eyes in a knifelike glare. Parker was proving to be a difficult challenge. He pointed a finger at him. "Keep your voice down, you fool!"

Ned continued at only a slightly more controlled volume. "I'm talking about hundreds of innocent lives, al-Masri. Murdered! That's what your Saudi businessmen are doing with the cash we give them. I'm talking about the fact that we – you and I – have been financing terrorist attacks against our own country!"

"And you arrived at that conclusion based on what? One piece of circumstantial evidence! That duffle bag may not have been the same one, you know. There really is no way we can know for sure."

"Oh, right!" Ned scoffed. "Let's see now…" he put a mocking finger on his chin and scrunched his forehead. "Who among the other handful of people in this company that have received my personal recognition award would have passed it on to a suicide bomber? Hmm? Perhaps Carol, the Senior Marketing Director and mother of three?" He looked back toward al-Masri and threw up his hands. "Or maybe David, retail sales manager of the year and respected member of the community?"

"Fine!" al-Masri spat through clenched teeth. "Then we won't give them any more money. We won't do any more business with them. You can even cancel the purchase order if you want. Then we wash our hands of it forever. No one needs to know about speculations that can't be proved."

Ned blinked back at al-Masri and shook his head. "No, James. That's not what we're going to do. You may not have any morals that rise above your greed, but I do." A look of resolution crossed the CFO's face, and al-Masri knew that his attempt at diplomacy had failed. He had prepared for this possibility, and was ready for what he must do next. He listened to Ned state his decision.

"I've got to report what we know to the authorities, and I'm going to do it right now." He turned toward the desk and the phone. "I'll take responsibility for planning what we did, so you should get off with less —"

Al-Masri reacted with lightning quickness. His foot struck high in the air. The blow landed with such force that Ned lurched sideways into a small wooden table, toppling it with him to the floor, and shattering the antique lamp that had rested there. He sat up slowly, looking dazed and confused, as if his mind couldn't grasp what had just happened. The side of his face was already turning a deep shade of pink, and he raised his hand to the painful area.

Al-Masri stood over him and looked down with a fiery gaze. "*You* will take responsibility for planning what we did? *You, Mr. Parker?*" He laughed a scornful laugh, as Ned got unsteadily to his feet. "You are so bloated with arrogance," al-Masri continued, "and self-righteousness. You think you're a king!"

Ned's eyes began to clear somewhat, and he frowned, even as he took a cautious step back. "What are you talking about, al-Masri?" His voice was unsteady.

"You think you're a king!" al-Masri smiled broadly and made a grand gesture with both arms. "You all do!" He let his arms drop to his sides, and his tone became serious. "But you're not. You are only a pawn, Mr. Parker." He lowered his voice almost to a whisper, "and the game is *mine*."

For the first time, Ned's eyes showed a hint of fear, and he glanced toward the office door.

Al-Masri continued with a sneer. "I planned what we did, not you. Every detail of it. Even the request for a bigger payoff than we originally agreed to was my idea. It's just as you told Whitman this morning, Ned. I am the best at what I do."

"So you are the king then." Ned slowly stooped to pick up the little table and some of the scattered clutter, positioning himself a few feet closer to the door in the process. "Congratulations."

"No, not the king. I am simply coordinating many of the various pieces in the game. Allah is king." At this Ned glared at him and straightened up with his hands resting on the table. "And as you know, Mr. Parker, sometimes pawns must be sacrificed for the sake of the king. Terrence Whitman is one such pawn, and you are another." He fixed an ominous stare upon the CFO. "You have outlived your usefulness as a pawn in my game."

Ned clenched his jaw and gripped the table with both hands. "Filthy traitor!" He lunged forward, lifting the table and shoving it with all his might.

Al-Masri easily stepped aside, grasped the legs of the table, and then noticed Ned's fist arcing through the air. Al-Masri tried to spin, but the table was awkward in his hands and the miserable old man was quick for his age. Ned struck a glancing blow, and al-Masri winced at the impact against his face.

Ned bolted for the door, and al-Masri pursued him with renewed fury. Before they had run five paces, he flung the wooden table into Ned's back. The CFO crashed to the floor, rolled to his feet, and whirled to face him, fists raised. Al-Masri paused just long enough to unleash a look of fierce hatred, and then his foot again shot through the air like a bullet. Ned raised an arm and attempted to dodge the attack, but was completely unable to defend against the multiple blows that followed.

◆

Angela finished putting Briana to bed and sat down on the couch with a good novel. The boys were playing games on the computer, and she hoped to spend some quiet time reading. She had been on edge ever since Terry had called her earlier in the evening. He told her about his meeting and the incident with the duffle bag, and Angela worried about her husband. Would he be alright? How long would his nightmares last? She felt powerless to help him deal with the situation, and wondered if she should suggest that he see a counselor.

"Jesus, please be with Terry," she prayed. "Holy Spirit, fill him with comfort, and be his counselor. Take his fear, and replace it with a complete trust and confidence in you."

Angela sat for a moment in silence, allowing her heart to listen for a response. Gradually she perceived a direction for her prayers – not a voice telling her exactly what to pray, but an impression on her heart that steered her thought.

"I ask you, Father God, to send your angels to protect Terry and bring him safely home. I pray that the plans of the enemy, which are bent on death and destruction, would be completely thwarted. Let those plans come to nothing! Put a shield of protection around Terry – and Mitch too – let it be a supernatural covering over them as they travel tomorrow. I trust you, my Lord and my friend, to bring them safely home."

Angela stopped and pondered for a moment the goings on in the spiritual realm. It was obvious to her that darkness was growing; that the spiritual battle between good and evil was intensifying. Simply watching the evening news provided proof of that. But now Angela was suddenly aware that the battle was coming to her family, personally. She was surprised that the realization did not bring with it fear. She felt a peace growing from somewhere inside, deep down. *Not a peace that the world gives.* She wondered what part of the battle would be Terry's and hers to fight.

Abruptly Angela was startled by the phone ringing. She got up to answer it.

"Hello?"

"Hi, Angela. This is Jennifer Mattley."

"Oh, hi Jennifer. How are you?"

"I'm okay. I just got off the phone with Mitch." Jennifer hesitated. "Did you talk to Terry yet today?"

"Yes, I did," Angela smiled. "Did Mitch tell you about the black bag in the CFO's office?"

"Yes, he said that Terry was pretty spooked over it. He's worried about him."

"I am too."

"How did he sound when you talked to him?"

"Oh, he was doing okay. I think he was embarrassed more than anything. He just needs time to get over what happened, that's all."

"Yes," Jennifer agreed, "it is completely understandable."

"Besides, I have a strong sense that God is taking care of Terry."

"Well..." Jennifer responded slowly, "that's kind of what I wanted to talk to you about, actually."

"Oh?" Angela was mildly surprised. Terry had told her that Jennifer believed in God, and even claimed to pray from time to time. She had been raised in a Baptist church, and her parents were to this day faithful church-goers. But Jennifer was not interested in church. She had told Terry that Christians were judgmental of anyone who did not fit into their mold, and therefore church was a place where people were never allowed to simply be themselves.

"Terry has told me," Jennifer began, "about how you sometimes have Bible studies in your home with friends from church."

"Yes. It's always pretty low-key. We usually study something from the Bible and have a time of prayer. Sometimes we sing songs."

"So... is it...." Jennifer sounded nervous, but she finally blurted out her question, "...do you ever let anyone else come that doesn't go to your church?"

Angela laughed in a friendly way. "Sure. Are you interested in finding some people that you can study the Bible and pray with?"

Jennifer sighed and took a moment to respond. "I have actually been praying more these days. With all these suicide bombings, I feel afraid to leave my house for work in the morning."

"I think prayer is the best thing we can do when we are afraid."

"I really have not known *what* to do lately. I finally thought that maybe I should go to church somewhere. You know? To get closer to God, or – I don't know – maybe just to meet other people that would pray for me. But then I heard on the news that most churches are not going to have their Sunday services now because of all the bombings. So I thought 'Well, that's that!'"

"It just goes to show that you are not the only one who is afraid.

It's a normal feeling these days. I know that I was absolutely petrified when I first got to the hospital and found out that Terry was there, unconscious." Angela paused, feeling like it was just yesterday. "I talked to God a *lot* during those hours in the hospital. I would sense his reassurance that everything was going to be okay, and I would feel better for a while. But then the fear and worry would return, and my stomach would be tied in knots. So I'd start talking to God about it again. I begged God for his mercy. I pleaded with him to bring Terry back, and to take care of us, and to give me the strength to get through that trial." Angela's voice now choked with emotion. "I felt so small and weak, Jennifer, but I know that God listened to every word. I know that he was there with me."

Angela stopped talking and reached for a tissue. It was the first time she had shared with anyone how she felt during those dark hours of waiting in the hospital. Jennifer was silent, and Angela thought she heard a sniffle over the phone. She waited, not knowing what else to say.

"Angela?" Jennifer spoke quietly.

"What?"

"How do you know that God really listens when you talk to him? I mean, does he really care about what *I* have to say?"

The world seemed to stop for a moment, as Angela realized the importance of the question. Jennifer was at a crossroads; she would either continue along the same path, or take a new road toward a deeper faith.

"Yes, God does care about you, Jennifer. And he gives his full attention to anyone who will believe in him enough to talk to him. In my experience, the more I get to know God, the easier it becomes to recognize when he responds back to me. Jesus said that his followers would become familiar with his voice, and not follow the voice of a stranger. I'm still learning what that is like, but I know it's the truth. If you keep talking to him, you will know it too."

Jennifer didn't respond, and Angela knew she was pondering the implications of a God who cared for her.

"You and Mitch should definitely come this Sunday and hang

out with us," Angela offered. "We are getting together with the Givens to have church at their house while our normal church services are canceled."

"Oh, I don't think Mitch will come," Jennifer responded quickly. "He's not as open as I am to God and church and stuff."

"Well, you should come then. I know that everyone would be glad to have you."

"Okay," Angela could hear the smile – the hope – in Jennifer's answer, "I think I would like that. What time should I be there?"

"Wonderful! Anytime around 10:30 is fine, and you can plan on staying for lunch too. Give me your email address and I'll send you directions."

"Okay, I'll be there. Thank you, Angela."

"You're more than welcome."

Angela wrote down Jennifer's email and hung up the phone. She thanked God for the unexpected gift of a new friendship.

Chapter 16

The next morning Terry and Mitch left the hotel at 7:00 a.m. They were anxious to get home and put the twelve hour trip behind them. Mitch drove the rental car to a gas station near the freeway and stopped at one of the pumps.

"I'll pump the gas," Mitch said. "You want anything from inside?"

"Yeah," Terry answered, "I think I'll go in and look for something to munch on."

"Okay, you can wait for me inside. I'll put it on my corporate card along with the gas."

Terry got out of the car and yawned as he stretched. Then he made his way into the snack food area of the gas station, and perused the isles of candy bars, chips, donuts, beef jerky, and countless other junk food items. He felt a weariness upon him like a heavy blanket, and he wondered when his last good night's sleep had been. He had rested most of the afternoon and evening the day before, only leaving the hotel to eat dinner with Mitch. But sleep had been elusive, visiting him for minutes rather than hours.

As Terry turned into an aisle near the back of the little store, he heard the jingle of the bell on the entrance door and realized that he had not yet decided on a snack for the road. He forced himself to focus on the shelf in front of him. He saw peanuts, assorted nuts, and various trail mixes. He reached for a good-sized bag of cashews, but his hand never completed the action.

"You! Get your hands where I can see them! NOW!"

Terry froze, every muscle taut like strained wire. The unfamiliar voice was rough, sounding intense but under control, commanding but not shouting. It came from somewhere near the front of the store.

"Now step away from the register," the voice continued, "and stay still!"

Terry very slowly rose up on his toes, peering over the shelf towards the front of the store. He glimpsed two men, one standing a few feet behind the counter, arms raised and looking very pale. Terry could see the other man from the side. He had light skin in contrast to his black long-sleeved shirt, dark sunglasses and black stocking cap pulled down over his ears. He was holding a hand gun and pointing it at the first man. Terry noted that there seemed to be no other customers in the building.

He did not have time to see more, as the man with the gun immediately turned and looked at him. Terry instantly ducked behind the shelf, and his breath began to come in short gasps.

"Sir!" the man barked. "You need to come stand behind this counter, and you won't get hurt!"

Terry thought hard, willing his mind to focus. *How can this be happening to me?* It was the only thought that he could draw out of his head for the moment.

"I mean it!" Terry realized with a jolt of fear that the voice was moving closer. "You will regret it if I have to come all the way back there, mister!"

He had only seconds to act. Looking up, he noticed for the first time a door leading into another room at the back of the building, not ten feet away. An "Employees Only" sign hung above it, and the door was slightly ajar. Something in Terry's heart – something other than fear – urged him to his decision. *Go!*

Terry bolted across the floor and burst through the door into the dimly lit room beyond, staying low the entire time. Without stopping he noticed a narrow aisle directly ahead, between rows of shelves, that led to a door marked with an "Exit" sign. He could hear cursing from the store behind him, and footsteps in pursuit. Straightening up, Terry accelerated towards the door. The distance was maybe thirty feet, and Terry realized with a wild panic that his very life might depend on making it through that door before the man with the gun reached the stock room.

What happened next happened much too quickly for Terry to consciously process. First, he saw the handle of the exit door turn and the door began to swing outward. At the same time he felt his right hand close around something on the shelf next to him, and his brain screamed in his head, *Don't stop!* The door was two-thirds of the way open when Terry slammed into it. The man on the other side of the door staggered backward with a cry of surprise. He was taller than Terry and held something at his side with one hand. Without any thought, Terry swung the object in his hand with all his might. The man's mouth dropped open and his eyes grew round with fear, as his face took the full force of Terry's attack. His head snapped back and without uttering a sound the man fell heavily to the pavement with a thud.

Terry whirled around to his right at the sound of squealing tires. It was the rental car, skidding to a stop. Terry started sprinting again as Mitch yelled, "Get in!" and opened the rear driver's side door, just in time for Terry to dive into the back seat. Mitch punched the accelerator and steered hard toward the parking lot exit. Peering out the back window, Terry saw the man with the gun running after them.

"Don't stop!" Terry screamed. "He's still coming!"

Mitch kept his foot on the gas and the vehicle careened wildly out into the street, bouncing Terry sideways in the seat. Thankfully there was no traffic on the side street to hinder their escape. A gunshot exploded from behind them. Then a second and a third loud bang.

"Is he *shooting* at us?!" shouted Mitch.

Terry's eyes were wide and he was shaking uncontrollably as he dove face down on the back seat. "Yes! Yes! Don't stop, Mitch! Don't stop!"

"Don't worry! I'm not stopping!" Mitch turned the car onto the entrance ramp to the interstate. Terry lay in the back seat for several moments, listening earnestly for the sound of gunshots. When he was convinced that it was safe, he slowly sat up in his seat to look around. He realized that they were on the freeway, traveling at high speed in the direction of home.

"Don't you think we need to report this to someone?" he asked Mitch. "The police?"

"No! We're going home. I'm sure someone called the cops while that maniac was chasing us outside."

Terry's heart and breathing began to slow down, and he noticed the renewed aching in his head and ribs. He tried to think through what had just happened. Suddenly he realized that he was still clutching something in his right hand, and he looked down.

"Mitch, I think I may have really hurt the guy who was coming in that door. We should tell someone what happened."

"Well, I'm not going back now! Call them on the phone if you want to tell them. Besides, I think an armed burglar deserves to get smashed with – hey, what did you hit him with anyways?"

"A tire iron." Terry set it on the floor. "But for all I know that guy might have been the manager of the place."

"The *manager*?" Mitch sounded shocked. "Didn't you see what he dropped when you hit him?"

Terry vaguely remembered the sound of something sliding across the pavement after the man fell. "Well, actually, no. I heard him drop something, but never had time to look I guess."

"It was a shotgun, Terry. Somehow I don't think the manager dresses every day in torn jeans and a faded sweatshirt and enters the back door of his gas station carrying a sawed-off shotgun. Do you?"

Terry didn't offer the obvious answer. Instead, he asked Mitch a question that had just occurred to him.

"How did you know to drive around back to get me?"

Mitch didn't answer.

"Mitch?"

"I don't know," said Mitch slowly. "I was tightening the gas cap on the car when I saw what was happening. I saw the guy holding a gun on the cashier behind the counter. Then I saw you just as you ducked down in that back aisle, and the guy started to move towards you. I panicked, and didn't know what to do. I was about to rush inside and scream at the guy or something, you know? Something that probably would have got us both killed." Mitch paused, and it seemed like he was thinking hard. Terry waited.

"Then my eyes saw that door in the back of the store, and something told me, 'He's going out the back.'"

The car grew quiet for a moment.

"Something told you?"

"Well, no, not really. It was like…" Mitch paused again, and Terry could see that he was having trouble describing what he had experienced. "It was like a strong, complete and clear thought. And it was a calm thought too – not the panicked racing thoughts that I was thinking right before that. And then I knew what I needed to do. I got in the car as fast as I could and drove around to the back. And the first thing I saw was that guy hitting the pavement, and you spinning around to look at me."

Terry suddenly grinned, and his fear abated. "God told you what to do! He was taking care of us!"

"No, no," Mitch groaned, "it wasn't like *that*. It wasn't like God talking or anything. It was just the right thought at the right time."

"You said that *your* thoughts were about to get us killed, remember?"

"Well, I guess I had a good one after all. The brain is capable of some amazing things when under pressure you know. There've been studies –"

"What do you think it would sound like anyway, if God told you something?" Terry interrupted.

"I don't know!" Mitch sounded exasperated. "It would certainly be more than a quiet thought inside my head. Right? I mean, it would be a big voice or something, so that you would know it was him, right? Otherwise – if you don't even know it's him – what's the point?"

"Mitch, the Bible tells of many ways that God spoke to people. God did sometimes speak with an impressive voice, but there were other times when he spoke directly to individuals with what the Bible calls a 'still, small voice.' At other times he spoke in dreams. This definitely sounds like the still, small voice thing happening." Mitch did not respond.

"Think about it," Terry continued. "If you hadn't come around back, we were in a world of hurt! If you had run inside shouting, one or both of us would have been shot. It would have delayed me going out the back, and the other guy with the shotgun would have got me from behind. And if you had simply stayed outside, and maybe called 911 on your cell phone or something, you would not have been ready to drive off when I came running around from the back. And the way that guy was chasing me, he would have caught us for sure."

Terry rapped Mitch on the shoulder. "Mitch, I had the same kind of thought from inside the building, after I saw the back door. It was exactly like you are describing, and it was a single word: 'Go.' Don't you see? Both of us had to take exactly the right action at exactly the same time to get away. And God made it happen." Terry leaned back in his seat with a smile. "Thank you, God, for taking care of us!"

Mitch scowled at the road as he drove. "Doesn't prove anything," he mumbled, "except that fate and luck were on our side."

"Ha, Ha!" Terry laughed. He was now feeling almost cheerful. "Think what you want, dude! Believe in fate, if you think it will stick with you. I prefer to believe in a good God who will always take care of me."

The expression on Mitch's face turned suddenly contemplative. "Terry, you said something a minute ago, about the way that guy was chasing you."

"Yeah, he was definitely after me."

"That doesn't make any sense!"

"What do you mean?" Terry sat forward and rested his arms on the back of the front seat.

"Those guys were trying to rob the store, right? So the first guy knew that his partner was coming in the back door. It doesn't make sense that he would run after you, and leave the guy at the checkout counter to call 911. He should have stayed in the front and got the money, knowing that his partner would stop you. That would have been their logical plan, right?"

Terry thought for a moment. "What are the odds that the guy coming in the back door was not the first guy's partner?" Terry did not really believe what he had just suggested, and Mitch definitely did not.

"Yeah, right. I'd say about a million to one. Even if that were the case, the first guy would still be smarter to stay in the store and try to get some money. The minute he leaves to chase you, the cashier is going to call the cops!"

"So maybe they were just stupid. After all, how smart can you be if you are robbing gas stations for a living?"

"Well, they had a coordinated plan. But it's like the first guy just completely lost his head or something." He smiled back at Terry through the rear-view mirror. "I guess maybe that's another example of fate taking care of us, right Terry?"

"Not fate," Terry mumbled. The bit of cheerfulness he had felt a moment before had vanished, and he was now troubled. About what, he could not yet determine.

Chapter 17

Marseille, France. Fifteen years ago.

Ibrahim kicked the dirt at his feet in the empty alleyway behind the dance club. The mid-morning hours brought little life to this section of the city, and he had no fear of being bothered. He wondered if Griz would come. What would he do if Griz didn't come? He shuddered, and decided to push that scenario from his mind.

Ibrahim had been on the streets for three days and nights since Paolo was killed. *No, not killed. Murdered. Executed by those who labeled him an extremist.*

Griz had been right after all, and Ibrahim was now a walking casualty in a war that he had tried to ignore. His only hope was that Griz still believed that Allah had brought them together for a purpose.

But would Griz risk meeting him? Ibrahim knew where Griz was staying, but he decided against going there. The police could be watching. Or even the Americans. Instead, he had wandered aimlessly for two days before showing up at a club often frequented by Griz' followers. There he spotted a familiar face, and asked for a message to be taken to Griz. Meet him in this alley today.

Ibrahim suddenly realized what the outcome would be. If he

were Griz, he would not meet a fifteen year old kid in an alley under these circumstances. Certainly Griz knew by now of Paolo's death at the hands of the authorities. He also knew that Ibrahim had been spared. The obvious conclusion was that they wanted Ibrahim to lead them to Griz. He looked over his shoulder down the alley. Were they even now watching? Could they be so invisible?

No, Griz would not come. Ibrahim would be left alone in the world, to die hungry and homeless and unknown.

And to think that just days ago he planned to attend college in the United States! He laughed at the bitter irony. Allah must have grown tired of his reluctance to follow a greater purpose, and had moved on to someone else.

Overwhelmed by despair, Ibrahim slumped to the dirty ground and cried.

Chapter 18

Smoky Mountains, Tennessee. Present day.

Josh sat on the front porch of the log cabin and sipped his coffee as he admired the scenic valley spread out before him. It was 7:00 a.m. on Thursday morning, and his wife, Mary, was still asleep. The Smoky Mountains were still cloaked in shadow at this hour, but the birds nevertheless greeted the growing light with song. Josh listened to the chirping music and permitted his mind to take in the peaceful beauty. He took another sip of the hot coffee and pulled his coat closer around him. He loved the mountains; the splendor and majesty of the wild, unspoiled by civilization. A pure reflection of the splendor and majesty of God.

For the moment Josh did not think of the events that had resulted in his being here. He had rehashed it all a thousand times in the past three days. He had questioned God with a thousand questions. Why couldn't he have stopped Ismail? Why had he been suspended? Why did God allow him to be put in a position of doing nothing? Why did God allow all those people to die? *Christian people.* These were the questions that had been occupying most of his waking thoughts, and would again soon enough. But for now, Josh simply enjoyed the moments of peaceful solitude in the mountains.

The cabin door opened, and Mary stepped out into the brisk morning air. Her shoulder length blond hair was uncombed and she looked every bit like she had just crawled out of bed. Josh watched her as she quickly zipped her flannel coat and sat in the chair beside him. She was beautiful, even now with no makeup and sleep in her eyes. He was glad to have this time alone with his wife, and he regretted that they had not spent more time together over the last few years. He knew that he had allowed their relationship to grow distant. Suddenly he remembered something from the Bible, *God works all things out for good to those who love him.* Josh smiled. A more intimate relationship with his wife would definitely be a good outcome of the current chaos in his life.

Mary gazed across the valley. "It's beautiful out here, isn't it?"

"Yes, it is." He reached out and gently squeezed her hand.

"I wonder how Carla is doing."

"Oh, I'm sure she's fine. She was thrilled to be staying with the Johnsons, and its only for three nights."

"I hope she misses us," Mary said, "at least a little bit."

"Of course she does," Josh chuckled. "Even if being thirteen won't allow her to admit it."

For the next several minutes they sat quietly, watching the sky grow brighter and the colors of the landscape grow richer. It was Mary who finally broke the silence.

"Have you come to any conclusions about anything?"

Josh sighed. "Not really. I sure don't understand how God works sometimes."

"That's when it takes faith to follow him, right?"

"Yeah, but he doesn't seem to be leading us anywhere fast, does he?" Josh looked at his wife and smiled.

"It's not so bad, is it?" Mary returned his smile. "Slowing down and spending some time together for a change?"

"No, it's not bad at all, and probably long overdue."

Mary shivered and stood up. "How about some breakfast? Ham and eggs?"

"That sounds wonderful."

Josh followed his wife into the cabin, and thought to himself that the day was beginning to show promise. Perhaps he could actually enjoy a few hours of relaxation before returning home tomorrow.

◆

Terry sat at lunchtime with Mitch and Jennifer in the company cafeteria. After yet another night of fitful sleep, he had contemplated calling in sick, but Terry knew that he needed to manage his team's efforts toward completion of the POS release. He had spent the morning trying to re-work the development plan to meet the timeline. Now that he was not concentrating on work, his mind was distracted.

"Terry?" Jennifer queried. "Are you okay? You seem troubled."

Terry looked up from his plate. "What? Oh, I'm just tired. Not sleeping much these days."

"Are you taking anything?" Jennifer sounded concerned. "Something to help you sleep?"

"Oh, no," Terry answered quickly, "I'll be fine. I just need to stop having a brush with death every other week, that's all." He gave a half-hearted laugh.

Jennifer was unconvinced. "Terry, you really should take an over-the-counter sleeping aid. With all you have been through, it's no surprise that you can't sleep. But if you don't do something, you're going to collapse from exhaustion."

Terry didn't respond, but instead took another bite of his hamburger and tried to think of something to talk about besides his well-being. Jennifer narrowed her eyes and looked as if she was about to continue her attempt to convince him that he needed drugs. He quickly swallowed his food.

"Mitch," he blurted out, "there is something you said yesterday that has me thinking."

"About what?" asked Mitch. Jennifer rolled her eyes, clearly irritated that Terry did not want to listen to her advice.

"Well..." Terry paused. He had not meant to divulge his

thoughts about the previous day's events, but now he didn't see how he could turn back from the subject. "Do you remember your comment that the way those burglars acted yesterday didn't make sense?"

"Yeah, chasing you instead of remaining in the store. What about it?"

"What if..." Terry stopped short. He suddenly realized that what he was about to say might sound a little unbelievable. "Never mind." He took another bite of food.

"You can't do that!" Mitch protested. "Tell me what you're thinking. What if... what?" Jennifer also leaned forward with interest.

"Well, don't think I'm crazy or anything, but what if those guys really weren't there to rob that store? What if they were there for..." Terry looked into the eyes of his friends, wondering if they would think he was losing his sanity.

Mitch gave him an exasperated look. "*For what?*"

"For me."

Mitch sat back in his chair, appearing puzzled. He looked at Jennifer, then back at Terry. "You mean... they might have been there specifically to..." Mitch leaned forward and lowered his voice. "...to kill you?"

Terry nodded his head and continued in hushed tones. "What are the odds that I would almost be killed twice in less than two weeks? I'm not a policeman, or in the military. I'm an IT manager for pete's sake! The odds must be staggering. So was it really just *bad luck*?" Terry peered into the two faces across the table. Jennifer and Mitch both looked at a loss for words.

"Think about this," Terry continued with increased intensity. "I was the only person to see that suicide bomber close up and live to tell about it. I gave the FBI a sketch of what he looked like. My sketch probably turned out to be a positive ID on some terrorist or something. And then a few days later someone tries to kill me! Is that really just a coincidence?"

"So you think," Mitch asked slowly, not sounding convinced, "that there's a connection between a suicide bombing in Louisville,

Kentucky, and a convenience store robbery in Florida?"

"Oh forget it." Terry started to get up from his chair.

"No, no, no! Sit down. I'm with you, dude. I'm just trying to understand your reasoning, that's all." Terry sat back down and Mitch continued. "So why would anyone care that you had seen the bomber? He's dead, after all."

"He could probably be connected to others who are still alive."

"Okay, I'm following you that far. But how would someone in Florida know that you had seen a terrorist up close? The terrorist certainly couldn't have informed anyone. You only told the FBI, CIA, and Homeland Security. Oh, and your family and friends."

"I don't know. Maybe there is someone inside the FBI or something. Who knows?"

Mitch looked doubtful. "They would have had to know that you were going to Florida, and where you were when you got there. Besides, terrorist sympathizers inside the FBI or the Department of Homeland Security sounds a little unlikely."

"Well," Jennifer said seriously, "there was that one FBI agent a few years ago who was caught leaking information to China or something. What was his name?"

The two men looked at Jennifer in silence.

"Well, it did happen!" Jennifer insisted.

Mitch forced a nonchalant laugh. "Come on, Terry, we're talking odds of ten thousand to one here. There's no reason to believe that someone in the FBI is after you."

"Maybe someone inside our company then," Terry suggested. "After all, the guy carried his bomb in a bag with our logo." He was about to take another bite of food, but stopped. "Yes! Everyone here knows what happened to me. Even Parker knew! If someone who works here has terrorist connections, that could explain – "

"Wait a minute," Jennifer interrupted. "That still doesn't make any sense. Terry, you already gave the description to the FBI. The damage is already done. They would have no reason to kill you now, right?"

Terry rubbed his eyes and tried to think through his headache. "You're right, that doesn't make much sense." He sighed heavily. "I guess it's maybe impossible to find a connection between the two events."

Jennifer gave him a sympathetic look. "Terry, you really should go home and get some sleep."

He ignored Jennifer's statement and looked at Mitch. "Tell me what you think of this idea. Should I call that FBI agent I talked to at the hospital, and tell him what happened to us yesterday? Just to see what he thinks about it? I had a good feeling about him."

"Hey, that's not a bad idea," Mitch agreed. "If he knows of any possible connections, he can look into it. If not, then you can stop worrying about it."

"Yes," said Jennifer, "and then maybe you'll be able to get some sleep!"

◆

Terry dialed the number on Josh Kepler's business card. He did not want anyone to overhear his conversation with the FBI agent, so he had found an empty meeting room from which to make the call. The phone rang only once before he heard a female voice on the other end.

"FBI Indianapolis Field Office, may I help you?"

"Yes, can I speak to Josh Kepler please?"

"Agent Kepler is not in the office. I can take a message, or transfer you to the unit chief."

"Um..." Terry hadn't anticipated this possibility. He did not want to talk to anyone other than the agent he had met. "When will he be back?"

"Agent Kepler is ... on assignment. He may not be back for several days, sir." Terry was frustrated. The prospect of talking to Agent Kepler about his situation had made him feel like he would get some good answers. Now he felt his hopes fading. At the same time he wondered why the woman had hesitated to answer. It was barely a pause, hardly more than a stutter, but it was enough for Terry to notice. He had the distinct feeling that she was trying to hide something from him.

Terry decided he did not want to give up just yet. "Well, he interviewed me a couple weeks ago about a case he was on, and told me if I thought of anything else I could call this number. He said that you would be able to put me in touch with him wherever he was."

"Sir, if you will leave me a name and number where you can be reached, I'll have someone get in touch with you right away."

Terry hesitated. *What should I do?* Something didn't seem right. He was sure that the agent had told him that the people at this number would know how to contact him. It was possible that Kepler was deep under cover somewhere and could not be contacted. *But why did the woman hesitate?* Terry remembered his conversation at lunch. Could the FBI be trusted?

"Sir," the woman said in a reassuring tone, "let me transfer you directly to Agent Kepler's unit chief. His name is Joseph Seeley, and he can take any information you have and get it to Agent Kepler."

"No!" Terry was now convinced that something wasn't right. "Look, I'll just call back later and see if he's in. Thanks." Without waiting for a response, Terry quickly hung up the phone. He sat for a few minutes in silence, contemplating the short conversation. *Why couldn't she just give me his number?*

Suddenly he felt foolish. Did he really think a unit chief in the FBI couldn't be trusted? *I'm getting way too paranoid.* He rubbed his tired eyes. Finally he stood up to go back to his cubicle, glancing upward and muttering, "God, I don't care if I *am* paranoid. I'm not going to talk to anyone but Kepler."

Chapter 19

Marseille, France. Fifteen years ago.

A shadow passed over Ibrahim, shielding him momentarily from the afternoon sun. He blinked. How long had he been sitting here?

Looking up, he slowly realized the silhouette against the bright sky was familiar. *Could it be?* When the man finally spoke, his doubt receded, and hope rekindled like a hot flame. Griz spoke.

"Hello, Ibrahim."

"Griz! You came."

Griz reached down a hand and lifted Ibrahim to his feet. His face was serious, masking any emotion that might be there. "We've been observing you for two days. The authorities aren't watching you."

Ibrahim's eyes widened. Griz had been watching him, a day before he had even asked to meet! Did that mean that Griz still cared about him? The flame within him burned hotter. Griz now looked deep into his eyes, as if he could search the depths of his soul.

"You and I have come to a crossroads, Ibrahim. What is it that you want from me?"

The words rushed out of him like a river. "I want a purpose! To have my part of destiny! I want to serve Allah's higher purposes without reservation!"

A smile broke through the serious features of Griz' face, and he put a hand firmly on Ibrahim's shoulder. "I am pleased to hear you say it, Ibrahim! I have always felt that Allah has great plans for you."

The flame within him now became white hot, and Ibrahim knew it was fueled with newfound purpose. And something else. He narrowed his eyes and spoke through clenched teeth. "And there's one more thing I want."

"What is that, little brother?"

"I want to wage war." The words came out of him like molten steel from a forge. "I want to bring Allah's fury down on his enemies!"

Griz beamed. "What do you know about Afghanistan, little brother?"

Ibrahim drew a blank on the question.

"There are camps there where you can receive the training you will need to become a great warrior. I plan to go there myself, very soon. I think we should go together."

Ibrahim could not believe his good fortune. In the span of a few moments he had been transported from the lowest valley of despair to a mountaintop of joy. His mind could not absorb the impact of the change. He could only smile in silence as he walked with Griz to a waiting vehicle. He had received a new beginning. A new life. Ibrahim vowed with all his might that he would not waste a moment of it.

♦

Atlanta, Georgia. Present day.

James al-Masri switched off the headlights of the rental vehicle as he braked to a stop in front of a small brick house in a quiet neighborhood. He observed a dim light coming from one room, and checked the time. It was 8:55 p.m. He sighed and leaned back against the head rest, closing his eyes for just a moment. It had been a busy day. He had driven far, and made several hasty arrangements, which he now reviewed carefully in his mind.

Satisfied that he had done all he could for the moment, al-Masri opened the door and climbed out of the vehicle. He looked up and down the street once, closed the car door softly, and proceeded to the front door of the house. Even in the dim light of the street lamp, the house looked shabby and run down. The paint was peeling from the shutters, and the bushes along the front were overgrown and unsightly.

Al-Masri knocked sharply on the door, and waited. Another light came on inside, shaded by the blinds drawn across the front window. The door opened, revealing a tall, slender man with dark skin, dark hair and eyeglasses. In appearance he could have been al-Masri's brother. Qasim smiled broadly. "Ibrahim!" The two embraced and went inside.

The interior of the house was unimpressive. The shag carpet was badly worn, and three old-looking wooden chairs comprised the only furniture in the front room. A small television rested silently on a cardboard box. Sitting in two of the chairs, the men looked at each other with serious expressions.

"You look well, Qasim," said al-Masri. "Allah will reward you for assisting me on such short notice."

"It is an honor, Ibrahim. Did you manage to make the necessary arrangements?"

"Yes." Al-Masri stared blankly at the floor, contemplating the plans that were now in process. "Everything has changed, Qasim," he said softly. "Life has become a great deal more precarious for me." He shook his head with a hint of a smile. "And all because of something as insignificant as a duffle bag."

"It is unfortunate."

"If the fool wasn't already dead," al-Masri stated flatly, "I'd have to kill him myself." Qasim shifted uneasily in his chair.

"But what's done is done. Now I simply have to make some adjustments." He looked knowingly at Qasim. "First you will help me leave the country tomorrow. Then I will be able to tie up the loose ends." He stood abruptly. "Let's try to get a few hours of sleep, my friend."

Chapter 20

Sunday morning began with intermittent snowflakes fluttering lightly from a cold gray sky. At 10:30 a.m. the Whitmans arrived at the Givens' house for their home church gathering. The children scrambled out of the mini-van and ran excitedly to knock on the door, while Terry and Angela gathered various items: Bible, guitar, music, and dessert for later. Upon entering the house, they realized that another family was already there, and recognized them as neighbors from down the street.

"Hi, guys!" called Pam in a lighthearted voice as she greeted Angela with a hug. "How is everyone this morning?"

Terry set his Bible on the counter. "We're all doing well."

Pam motioned toward their other guests. "I know you've met our neighbors a couple of times before. This is Dave and Sheri Lydon, who live three doors down the street." Dave and Sheri shook hands and exchanged hellos with the Whitmans. Dave appeared to be slightly older than Terry, a thin soft-spoken man with graying hair. Sheri was tall for a woman and a little overweight, with wavy brown hair, brown eyes, and a pretty face. Terry remembered them to be a friendly and likeable couple.

"Dave called Roger last night," Pam explained, "and wondered if they could come over and have church with us this morning, since their services are canceled too."

"Oh, that's great!" said Terry enthusiastically. "Glad you came."

Dave appeared somewhat relieved. "I was hoping we wouldn't be intruding," he said quietly.

"Yes," Sheri added in a more lively voice, "it's not normally something we do – inviting ourselves over to someone's house up the street." She laughed in a cheerful fashion, and Terry noted the obvious contrast between the Lydons' personalities.

"No problem at all. We invited a friend of ours as well, and she was planning to come too."

"Did I see some extra children running around?" asked Angela.

"Yes," answered Sheri, "we have two girls who are fifteen and thirteen, and our son is ten."

"The girls are wonderful with the younger kids," offered Pam. "We have had them baby-sit a couple of times for us."

Just then the doorbell rang. "Oh good!" Angela hurried to open the front door. "Jennifer made it."

Some forty minutes later the children played happily in the basement, their lesson finished. They were presumably kept quiet by the presence of the older girls, which gave the adults an opportunity to spend some time singing songs of worship to Jesus.

Terry played his guitar and chose the songs as he went, flowing from one to the next. He finished with a chorus that caused his own heart to reach out to God more intensely than it had since he regained consciousness in the hospital two weeks ago. His voice filled with emotion as he led the others through the refrain.

Lord, I trust in you as I draw near
I bring my life, the hope, the fear
With a child's faith I do believe
That you will hold me here

I sing to you as I feel you near
You renew my life and remove my fear

With a child's faith I do believe
That you will hold me here

With a child's heart I do believe
That you will love me here

The song ended, and the room became quiet. Terry looked around the group, feeling the intensity of God's presence. He observed that most everyone's eyes were still closed. Pam's face wore a tranquil smile, and Roger was silently mouthing words of prayer. Tears were glistening on Angela's cheeks. The Lydons had their hands upraised, and appeared to be waiting, or perhaps listening for something.

Terry caught Jennifer's eye and he noticed that she appeared to be somewhat uncomfortable, as if she were wondering what was supposed to happen next. Terry smiled reassuringly, realizing that she was likely not accustomed to this type of worship – expressive worship that treated God as if he really was in the room listening. Worship offered not just to a benevolent and all-powerful being, but also to a close friend. *God, help Jennifer to catch a glimpse of who you really are today.*

Roger opened *The Message* Bible and began to read.

Light, space, zest –
    that's God!
So, with him on my side I'm fearless,
    afraid of no one and nothing.

When vandal hordes ride down
    ready to eat me alive,
Those bullies and toughs
    fall flat on their faces.

When besieged,
    I'm calm as a baby.

When all hell breaks loose,
  I'm collected and cool.

I'm asking God for one thing,
  only one thing:
To live with him in his house
  my whole life long.
I'll contemplate his beauty;
  I'll study at his feet.

That's the only quiet, secure place
  in a noisy world,
The perfect getaway,
  far from the buzz of traffic.

God holds me head and shoulders
  above all who try to pull me down.
I'm headed for his place to offer anthems
  that will raise the roof!
Already I'm singing God-songs;
  I'm making music to God.

"That's Psalm twenty-seven, verses one to six," Roger finished. "I think we should pray for you, Terry, to have God's peace in your heart so you can sleep again."

Terry felt embarrassed. He looked down, avoiding eye contact with the others, but inside he was glad to let someone pray for him. His nightmares visited him relentlessly, and fatigue was his constant companion. Terry did believe that God could bring peace back into his soul.

"Okay, I'd appreciate the prayers."

The group gathered around Terry's chair, some of them placing a hand on his shoulder. They prayed, taking their time, agreeing together and asking God to help their friend. Some of them prayed out loud, specific things that they felt in their heart.

Suddenly someone gasped, and everyone looked up. Jennifer had stepped back from the group and was standing wide-eyed with both hands over her mouth.

Terry leaned forward in concern. "What's wrong?"

Jennifer shook her head in silence, and Terry noticed that tears were brimming around her eyes.

Angela moved to her side and put an arm around her. "Jennifer? Are you okay?"

Jennifer took her hands away from her mouth, and spoke in a small voice with an awkward smile. "I think so." Everyone looked at her with puzzled expressions. Suddenly she turned toward Terry and grinned.

"I'm supposed to tell you something."

"What?" Terry asked, surprised.

"I was listening to everyone pray for you, encouraging prayers and all, and I suddenly asked God 'What can I say to Terry?'" Jennifer stopped and giggled. "I immediately told myself, 'That's a stupid thing to ask God!' But then I saw a picture in my mind of a cell phone, clear as day. And then…" her voice trailed off for a moment and when she finished the sentence it was almost in a whisper. "…he spoke to me." Jennifer suddenly appeared cautious, and looked quickly around at the others, as if doubting whether they would believe her.

Angela happily squeezed her arm. "That's so awesome!"

"Very cool!" Roger agreed.

"Well, what did he say?" asked Terry. "You better tell me, before you forget!"

Jennifer rolled her eyes. "Yeah, like I'd ever forget the first time *God* spoke to me!" The others laughed. "As I was seeing this cell phone," Jennifer continued, "I heard him say, 'Terry needs to follow his heart. I will take care of him.' That was it."

Roger turned to look at Terry. "What's that mean?"

"I know exactly what it means," Terry responded. "I had almost talked myself out of it."

"Yep!" Jennifer agreed. "You better try to call him again first thing tomorrow."

Roger looked bewildered. "Call who? Am I the only confused person in the room?"

Terry grinned at his friend. He felt renewed energy flowing through him. It was as if some deep reservoir in his soul had been filled. *God will take care of me.*

Soon after Terry had recounted his attempt to call Agent Kepler, and promised that he would try again in the morning, Roger turned on the television to check the national news. Everyone was anxiously wondering if there would be more deadly attacks. Roger quickly found a special live edition of the popular news talk show with George Keene and Steve Sorensen.

"So to summarize once again," said George as he looked into the camera, "it's now past noon on the east coast and there are no terrorist attacks to report. There have been two arrests in St. Louis, Missouri, where local authorities stopped a van that was driving in the vicinity of a church. There is no word on whether the two men arrested are actually suspected of being terrorists or not. We do know that the church there in St. Louis had canceled all meetings today – as most every church in the nation has done I think, Steve – and presumably there was no one there."

"We have also been informed," added Steve, "that the Department of Homeland Security, in conjunction with the FBI, has made dozens of arrests this week of those suspected of having links to terrorist activity. So there has been a lot of movement on this, and we are hoping – if the relative calm continues today – that this will be a sign of some success in stopping these murderers."

"But the question still on everyone's mind, Steve, is how can this happen in our country? How do these terrorists get into the country and live freely among us until they decide to blow themselves up?"

"That is definitely one of the pressing questions that our nation is facing, George. The United States stands for freedom and an open way of life, and it is relatively easy for people to get in. Listen to this statistic. In just one year over four hundred million people enter the country at more than four thousand terminals and ports of entry. The number is staggering, and our Government has decided, at least in the short term, that it will take drastic measures to make it harder for terrorists to come here. Security at our boarders has been tightened to unprecedented levels. Right now, if you are not verified as a United States citizen, or have a U.S. citizen here that you are visiting, the customs inspectors will not let you pass. They are literally turning people back at the borders and in the recently opened airports."

"Many people are of the opinion," George interjected, "that this is going too far. Most of those being turned away are *tourists*, not terrorists, and there is no valid reason to stop them."

"The valid reason, George, is that we are at war. Most people understand that, and are supportive of locking down our borders."

"What about the terrorists who are already in the country, Steve? Obviously there is an organized effort within our borders, and it stands to reason that they are still out there. Maybe only five people at this point. Maybe fifty. Maybe more. The speculations vary. Why haven't we heard of any credible arrests?"

"Well, there have been arrests, dozens of them in the last week, according to the DHS."

"Only suspects at this point," George answered. "If they had found and arrested a genuine terrorist, they would have released a name and a picture by now. They are doing little more at this point than rounding up a lot of Muslim people for questioning." George turned toward the camera. "Let's take a look at the following report from Louisville, Kentucky, where it was just sixteen days ago that a terrorist blew himself up in a crowded toy store."

Everyone in the Givens home suddenly straightened up and leaned in toward the television with interest. "Hey," said Terry, "they're talking about Louisville on the national news again."

"The past sixteen days," the reporter began, "have seen drastic changes in the lives of some people in Louisville, Kentucky. Specifically those who live in the Heartland Community Apartments, a low-income housing area that boasts a twenty-seven percent Arab population. It is the highest concentration of Arab immigrants in the state of Kentucky, and for many of them life may never be the same."

Terry watched as the report told of discrimination against the local Arab population. The stories ranged from name-calling on the street to bricks thrown through windows and threats of violence. When one family turned to the local authorities for help, they were subjected to intense questioning about their background and beliefs. Several men and women in the community had been questioned by Homeland Security agents, and a few had been held in jail cells for more than twenty-four hours. Terry's heart felt heavy as he observed the faces on the screen, filled with anger and fear as they recounted their tale. None of the handful of residents who were detained had been arrested. No evidence of terrorist connections had been found.

"It is a sad truth," the reporter concluded, "that many in this country will now find themselves suspects of terrorism, based solely on appearance and ethnic background. But for most Americans this week, that is an acceptable situation given the current circumstances."

Chapter 21

Terry arrived at the office early Monday morning. For the first time since the attack in the toy store, he had slept through the night without dreaming. It was truly an answer to the previous day's prayers. He felt better than he had in a long time, with a new level of energy to face the challenges of the day.

Terry worked diligently to keep the POS project moving forward at an accelerated pace. His current tasks included sending regular updates to the Project Management Office, ensuring that all interfaces between the POS system and other systems were being tested, and proof reading the training guide to ensure technical accuracy. It was not until mid-morning that he remembered to make the phone call. He took a break from his work to find a vacant meeting room and dialed the number on the business card for the second time.

"FBI Indianapolis Field Office, may I help you?" Terry recognized the same female voice.

"Is Josh Kepler back in the office today?"

"One second, sir, I'll transfer you."

"Okay, great." Terry felt relief, as he heard the phone ringing again. But it was short-lived.

"Unit Chief Seeley." The voice was gruff and impatient.

"Uh ... I've been trying to reach Agent Kepler. Do you have a number for him?" Terry winced. He realized that the unit chief was probably not going to hand out phone numbers to unidentified callers.

"Agent Ke--," the unit chief stopped himself from repeating the name, and quickly continued. "He's not in this week. If you will tell me your name and number, and what this is about, I can have another agent contact you if need be."

Terry decided he had no other choice at this point. "My name is Terry Whitman. Agent Kepler interviewed me after I witnessed the suicide bombing in Louisville a couple of weeks ago. He told me to contact him at this number if I thought of any other pertinent information."

"Okay, Mr. Whitman," the unit chief sounded only mildly interested, "go ahead then. I can take down your information and get it to the people who are working that case."

"Well ... it's not really new information about that bombing. It's more along the lines of ..." Terry was having trouble coming up with the words to explain himself. "Some other things have happened since then that don't make sense, and they could be related somehow. I was hoping to go over it with Agent Kepler and get his thoughts."

There was an awkward pause before Seeley responded with a tone of continued impatience. "Sir, our agents are all very busy right now. If all you want is advice, I suggest you talk to your local--" Again the unit chief stopped in mid sentence, but this time Terry heard muffled arguing on the other side of a hastily covered receiver.

"Look!" Terry yelled into his end of the line. "I might not have any concrete information, but I was almost murdered again last week! Maybe that's just a stupid coincidence to you, but to me it's my *life*. I think it's more than a coincidence that I almost got blown away with a shot gun just a week after giving the FBI a detailed sketch of a terrorist!" Terry was surprised at his own forcefulness, but he suddenly knew exactly what he wanted to say. "Now if you are interested in the details, I'm willing to give them. But *only* to Agent Kepler. He's the one I want to deal with." Terry stopped and heard only silence in response. "Well?

Do you want to have him call me, or should we just forget the whole thing?"

Seeley finally answered, and though Terry would not have believed it possible, the unit chief now sounded more irritated than ever. "Mr. Whitman, it pains me to say this, but Agent Kepler has actually stepped into the office this morning. I'm going to put you on hold and transfer you to him."

"Thank you." *Now we're getting somewhere.*

Terry recounted to Josh the details of the convenience store robbery and his fear that it may have been an attempt on his life. He also offered his thoughts that someone from the company might be involved somehow, noting that the CFO had commented on his earlier brush with terror. The bomber had, after all, been carrying a bag with the Kellor Computing logo, and practically everyone in the company knew that Terry had seen the man close up.

He decided to leave out the incident with the duffle bag at Parker's office. He was still embarrassed by the way he had panicked at the sight of an empty duffle bag, and it certainly was not unusual to find company logo items around the headquarters building.

Agent Kepler listened with interest, asking several questions along the way. When Terry finished his account he felt that the agent had given serious attention to his concerns. "Do you think I'm just being paranoid?" he asked.

Josh chuckled. "Maybe, but a little paranoia these days is probably not a bad thing, Mr. Whitman. I'll try to juggle some things here so I can do a little digging for you. Most likely I'll be able to get back with you in a couple of days and tell you that you've had nothing more than a string of bad luck."

"Great." Terry felt a wave of relief. "I really appreciate you taking the time to talk to me, Agent Kepler."

"Hey, please call me Josh. And it's not a problem at all. I'll talk to you soon."

"Okay, bye."

♦

Josh and his unit chief both hung up the phone after Terry said goodbye. Seeley glared across his desk, and Josh knew what was coming.

"You'll try to juggle some things? You don't carry a badge right now, Kepler! What were you thinking?"

"Well he's comfortable talking to me, right? Even if you don't let me do the investigating, I could be the one to call him back and tell him whatever we find out."

"There is no *we*, Kepler! You don't work here! You shouldn't be here talking to paranoid people in Kentucky, and you will *not* be here later this week to call him back! Do you understand me?"

Josh frowned as he looked into Seeley's face. He suddenly realized that his chief must be very frustrated indeed, having to submit the unit's investigations to the Homeland Security guys. He decided not to argue. "Yes, sir. I understand. I guess I better be going." He stood up to leave, then added, "Will you at least let me know what we … er … I mean, what you all find out about the Louisville case?"

"There won't be any finding out. That case is back burner."

"What?" Josh couldn't accept this. "It's possible that there is more than meets the eye on that one. If I were still on that case, I would definitely make some phone calls to the authorities in Panama City and–"

"KEPLER!!" bellowed Seeley, rising from his chair. "You are not still on that case, or any other for that matter!" He straightened up and sighed, softening his tone. "I am only authorized to investigate direct leads in terrorist cases. This was an attempted robbery in Florida, with no clear evidence to link it to any terrorist act. I can't put an agent on it."

Seeley sat down heavily in his chair and began to organize the mounds of paper on his desk. "Of course if you want to go to Florida yourself, Kepler," he said without looking at Josh, "and ask some questions in a very *unofficial* capacity, I certainly wouldn't be able to stop you from doing that much."

Josh grinned. "Okay, I understand, sir." He turned and opened the office door to leave.

"If you find anything important, Kepler, I'd appreciate a phone call."

Josh hurried through the office toward the exit. He felt as if his life had just been given back to him.

◆

The first half of the week went by quickly for Terry. It was imperative that his team produce a final build of the POS system by the weekend, and there was a long list of defects from the Quality Assurance team that needed to be resolved. All of the developers worked long hours, and in between his management duties, Terry even fixed some of the bugs himself.

On both Monday and Tuesday evening he arrived home late to discover his house in various stages of Christmas decor. Angela and the children were busy creating a festive abode, replete with Santa figurines, elves, snowmen, wreaths, and tiny winter village displays. If it weren't for these transformations, Terry wondered if he might have forgotten Christmas altogether this year. The weather remained unusually warm, and the absence of snow on the ground contributed to the feeling that it could not possibly be a mere two weeks from the holiday.

Terry left work on Wednesday with just enough time to make it home for dinner. His mind was occupied with various aspects of his to-do list at work, which he had started to call his "undone list". The irritation he felt at the state of the POS software was mounting. He knew that there would be several priority one issues in the system when it shipped, and that did not sit well.

Terry sighed as he glanced in the rear view mirror. *Is that the same pickup truck?* He surveyed the maroon vehicle behind him. He vaguely remembered a similar truck pulling out of the parking lot behind him as he left work. Squinting into the mirror, he attempted to make out the face behind the wheel, when suddenly his cell phone started to ring.

"Hello?"

"Hi, sweetie," he heard Angela say.

"Hi there! How was your day?"

"It was fine. The boys did well in their studies today."

"That's great. Will you be finished with their lessons this week?" He knew that Angela wanted to have their home schooling studies finished a few days before Christmas.

"I think so, but they will probably have to finish their last writing assignment next week, which is fine." Angela changed the subject. "So, I take it you are on your way home for supper?"

Terry smiled. "Yes, I might be there a couple minutes late, but no more than that."

"Good. You have to eat supper with us at least one night this week. We all miss you when you're not here."

"I know. I'm looking forward to it myself. It's so strange, but food just seems to taste better when it's still hot! I'll be there in about twenty minutes."

"Okay, we'll see you then."

Terry ended the call and thought of his family. He was truly grateful for the blessing they were, and knew Angela and the children would be disappointed if he worked any extra days during his holiday vacation. The thought only added to the pressure he felt. *I've got to get this POS system finished, or my career may be over.* He glanced in the mirror, vaguely noting that the maroon pickup was still visible. *Angela will just have to deal with a few more weeks of disappointment.*

Ten minutes later Terry exited the freeway, and noticed the pickup did likewise. His pulse quickened. Another turn, and then another. Watching the truck in the mirror, Terry suddenly scolded himself for worrying. *You've slept good for three nights, Terry. Don't give in to the fear again.*

He was approaching the turn into his subdivision, when something happened that both calmed and heightened his apprehension. God spoke to him.

Don't turn here.

In the handful of instances that Terry had heard God's voice, it was never this clearly audible. Instinctively he turned his head and looked to the empty seat next to him in surprise.

"What?"

There was no answer. Terry didn't need one. He drove straight past his subdivision, and watched as his pursuer did the same.

"Now what, God?" Terry asked out loud.

Silence. Terry's brain was working hard, and he tried to latch on to an idea. Any idea. He passed two more subdivisions, and approached an intersection with a small gas station. A thought finally stuck in his head and he pulled into the gas station, stopping at a vacant pump. He began to pump gas into his car, and inconspicuously observed the maroon truck come to a stop in a parking space near one end of the building. The driver did not get out of the vehicle.

Terry's jaw tightened and his hand suddenly clamped into a fist. He was tired of feeling like his life was in danger. Jamming the gas nozzle back into its holder, he hurried into the gas station.

Great. The window facing Mr. Maroon Truck is behind the checkout counter. Terry didn't care. He strode around the counter and pushed past the attendant, a gangly college-aged boy who protested loudly. Not slowing his pace, he marched to the window, pointed a finger directly at the man behind the wheel, and fixed him with a fierce stare. The man looked younger than Terry, with a shaved head and a goatee. His dark eyebrows rose in alarm.

"Stop following me!" Terry hollered, making sure to mouth the words clearly through the window. He was pleased with the result. The man quickly put his head down, started the engine, and roared out of the parking space without another glance in his direction. Watching the truck's retreat, he let out a long sigh and breathed easier.

Thanks for the tip, God. Terry smiled for a moment, wondering at the unambiguous way in which God had spoken. He was grateful that his prayers for protection were being answered. Still he couldn't help but feel apprehensive. What were the intentions of the man in the truck?

When Terry arrived home, he found his family seated at the table and eating their first helpings of food. Angela gave him a quizzical look.

"Did you run into traffic?"

"You could say that." Terry did not want to share the events of his drive in front of the children. As he prepared to sit down at the table, the phone rang.

"I'll get it," Terry announced as he picked up the cordless receiver. "Hello?"

"Terry, this is Josh Kepler." Terry immediately noted the seriousness in the agent's voice.

"Hello, Agent Kepler."

"Did you hear any interesting news at work today?" Josh queried.

Terry thought for a second. "No, I don't remember anything."

"Ned Parker has been missing since the day you met with him. They've kept a lid on that for a week."

Terry was shocked. "What?"

"They just found his body today, Terry. He was murdered."

Chapter 22

The next morning Terry turned on the news as he readied himself for work. Within minutes he was looking at a picture of Ned Parker in one corner of the screen as the news anchor relayed the few facts about his death. The CFO had indeed been missing for a week, and his badly beaten body had been found the previous morning behind a little used warehouse in Panama City. He had a broken neck, and apparently had died of severe internal injuries. The authorities had few leads to follow and offered no motive for the gruesome murder. There was no official statement from Kellor Computing Group, though the company's stock was down sharply in pre-market trading.

"Why can't you work from home today?" Angela's voice was terse. He avoided her eyes as he answered.

"I told you already. I can't direct the efforts of multiple people over the phone." He hoisted his laptop bag over his shoulder and moved toward the door, but Angela blocked him.

"Terry, even Josh said you should stay home. You don't know why that man was following you yesterday." She put her hand on his arm.

"Angela, it's just today. Josh will be here tonight, and then--"

"Terry, please!" She was on the verge of tears, begging him. He couldn't deal with this pressure! Didn't she understand that his career was teetering on the edge of failure? He tore away from her grasp.

"Angela, stop! My responsibilities won't wait until tomorrow."

He was through the door without looking back, ignoring what sounded like a stifled sob behind him. *Women are so emotional!* Certainly he could handle getting to work and back. Just like he had yesterday. And the day before that.

Later that morning Terry arranged to have lunch with Mitch and Jennifer at a restaurant near the office. As they waited for their food he recounted the events of the prior evening. His friends were enormously concerned over the fact that Terry had been followed most of the way home. They were also amazed to find that he had known about Parker's murder before anyone else.

"What did Josh say about it?" asked Mitch in a hushed voice.

"I don't know if there are any official suspects yet or not, but Josh found out that al-Masri was maybe the last person to see Parker at the office that evening. And he's disappeared now too."

"What do you mean, disappeared?" asked Jennifer.

"Josh wanted to talk to him, but evidently he left unexpectedly last week on the day after our meeting. He called in to the office last Wednesday and said he had urgent business back in Europe. Josh confirmed that he took a flight early Thursday morning from Atlanta to France."

"France?" asked Mitch.

"Yeah, evidently he grew up there or something. Josh contacted the Kellor offices in Europe yesterday and no one had heard from al-Masri yet." The waitress arrived with their salads. "That's all I know for sure," Terry concluded.

They chewed their food in silence for several minutes before Mitch spoke.

"So let's just review the facts for a minute, Terry. You bump into a suicide bomber right before he blows up a store here in town. That bombing turns out to be just one of many. You provide a detailed sketch of the terrorist to the FBI, CIA and Homeland Security. I have to believe that all those agencies are circulating your picture and tracking down any links to that man, right?"

"Right so far," Terry answered.

"Then we go to Panama City, and you personally meet with Parker and al-Masri, where you tell them that the bomber in Louisville was toting a Kellor Computing bag, right?"

"Yeah." Terry knew where Mitch was going. He had already gone down this path in his own mind.

"And the very next day," Mitch continued, "Parker is dead, al-Masri is fleeing the country, and you narrowly escape being killed by two gas station robbers. Does that about sum it up?"

Jennifer had stopped eating and was looking at Terry with a wide-eyed expression.

Terry took another bite of his salad. "Well, you forgot to mention that within one week of *not* getting killed in Panama City, I'm being shadowed by someone as I drive around town." He laughed and added, "But that's just a minor detail."

"How can you laugh?" Jennifer sputtered. "This is not funny! What are you going to do, Terry?"

Terry decided to return to a serious tone. "Well, Josh was actually very concerned to hear about my shadow. He is going to fly here tonight to look into it himself. Today he is trying to find out more details about Parker's death, and he also has a CIA contact in Europe trying to find al-Masri. So I'm just waiting for him to get here, and we'll see what happens."

Mitch took a drink of his water and looked thoughtful. "Terry, when you first told me about the duffle bag in Parker's office, you commented on his reaction. Do you remember what it was that seemed strange to you?"

"Yeah, I do." Terry took a second to recollect. He had an uncommon ability to remember exact words of a conversation long after it took place. "When I saw the duffle bag sitting on that table, I said that the terrorist had his bomb in that bag. Meaning, of course, the exact same model and color. Well, everyone went silent for a minute, but Parker's reaction was different."

"How do you mean, different?" asked Mitch.

"He seemed to get flustered, and he even stammered when he questioned what I meant." Terry looked from Mitch to Jennifer. "I've never heard that man stammer before – he's got a silver tongue."

"What did he say to you," asked Jennifer.

"He said 'Surely you don't ... I mean ... not that *exact* bag, of course.' Which struck me as a really stupid question. Al-Masri seemed to think so too, because he was suddenly very irritated and said 'Well of course not this *exact* bag!' and he proceeded to yank it open to show everyone it was just an empty duffle bag. It was a weird moment." Terry paused in thought, and then concluded, "I think it was just hard for them to know what to say when they saw me panic like that."

"Or possibly," Mitch reasoned, "that bag *did* mean something to Parker. Something that he did not expect to be confronted with in that moment. Why else would he get nervous enough to begin stammering silly questions?"

Jennifer put her fork down and looked at Mitch. "It sounds like al-Masri got irritated at Parker, doesn't it? Maybe he knew that Parker was about to give something away!"

The two of them looked across the table at Terry. "I suppose that's possible," he offered. "But you are suggesting that both Parker and al-Masri had something to hide, something that related directly to the terrorist bombing in Louisville. A vice president and the CFO of our company? That's hard to believe."

"Not so hard for me," Mitch stated. "Al-Masri is from France, right? And we all know that the United States and France aren't exactly close friends. And beyond that, which country did al-Masri orchestrate a huge sale with? A deal that seemed to come out of nowhere and save our financial numbers for the quarter?"

"Saudi Arabia," Jennifer answered.

"Exactly," Mitch declared. "A nation of wealthy Arab businessmen who have financed terrorist activity for years."

"Okay, I'll give you al-Masri," Terry conceded. "But Parker? I don't buy it. He would not knowingly support terrorism."

"And now he's the one who's dead, isn't he?" Mitch let the question hang heavily in the air between them.

Jennifer looked frightened, and started to say something, but stopped herself as the waitress arrived with their entrees. As soon as they were alone again she blurted out, "Terry, why did you come to work today? They could still be following you!"

Terry rolled his eyes. *Not again.* "I don't think they know where I live, at least they didn't find out last night."

Mitch shook his head and looked serious. "Jennifer is right; you should have stayed home today. They won't make the same mistake twice. Tonight you won't be able to see them following you. They might even use multiple cars." He leaned forward and looked intent. "You've got to let someone else drive you home tonight, and I'd even suggest going out the back entrance."

"Come on, guys. You're over-reacting! This isn't a spy movie! There's no reason to believe that someone out there is going to try to kill me on the way home tonight, and Josh will--"

"Terry," Jennifer interrupted, "will you be reasonable! Did Josh actually tell you to go to work today like normal?"

"Well…" Terry decided not to answer. "Look, how about this? I'll leave an hour early today, and I'll move my car around to the back parking lot and go out that way. But that's all I'm going to do."

Mitch still looked doubtful. "Okay, but I will move your car to the back. Jennifer can make sure you are out of the building by four o'clock, and you have to swear that you will call me on my cell as soon as you get home tonight. Got it?"

"All right, I promise."

"Good," said Mitch. "And I'm going to check on something myself this afternoon."

"What?" Jennifer asked, with a note of concern.

"There's a director who regularly exercises in the company fitness center, and I've seen him carrying one of those black leather duffle bags like Terry described. I'm going to find out if there is anything special about that bag."

"Like what?" Terry inquired.

"Who knows? Probably nothing. But there has to be a reason that Parker reacted the way he did, referring to 'that *exact* bag.' And it's worth asking."

"Yes," Terry agreed, "definitely worth asking."

♦

The afternoon passed swiftly and before Terry knew it, Jennifer was urging him to shut down his laptop and go home. He was in the middle of typing an important email message, but Jennifer became so agitated that she threatened to pull the computer's plug from the wall. When Terry calmly reminded her that the laptop would simply continue to run on battery power, her face turned red and she gave him a furious look.

"You promised, Terry," she said through clenched teeth. He decided that it would be wise to comply.

Jennifer accompanied him to the back door. At her request, they took the stairway rather than the elevator, though Terry felt that this was unnecessary. As they proceeded down the stairs, he realized that he had not heard from Mitch since lunch.

"Did Mitch get to talk to that director this afternoon?" he asked.

"No, the guy was in meetings until four. Mitch was going to try to talk to him as soon as he could after that."

They reached the exit door which was located near a back corner of the building. Jennifer turned toward Terry and handed him the extra key to his car.

"Here is your key. Mitch parked it straight out from this door, three rows back. Remember that you promised to call him as soon as you get home."

"I will." Terry looked into Jennifer's face, and realized that she was genuinely worried. He thought of Angela, and wondered if he should have stayed home today after all, but quickly dismissed it from his mind. He smiled and said, "I'll give you a call too, if you want."

She smiled back at him and looked a little less apprehensive. "Thanks, that would be good." As he walked out the door, she added, "I'll be praying for you, Terry." In that moment he realized that he was thankful for the extra prayers.

It seemed as though the drive home would be completely uneventful. The rush hour traffic was not yet in full swing, and as Terry exited the freeway near home he began to think that everyone's worries had been unfounded. He turned onto the local highway and proceeded to a four way stop. Enjoying a worship music CD, he thought about meeting Josh later in the evening, and whether the agent would have any new information about Parker or al-Masri.

And then his heart leaped into his throat.

Before he could react, a light blue sedan swerved crazily toward him while driving through the intersection from the opposite direction. The impact crunched the front bumper of his car, jolting him in his seat. He heard glass from the headlamps tinkling on the pavement. Looking out the front window, he saw the driver in the sedan – a man with a dark complexion and waves of black hair – holding a hand to his forehead.

Stunned, Terry climbed out of his own vehicle and walked toward the other car.

♦

Mitch knocked lightly on the office door, and the director looked up from behind his desk. He was a thin man with gray hair and a bald spot, wearing narrow-rimmed glasses that rested too far down his long nose. He smiled. "Hello, what can I do for you?"

Mitch stepped into the office and held out a hand of greeting. "Hi, I'm Mitch Hughes. I don't think we've met before."

"I'm Tom Maddox," said the director as Mitch shook his hand.

"This may be a strange question, Mr. Maddox, but I've seen you down in the fitness center a couple of times and noticed that you have a nice looking duffle bag with the company logo on it."

"Oh," Mr. Maddox reached behind his desk and lifted up a black leather bag. "You mean this?"

"Yes, that's the one. I was just wondering if you ordered that from the company catalog, and how much you paid for it."

"Oh, you can't get this bag from the company catalog." Mr. Maddox smiled as he surveyed the nicely embroidered logo.

"You can't?" Mitch asked with heightened interest.

"No, the duffle bags sold in the company stores are not this nicely made." He turned the black bag around, so that the logo was facing Mitch, and set it down in front of him on the desk. Mitch looked closer, and noticed that there were words stitched into the bag below the picture.

"Carrying the Weight" Award #7
presented to Tom Maddox
by Ned Parker, CFO
August 24, 2005

Mitch read the inscription twice before it's meaning began to take full shape in his mind.

"It's Ned Parker's personal recognition award," Mr. Maddox explained. "Or at least it was. There were maybe only fifteen of them that he gave out over the years. It sure is hard to believe that he's dead. Why just a few weeks ago I was in Panama City talking with Ned…"

The sound of the director's voice faded as Mitch heard his own heart beating loudly in his ears. His mind reeled under the weight of the discovery. Terry had actually provided eyewitness testimony to the FBI that directly linked the terrorist bombing in Louisville to the highest levels of management at Kellor Computing. *And not one of us realized it!* He began to back out of the office, reaching for his cell phone.

"Thank you Mr. Maddox," he interrupted the director's rambling. "I just remembered I have to make an important call." He stopped outside the office door and selected a number. The phone rang several times, and Mitch cursed in frustration as he heard Terry's recorded voice instructing him to leave a message. He spoke urgently into the phone, "Terry! Call me back as soon as you get this!"

♦

Terry peered through the passenger window of the blue sedan. "Are you alright?" he called through the glass. The driver was an average sized man, and Terry noticed a scar below his right eye. He blinked back at Terry, dazed, and then looked down at his hands as if checking for blood. Terry was about to try the door when he heard tires squealing behind him. He whirled around to face the sound, his muscles tensing. A familiar maroon pickup truck slid to a halt not twenty feet away.

"Oh, God, no," Terry prayed under his breath. His mind did not want to believe that it was the same truck, until his eyes observed a bald man with a goatee and dark eyebrows jumping down from the driver's seat. The muscular man easily stood over six feet tall and wore a snarling grin on his face. A second man climbed out of the passenger's door on the other side of the truck.

Before Terry could take a single fleeing step, an arm closed around his neck from behind and he realized with a shock that it was the driver of the sedan. Terry instinctively tried to twist around, preparing to fight back with all his strength. But suddenly he felt the cold steel of a gun barrel pressed against his right temple, and heard an Arab sounding voice speak threateningly just an inch from his ear.

"You can die now, or come with us. Your choice."

Terry stopped resisting and looked for anyone who might be close enough to help him. Across the intersection, another car had stopped and a woman was looking at him from the driver's seat with a terrified expression. Two men were standing near their vehicles at the gas station on the corner. They craned their necks, watching, but made no move from where they stood. Terry peered at them, longing, praying for them to run to his aid.

"Good choice," the voice said in his ear. Terry glimpsed the bald man at his side and a dirty rag was pressed violently over his face. He struggled again, panicking, forgetting the gun. A fist pounded into his stomach, and he cried out into the rag. Then gasping for breath, his nostrils and throat burned and his entire body swam to the edge of darkness. Indistinguishable sounds reached his ears as if through a tunnel, and all went black.

Chapter 23

Jennifer was working at her cubicle when Mitch appeared and quickly recounted his conversation with Mr. Maddox. He concluded with the fact that Terry was not answering his cell phone. Jennifer felt a rush of concern.

"He should have been home by now, Mitch. He promised he would call us. Do you think we should call Angela?"

"No. I think we should go over there."

"Just show up at their house?"

"Yes. If Terry is there, we can tell him about the duffle bag and figure out what to do next. If he is not there, we will have to tell Angela. And we can provide information to the police so they will start looking for him right away."

Jennifer admired Mitch's calm demeanor. She felt like her insides were tied in knots. "Okay." She shut down her computer. "I'll follow you over there." As Mitch walked away from her cubicle, she called after him, "Try him on his cell phone again!"

◆

Josh settled himself into a chair at his departing terminal. The security line was shorter than he had anticipated, and he now had an hour to wait before boarding the plane. He dialed a number on his cell phone and waited for his unit chief to answer.

"Seeley," came the gruff voice.

"Hey, it's Josh."

"What have you got, Kepler?"

"Nothing new on Parker's death. Al-Masri's disappearance definitely makes him a suspect, but there's nothing new on him either. Our CIA contact in Europe hasn't found anyone who knows his whereabouts, even going by his middle name – Ibrahim. Apparently no one in France has seen him yet."

"Or if they have," grumbled Seeley, "they aren't telling. Al-Masri grew up there. I'm sure he would have a thousand places to hide and friends that would help him."

"Something about it doesn't feel right. Why did he drive all the way to Atlanta to catch a plane?"

"Atlanta is a hub. He probably had to connect through there anyways. Depending on flight availability it may have been quicker to drive the first leg."

"Yeah, maybe."

"You think he met someone there?"

"I don't know, but I'd sure like to go to Atlanta and poke around a little."

"So, go ahead."

"I can't. I'm about to get on a plane for Louisville."

"Louisville?" Seeley sounded surprised. "New lead to follow?"

"You could say that. I called Terry Whitman yesterday after I talked to you, to tell him about Parker. It turns out that someone is following Terry home from work."

"How does he know it wasn't just someone that lives near him?"

"Well," Josh replied, "he pulled into a gas station, and the guy just parked his truck and waited. So Terry confronted him, told him to stop following him, and the guy drove off."

"Hmm, a little suspicious."

"Yeah, the local police probably won't look into something like that, but I'm starting to worry that Whitman really is in danger. There's just too much going on around him lately. I can't figure it yet, but somewhere there's a connection between the terrorist bombing in Louisville, Parker's murder in Panama City, and the burglars that tried to kill Whitman instead of burglarizing. I'm going to Louisville to keep an eye on Terry and see what else might turn up."

"Alright," Seeley agreed. "Are the locals investigating the terrorist angle of Parker's death?"

"No," Josh laughed dryly, "they just looked at me funny when I tried to explain it to them."

Seeley sighed. "That's not surprising. I doubt I could convince anyone here to let me send an agent to investigate that angle either. At this point we are still guessing."

"Speaking of which," Josh changed the subject, "do you have any information on my employment status?"

"No, and I have stopped asking for the moment. Everyone here is extremely busy, Kepler. It may take weeks for them to proceed through the red tape and bring you back to work."

"They can't just let me sit for no good reason!"

"Kepler, if your guess about the Whitman case turns out to be right, then you are exceedingly more useful now while you are suspended. At least you are still getting a paycheck. Just go with it and consider it good planning by that God of yours."

Josh laughed out loud. "For someone who insists that they don't believe in God, you seem to think about him more often than most."

"Gotta go, Kepler," Seeley growled. "Keep me posted."

"Okay, chief."

♦

Jennifer watched Mitch ring the Whitman's doorbell, and they waited for someone to answer. When the door finally opened, it was Angela who greeted them with a surprised smile. "Well, hello there!

What are you guys doing here?"

"Is Terry here?" Jennifer asked, trying her best to sound calm. Angela's smile disappeared.

"No, he's been getting home later and later these days. What's wrong?"

Jennifer looked at Mitch, not knowing what to say.

"Can we come in for a minute?" Mitch asked.

"Of course." Angela led them into the house and looked at them with a worried expression. Jennifer could hear the children playing somewhere in the basement.

"Did you know," Mitch began, "that Terry was followed home last night?"

"Yes, he told me."

"Well, we convinced him to leave an hour early today so that he could avoid any more trouble. He should have been here by now, and he is not answering his cell phone."

Angela forced a worried smile and said, "He probably stopped at the store for something."

"I don't think so." Mitch sighed heavily. "There's more that I need to tell you, Angela. We should sit down."

Mitch proceeded to tell Angela about his conversation with the director at work, and the obvious implications of Terry spotting the duffle bag in the hands of a terrorist. He expressed his concern that someone might want to keep Terry from telling anyone else about what he saw.

Angela responded with urgency, "We have to call the police."

"Let me do that," Mitch said as he stood to his feet. "I will need to tell them everything."

As Mitch talked with the police, Jennifer sat on the couch next to Angela and observed her initial emotion give way to a look of forced composure. She reached out and took Angela's hand. "Remember what God told me to tell Terry on Sunday?"

Angela looked at her and smiled weakly. "Yes," she nodded. "That God will take care of him."

Jennifer fought back tears. "I guess that was as much for us as it was for him, wasn't it?" The two women embraced, saying nothing more.

When Mitch hung up the phone, he looked pale.

"What is it?" Angela asked.

"There were witnesses who saw Terry kidnapped near the freeway exit." Angela covered her mouth with her hands and stifled a cry. Jennifer put a hand on her shoulder as Mitch continued, "They are looking for a maroon pickup and a blue sedan, as well as Terry's car, which was also taken. They told us to stay here and they would send someone over within the hour to talk to us."

The phone rang, and Angela jumped from the couch to answer it. "Hello? Terry?" She listened to the response. "No, he isn't here right now. Who is this?" When Angela heard the name, she nearly shouted, "Agent Kepler! They've got Terry!"

In a tumbled frenzy of words, Angela described the events of Terry's disappearance. She tried to explain the significance of the duffle bag, but in her haste she became confused about the details of Mitch's conversation with the director. Exasperated, she held out the phone to Mitch. "Here! Tell him!"

Mitch calmly filled in the details for the FBI agent, and then listened to the reply. He shook his head and spoke into the phone. "The police told us to wait here, that they would be coming over to talk to us." He paused again, and then turned to Angela, "He says that you can't stay here right now."

"What?" Angela responded in surprise. "What if Terry comes home, or tries to call?"

"It's too dangerous," Mitch answered. "They might try to take you too. Terry will call you on your cell phone if he can. Is there someone that you and the kids can stay with tonight?"

"Yes, the Givens."

Mitch spoke back into the phone, "Agent Kepler, we'll get them over to their friends' house right away."

♦

Josh drove the rental car through the cold night, following the directions that Mr. Givens provided him after his plane had landed in Louisville. It was 10:45 p.m. The freeway leading out of the city was nearly deserted, and Josh occupied his thoughts with the events of the past few days.

Of course he had called Seeley immediately after talking to Angela and Mitch, to inform the unit chief of Terry's abduction. He had asked Seeley to assign an agent to the case in Atlanta. Josh could not say why, but something inside was telling him that al-Masri had visited Atlanta for a reason. *Are you really back in France, al-Masri? Or are you still here, trying to clean up your mess?*

Once Seeley understood that the duffle bag now linked Ned Parker to a terrorist bombing, he agreed that he could legitimately assign an agent to help with the case. But he hesitated to do so. Josh smiled as he remembered his boss' gruff response.

"The moment I officially activate this case, it will be assigned to a Homeland Security agent, and you will have to come home, Kepler. Is that what you want?"

"No," Josh had responded. "I won't go home, not until Whitman is safe." He felt that he owed Terry that much, for not recognizing the duffle bag clue in time to prevent his kidnapping.

Seeley sighed and cursed under his breath. "I've asked several times that they reinstate you, Kepler, but they won't do it. They've got to follow their inane process." He cursed again, louder this time. "There are not nearly enough agents for the workload as it is! I'm not even sure this case would become a priority."

Seeley paused for a moment in contemplation. When he spoke again, Josh was surprised by what he heard. "I can divert an agent for two days, Kepler. I won't tell him what case he's working on. All he needs to know is that al-Masri is a suspect. I'll have him positively verify whether al-Masri flew out of Atlanta, and whether he contacted anyone there before he left. Will that do?"

Josh had jumped at the offer, and Seeley straight away gave him a word of warning. "Kepler, if you crack this case, I think we'll be alright. But if something goes wrong, it will be both our jobs. You realize that?"

"Yes, sir. Whitman's life is hanging in the balance now. It's worth the risk."

Seeley's final words still rang in Josh's ears. "If your hunch is right, as they usually are, then there are probably multiple lives hanging in the balance on this one, Kepler. Keep that in mind."

As Josh parked the car in the Givens' drive, he said a silent prayer for Terry. He then walked to the front door and rang the doorbell, asking God to give him the right words for Terry's loved ones.

The door opened and Josh was greeted by a tall man, not quite as large as himself, with thick black hair and a warm smile.

"Hello," the man said, "I'm Roger Givens."

"Josh Kepler."

Mr. Givens was eager to welcome him. "Please come in. We've been waiting for you."

Josh followed Roger into the living room, savoring the warmth of the fireplace and the smell of fresh-brewed coffee. He was introduced to Roger's wife, Pam, who offered to take his coat, and then to Terry's wife, Angela, and their friend, Jennifer. Josh was surprised at the atmosphere in the house. Rather than being greeted with the expected barrage of fearful questions, these people demonstrated a peaceful composure that was unusual under the circumstances. Pam brought him a cup of hot coffee and offered him a chair.

As he sat down, Angela asked simply, "What do we need to do, Agent Kepler?"

"Well," Josh began slowly, "I usually tell people in these types of situations that it is important to remain calm, and not dwell on worst-case scenarios." He looked around the room at the faces. "But it seems that you don't need that advice just yet." He smiled and took a sip of coffee. "I also tell people that prayer is always good."

Angela looked knowingly at Pam. "We've been doing a lot of

that tonight already."

"That's good to hear," Josh smiled at them. "Did the police discover anything new this evening?"

"No," Roger answered. "They are still looking for the vehicles. They were here earlier, and showed us sketches of the abductors, but none of us recognized them."

Josh looked at Roger with interest. "Where is Mr. Hughes? Did he get to see the sketches?"

Jennifer's expression turned momentarily sad, "Mitch left a couple hours ago. He did see the pictures though, before he left."

"Was he sure that James al-Masri wasn't one of them?"

Jennifer looked puzzled. "I don't think Mitch ever met al-Masri, but I thought Terry said that he flew back to France last week. Do you think that al-Masri is the one who took Terry?"

"I don't know yet. The evidence thus far suggests that he went to France a week ago. We are trying hard to find him, but until we do I'm not ruling anything out. He could have easily returned to the country under a different name by now, and it still may be possible that he never left. Wherever al-Masri is hiding, I have a feeling that he is deeply involved in whatever is going on."

Roger cleared his throat and spoke softly, "And what exactly do you think is going on, Agent Kepler?"

Josh smiled at Roger. "Please, call me Josh." He shifted in his chair and took another sip of coffee. "The duffle bag links the terrorist bombing of the toy store with the highest levels of management at Kellor Computing. Simply put, that bag originated with Ned Parker and ended up in the hands of a terrorist suicide bomber. Since Parker is dead, I'm betting that he was not knowingly involved with terrorists. My guess is that when Terry mentioned to Parker seeing the bag in the hands of the terrorist, Parker probably confronted someone about it. That confrontation resulted in his own death, as well as an attempt to stop Terry from telling anyone else."

Jennifer nodded. "That's pretty much what Mitch and I thought. Al-Masri is definitely the prime suspect in that scenario."

Angela had been listening intently to the conversation, maintaining a calm expression, though her hands were clenched tightly in her lap. "But if he really is in France," she said, "then he can't be responsible for kidnapping Terry, can he?"

"Not directly," Josh answered. "My guess is that one or more people within Kellor were giving money or supplies to a terrorist cell. What I don't know is whether the Kellor person was simply a supplier, or more directly involved in the terrorist activities. It could even be that they are one of the leaders or organizers of the cell. If that person is al-Masri, it would have been easy for him to leave instructions to others before leaving the country."

"So what can we do next," Angela asked, "to find Terry."

"Nothing more tonight," Josh answered. "First thing tomorrow I will go to the police and see what leads they have. I will be able to make some decisions from there." Josh looked at Angela, "Who knows that you are staying here?"

"Only ourselves and some extended family."

"Good. You need to keep a low profile here for the time being. And I will need a key to your house, and directions to get there."

Angela reached for her purse. "Why? Do you really think someone will do something to our house?"

"It's unlikely, but there's no way to be sure. Can you check your answering machine remotely?"

"No," Angela responded as she handed him the key.

"Then I will stop by the house a couple of times a day to check your messages. You will want to keep your cell phone charged and with you at all times."

Josh exchanged cell phone numbers with all of them, discussed a few more of their concerns, and left. Driving to his hotel, the clock on the dash showed 12:15 a.m. He sighed. *Not much time for sleep these days.*

Chapter 24

Terry's mind approached the first levels of groggy thought. The earliest perceptions were auditory. A droning sound, and voices echoing as if from the other end of a long hall. The sounds remained unfocused and unintelligible, part of a dream.

With the passing of time, Terry discerned that he was moving, perhaps floating. The droning steadily increased in volume, but the voices ceased. Slowly he became aware of something else. Pain. A sharp sting in his wrists. A dull ache in his head and back. Terry's brain struggled to free itself from a thick fog. He tried to move his arms and found that he couldn't. The drone was now louder in his right ear, and Terry realized that the right side of his face was pressed against a hard surface. It occurred to him that he must be lying on the floor, and it seemed as if the floor was in motion.

Terry slowly opened his eyes, and was greeted by a blurry darkness. He blinked and strained to focus his sight, to no avail. Was it nighttime? He couldn't be sure, and his brain seemed to be operating in slow motion. His face itched from the vibration in the floor, and Terry cautiously tried to turn over on his back. Pain shot through his wrists and shoulders and head, bringing a measure of clarity back to his mind. His hands were bound tightly behind him. Terry groaned as he made an effort to look up from the floor. The voices suddenly returned, and this time Terry recognized that they were not speaking English. He thought it sounded Arabic, but couldn't be sure.

In an instant the dark outline of a man's shoulders loomed above him. Terry opened his mouth to cry out, and felt another cloth pressed roughly over his face. He held his breath and strained mightily with his hands against whatever bound them. He kicked his feet upwards, and realized to his dismay that they were also securely bound. There was little he could do except hold his breath long enough to think a desperate prayer.

God, please help me! Are you going to let them kill me? Jesus, take care of Angela and the children. Please! Help me!!

Terry's lungs ran out of oxygen. Involuntarily gasping for breath, his nose and throat burned, and his eyes watered. Strong hands suddenly clamped his legs down, and the cloth was pressed so tightly against his face that he wondered if his nose would break. *Oh, God!! Please!!* His head spun wildly and he felt the floor lurch beneath him as consciousness fled.

◆

Josh spent the early part of Friday morning at the local police station, going over the police reports of Terry's abduction, and speaking with the officers that had done the initial investigation. He made copies of the three composite sketches of the abductors, frustrated that al-Masri's picture was not among them. After two hours of querying the FBI Criminal Database, Josh found no matches.

During the course of the morning, the police located two of the three vehicles they were looking for. The maroon pickup truck and blue sedan were discovered in a narrow alley behind a shopping strip. Josh asked for the license plate information of the vehicles as soon as they were found. When the police chief informed him that the sedan had Atlanta plates, Josh finally had evidence that corroborated his theory that al-Masri was somehow involved. The pickup truck had local plates, and not surprisingly both vehicles turned out to be stolen.

Early in the afternoon Josh received a call on his cell phone. He looked at the number and saw that it was Seeley.

"Hello, chief."

"Anything new in Louisville, Kepler?" the chief asked in his usual gruff voice.

"Yes, as a matter of fact. The sedan that was used in the kidnapping was stolen in Atlanta on Saturday. The eyewitness descriptions here don't look like al-Masri, but I know he is involved in this."

"Don't be too hasty, Kepler. I just got off the phone with our agent in Atlanta. He looked at airport security tapes, comparing them to photos of al-Masri."

"And?"

"Al-Masri got on that plane to France, Kepler."

Josh didn't want to believe it. "Maybe it was someone that looked like him."

"Only if it was his twin brother," retorted Seeley. "Besides it was al-Masri's signature on the credit card bill for the rental car, which he returned at the airport ninety minutes before his flight. The rental car agent recognized a photo of al-Masri."

"Were there any other charges on his credit cards?"

"No, we checked all of his known cards, and the rental car was the last recorded charge. There were no transactions of significance before that, other than the charge for the flight itself."

"No cash withdrawals?"

"None. Face it, Kepler, al-Masri is not the one you need to be looking for."

Josh ignored Seeley's conclusion. "Who did he contact in Atlanta?"

"No one that we can determine."

"There has to be someone, chief. He rented the car Wednesday morning, right?"

"Yeah."

"It doesn't take that long to get to Atlanta. Al-Masri had to spend the night there before going to the airport on Thursday morning. I don't think a vice president of Kellor Computing Group would sleep in his car on the side of the road, and there is no record of a charge for a hotel."

"He could have paid cash for one night in a hotel."

"No, he stayed with someone in Atlanta." Josh was sure of it. "It's too much of a coincidence that al-Masri spent Wednesday night in Atlanta, and two days later a car is stolen there and shows up in Louisville to kidnap Terry. If al-Masri left the country, then he gave orders to someone else before he left. We've got to find out who he made contact with, chief."

"I'll keep our guy looking for another day," Seeley consented, "but without any leads it's unlikely that he'll uncover anything."

"Do you know if there has been any sighting of al-Masri in France yet," Josh queried, and then added sarcastically, "or anywhere else in the known world?"

"No, but I have asked the CIA to get me any information on bank or credit card transactions that al-Masri might have made in Europe in the last week. I should have an answer on that by tomorrow. What are your next steps, Kepler?"

"Well, I don't have a good feel for whether Terry's abductors are still in town or not. They ditched the cars very quickly, in a well-hidden location, and one of them was a local vehicle. That suggests that at least one of the kidnappers may have been living around here. The suicide bombing here also suggests a locally operated cell, but that's just a guess. There are no leads other than the eyewitness sketches that the police got. I'm thinking about allowing Angela to make a plea on local television, to see if we can find anyone else that may have seen something."

"Angela? Is that Whitman's wife?"

"Yeah, sorry. She wants to go on TV and make a plea for Terry's release. We could show the pictures at the same time and ask folks to call in with any information. The local news stations started carrying the story today, I'm sure they would be willing."

"Alright, are you going to mention the duffle bag?"

"I don't think so." Josh had already decided against it.

"You might want to," Seeley suggested. "If you are correct that they took Terry to keep him from talking about the bag, then they would know they got to him too late, and the damage is already done. It might throw a wrench in whatever they are planning next."

"Yes, and then they would kill him for sure, wouldn't they?"

"Maybe."

"Right now they don't know who he has told about the bag. They may want to question him on that and figure out exactly what he knows, and who he talked to. That could keep Terry alive for a couple more days."

"Maybe. And then again, this may not even be what we think it is, Kepler."

Josh sighed. "I hope that's the case, chief. If Whitman really is in the hands of a terrorist cell, their best move would be to get rid of him quickly."

"Let's not think about that yet," Seeley's voice was quiet. "Just stay with it and keep me informed."

◆

Angela waited anxiously inside a small office in the county courthouse building. In a few minutes she would proceed through the door and down the main hallway to the lobby and read her statement. Members of the press were setting up cameras and microphones in preparation. Roger and Pam sat quietly with her as they waited. They had insisted on driving her to the courthouse, leaving their children with the Lydons.

Angela thought of her own children, now on their way to Illinois with her parents where they would be safe. Josh had tried to persuade her that they would all be safer if they went away for a while, but she had insisted on remaining in town until Terry was found. Josh grudgingly agreed, but only if she continued to stay with the Givens and not venture out alone. Now Angela second-guessed her own stubbornness. The reality of being without both Terry and the children pierced her heart with sorrow and loneliness. Inwardly, she pleaded with God for strength to bear the weight of it.

There was a soft knock on the door, which then opened enough for Josh to look into the room. "Angela, it's time. Are you sure you want to do this? The police chief will gladly make a statement without your part."

Angela stood resolutely and walked through the door. Roger and Pam followed. The police chief was ready to accompany them.

"I'll be waiting here when you are done," Josh said.

Angela turned and gave him a questioning look. "You aren't coming?"

"No. The police agree that it's better for us to keep the FBI presence at a low profile for now." He put a reassuring hand on her shoulder. "You will do fine, Angela. I will be praying for you."

Angela smiled. "Thank you."

She turned and looked at her friends, drawing strength from their presence, and then preceded them down the wide hallway to the lobby. As soon as she entered the spacious room, cameras began to flash and click feverishly, stopping her in her tracks until the police chief gently took her arm and directed her to stand beside a small podium. Roger and Pam stood behind her, and the chief stepped up to the podium microphone. As the cameras rolled, he addressed the small group of people.

"Yesterday at approximately 4:30 in the afternoon, Mr. Terrence Whitman – age thirty-four – was forcibly abducted at the intersection of Highway fifty-three and Blue Lake Road. Witnesses at the scene provided descriptions of the three men who committed this crime." He held up the pictures one at a time and allowed the video cameras to capture the images. "We will be providing copies of these sketches to the press, as well as photographs of Mr. Whitman." The chief paused as he placed the pictures back into a folder.

"In the last twenty-four hours we have found the vehicles that were driven by the suspects. One of them was stolen here in Louisville, and the other was stolen a week ago in Atlanta, Georgia. At this time we have no information on the whereabouts of the suspects or Mr. Whitman. No one has contacted us with regard to his condition, or to request a ransom, or to make any other demands. We do not have a motive for this crime. We are asking anyone who might have information on the identity or the whereabouts of these three men, or the whereabouts of Mr. Whitman, to please call our anonymous tip hotline at the number displayed on your TV screen."

The chief gathered his papers from the podium. "And now Mrs. Whitman would like to make a statement. I would ask that you please respect her wishes and wait to direct any questions to myself after her statement is finished."

As Angela moved behind the podium and unfolded the paper to read her statement, the small audience remained respectfully quiet, with the exception of a few clicking cameras. Angela's heart beat fast, and she silently prayed that the right people were listening.

"I come before you today," she began, "as a wife and a mother in turmoil. I don't have a lot of words to say. I simply want to make a plea on behalf of myself, my three young children, and our extended family and dear friends. To everyone who can hear my voice," she paused and looked into one of the television cameras, "if you know *anything* about the men in the pictures, no matter how insignificant the information may seem, please call the hotline. Do the right thing. Dare to get involved." Angela looked down at her written statement. "And if you don't have any information to give, please offer your prayers with me for Terry's safe return. Prayer does make a difference." She looked back into the camera and continued.

"And to those who have taken my husband," her voice trembled with emotion, "if it's money you want, I would sell everything I own..." she stopped and put her hand over her mouth, willing back the tears, "...in exchange for Terry's life." She paused again, and took a deep breath. "But I implore you – I urge you – to do the right thing. Let him go!" Though her eyes welled over with tears, her heart burned with intensity as she looked through the camera and into thousands of homes across the community.

Angela then turned and walked away from the podium. Roger and Pam followed her from the lobby as the police chief began to answer questions from the reporters. Pam placed a hand on her shoulder as they passed through the double doors into the hallway. "You were wonderful, Angela."

Before she could answer, she noticed Josh approaching them with an excited grin on his face.

"That was incredible, Angela. And we've already got a good tip on the hotline."

Angela felt hope rise up within her. "What is it?"

"Someone recognized one of the suspects and gave us an address. I'm going over there right away to check it out. You all should go home and wait for me to call."

Angela nodded. "Please be careful, Josh."

"Don't worry. I'll have plenty of backup on this one."

Chapter 25

Josh slowed his vehicle to a stop in front of the two-story brick apartment building, directly behind a pair of police cars that had already arrived. The Heartland Community Apartments offered some of the most affordable living in the city, and the development was a virtual melting pot of immigrant cultures. Josh removed the key from the ignition and surveyed the scene as he climbed out of the rental. It was almost dark, and plenty cold enough to see his breath. Only a fading glow remained in the sky to the west, visible through the bare branches of the tall oak trees lining the street. The brighter stars were already twinkling in the crisp evening air. He shivered.

A fourth patrol car stopped on the other side of the street, as an officer approached Josh. Captain Ogleby was in charge of the local investigation.

"You ready for this, Agent Kepler?"

"Sure, which one is it?"

"Lower right hand apartment. What do you think the chances are that Whitman is in there?"

"Slim." Josh surveyed the apartment building in the diminishing light. A sidewalk ran from the street to the middle of the building, and two steps led to a window-less double door. Yellow light shone from behind the curtains of three of the four dwellings. The upper left apartment appeared dark and unoccupied. "How are the entrances to the apartments laid out?"

"One stairway to a second floor landing," the captain answered. "The doors leading into the upper apartments are on either side of the landing. The entrance to the lower right is at the back, directly under the staircase."

"Who is the renter?"

"Ziyad Hendawi, an immigrant from Iraq. Been here almost three years. No rap sheet."

Josh rubbed his jaw in thought. The caller to the hotline had claimed to have seen one of the suspects – an Arab man with a scar on his face – coming and going from this apartment several times over the last month, but doubted that he lived in the building. The caller had not seen evidence of anyone being held in the apartment against their will.

"Okay," Josh sighed, "there's really nothing to do at this point but knock on the door and ask Mr. Hendawi some questions, right?"

"That's what I was intending."

Josh nodded to Captain Ogleby and pulled the zipper of his jacket closer to his neck.

The captain motioned to his men, and four officers approached the front of the building. When they reached the doors, two remained on the front steps and held the doors open, while the other two proceeded inside. Josh waited, aware of the cold December breeze rustling through the branches above his head. His eyes were trained on the front of the building, the doors, the lighted windows.

Without warning, the night air was pierced by a sharp, crackling sound from within the building. *Machine gun fire!* Instinctively Josh went into a crouched position, and his own gun found its way into his hand without need of conscious thought. The machine gun was answered by multiple shots from a hand gun in rapid succession, and the two officers at the front rushed inside. A door slammed and the machine gun fire stopped, replaced by shouts of "Officer down! Officer down!" The windows on the lower right went dark.

Josh noticed Captain Ogleby and his partner stand and take a few crouching steps toward the building, guns drawn. He side-stepped to the back of his rented sedan, extending his arms and resting his elbows on the trunk of the car, aiming at the front windows, providing cover. The double doors burst open, and two officers came through, carrying a third between them. In his peripheral vision, Josh saw the captain and his partner run across the lawn, and he simultaneously noticed a movement at the window. The curtain had been drawn back ever so slightly.

"WINDOW!"

Josh's shout rent the air only a second before the earsplitting sound of renewed machine gun fire. He felt his gun recoil in his hands with each shot, and the explosions pounded his ears. He aimed slightly behind the visible fireworks from the machine gun barrel until his own gun went silent, emptied. Shots continued to come from the officers in the yard, and Josh loaded a fresh clip without taking his eyes from the window. He aimed, finger on the trigger. But the shooting had ceased as suddenly as it began, and the window was silent. Curtains flapped gently as the breeze flowed through the frame, now devoid of glass.

An agonizing moan came from the yard, and Josh finally allowed himself a glance away from the dark window. Now there were two officers down, and a third was limping badly toward the street, helped by his captain. One of the wounded officers writhed in pain as he was dragged toward the street, while the other did not move at all.

Josh heard the captain radio for help, while he kept his gun trained on the building. Questions raced through his mind. Why had they immediately started shooting? Were they hiding something inside? Someone? *Terry!* The thought went off in his head like a siren.

If Terry was inside, chances were good that he would not be allowed to get out alive. Unless all of his captors had been shot. He looked to his left. The officers were all safely behind their cars. Three of them were physically okay, but looked as if they were in shock. Their eyes were wide as they tried to make their wounded comrades comfortable. Only the captain was watching the house, gun drawn and in a similar position to Josh. What could they do? It would be foolish to charge the apartment at this moment. Backup was on its way. Josh returned his watchful gaze to the apartment and wondered at how quiet the street had become. The breeze rustled in the branches again, and he imagined that neighbors were hiding in silence, not wanting to be drawn into the deadly drama.

What if Terry *was* inside? What if someone was deciding at this very moment to end his life?

Josh took a breath and yelled, "Terry Whitman! This is Josh. If you can hear my voice, let me know you are in there."

Silence from the brick building. If Terry were there, would his captors let him speak? Maybe for their own safety's sake?

"Come on, Terry," Josh continued, "speak up if you are there. We don't want to come in shooting and accidentally kill an innocent hostage."

Still nothing. Josh looked over at Ogleby and spoke in a low tone. "There may be explosives in there. We have to get everyone else out of that building." The police captain's eyes widened a little, but he nodded his head, and Josh continued, "I'll go in, but I'll need someone with me for cover."

Just then a voice drifted through the air.

"Hello?" The voice was male, Hispanic. "Señor Josh, sir?" He sounded timid and shaken. Josh instantly turned back toward the building.

"Yes? Who is there?"

"Señor Alovar." The voice came from the upper right apartment, and Josh noticed a curtain being pulled back from one of the windows. "I see two hombres climb out of the back window. They are gone, Señor Josh, sir. They run fast, sir."

"Mr. Alovar," Josh responded, "do you know if there is anyone else still in the apartment?"

"I don' know, sir. I don' hear nada now."

"Okay, Mr. Alovar, thank you. Muchas gracias. I need you to bring your family out of the apartment now, Mr. Alovar. For your safety. Comprende?"

"Sí, señor."

"Bueno, Mr. Alovar," Josh spoke slowly and clearly. "Wait for me to come inside. When I knock on your door, then you can bring your family out with me. Do you understand?"

"Sí, señor."

Josh stood up from behind his vehicle. There were now shadows peering at him from the curtains of the lower left apartment as well. "And the same goes for anyone else in the building," he yelled. "When I knock on your door, you need to come out so you will be safe." Josh motioned to Ogleby, and they started toward the building. A young junior detective followed the captain. *God, don't let a bomb explode while we're in there.*

They ran, crouched, to the front doors and went through, guns aimed down the short hallway by the stairs. Josh took in the scene and observed no immediate threat. "Cover that door," he said to the captain as he bounded up the stairs to the landing. He knocked on Mr. Alovar's door and without waiting hurried to knock on the other door as well.

The first door opened and Josh watched a family of three hurry through. Mr. Alovar was short and thin, while his wife was short and round. Their son looked to be about twelve years old. Fear showed on their faces, in their eyes. Mr. Alovar closed the door as Josh pounded again on the door across the landing. "Last chance to come out!" He only waited another second, and then he led the Alovar family quickly down the stairs. "Wait here at the door, he instructed."

Josh proceeded to the door on the bottom left, knocked, and repeated his call. "Please come out so you will be safe." He kept his weapon aimed at the door on the right, and noticed that a handful of bullets had ripped into the wood during the first gun battle. Captain Ogleby had moved past the bottom of the stairs and was crouched on one knee, arms extended, both hands wrapped around the butt of his pistol.

"Come on!" Josh pounded impatiently on the door again. He knew there were people inside, probably scared to death and quite possibly not able to speak English. *Likely fearful of the police, considering the current social climate.*

Josh's thoughts were stopped cold by the last thing he expected to hear. A female voice, likely Arab, shrill and shaking, emanating from the door on the right. "Please! Please!" Josh spun around and dropped to one knee, facing the bullet-ridden door with his finger now on the trigger, his breathing all but stopped.

"Please!" the desperate voice continued. "Don't shoot! He's dead. He's shot."

The door knob turned and the latch clicked free. Josh felt adrenaline surge into every muscle in his body, sharpening his senses. "STOP! Do not open the door!"

"Pleeeeeease!" the voice was a wail. Through an inch-wide opening, a hand slowly appeared from behind the door. Small, thin fingers, shaking. "Please! He's dead!"

"Ma'am! Step back from the door!" Josh demanded. "Step back inside!"

There was a muffled whimper, and the hand retreated. Looking sideways towards the front door, Josh motioned for Ogleby to go. "Get those people to the street, and then get back here." He waited for a few seconds and the captain returned again with the young officer.

"Ma'am," Josh asked through the door, "are you standing away from the door?"

"Yes." The voice was quieter now, more controlled.

"Are you alone in the house?"

Hesitation, then, "Yes, he's dead."

"Okay. We are coming in now." Josh stepped to the side of the apartment door and pushed it open, being careful not to step into the open doorway. No gun shots. He cautiously stepped into the dark apartment, senses on full alert. The captain followed.

Flipping a light switch, Josh quickly surveyed the small apartment's kitchen and living room. He felt the cold outside air, as the curtains still flapped in the breeze blowing through the shot-out front window. A male body lay on the blood-stained floor below the window. Beside him lay the machine gun, now harmlessly silent, with empty shell casings littering the floor. A dozen small and medium sized cardboard boxes sat against the wall next to the window. Josh warily eyed a dark hallway leading from the living room to the rest of the apartment. Ogleby moved quickly to the body, followed closely by the junior detective, and Josh turned his eyes to the woman standing by the refrigerator.

She was young, probably not more than eighteen. And beautiful, with long dark hair, dark skin, and dark eyes now bloodshot with tears. She wore a coat that obviously belonged to someone much taller, and she shivered as she thrust her hands into the pockets. Something twitched in Josh's mind, a warning signal sent to his brain from the recesses of his instincts. He lowered his gun a little, but his eyes bore into the woman.

"Could you please sit down, miss, and put your hands above your head."

She looked distraught, confused. "Please, I don't understand." She removed her hands from her pockets and raised them to shoulder height, but did not sit down.

The captain looked up. "This one's dead, Kepler, and look at this."

Josh didn't take his eyes off the woman. Something didn't feel right. He was uncomfortably aware of the dark hallway to his side. "What is it?"

"Most of these boxes are ammunition," Ogleby answered. "But a couple of them contain explosives."

Josh felt his heart beat faster. Explosives. This was it then. Not just a place where a kidnapper had visited on occasion. But an actual safe house for terrorists, perhaps the headquarters for a terrorist cell. This was a bigger jackpot than anyone could have expected. He spoke to the officers without looking their way. "You two need to secure the rest of the house, *now*."

At that moment the woman's eyes changed, became ice cold and strangely serene. She took a step away from the refrigerator and lowered her hands. Josh's gun came up in a flash, "Hey!"

She froze, and glared back at him.

"Stay where you are, and keep your hands where I can see them!" The warning signal in his brain now became a clear thought.

Don't let her move again. He saw her body go tense, as if she was readying to spring. "Please understand," Josh warned her, "that if you make any sudden moves I will shoot you."

The young detective stood to his feet by the window. "Hey, Kepler, take it eas–"

The girl's beautiful face twisted into a snarl and she plunged her hand into a coat pocket. Josh pulled the trigger twice before the motion was complete, and her head snapped back as the bullets passed through her brain. Blood splattered on the white kitchen appliances as she fell back and toppled a small table with a crash.

Ogleby lunged toward Josh, shouting, "What the–!" But he pulled up short, mouth gaping, as the woman's body hit the floor. Her coat came open, revealing a generous quantity of explosives attached to a belt around her waist. Her hand came out of her pocket last of all, and a small black detonator slid across the kitchen tiles.

Josh turned to look at the pale-faced police captain.

"This is not everyday police work, Ogleby," he said. "This is war. It's a war that has now come to the streets of your city. You'd be wise to learn the rules of engagement."

The junior detective looked like he might get sick. "But how did you know?" His voice trembled. "She was so young."

"Come on," Josh said forcefully, "we've got to secure this place. Now!"

♦

Much later that night, Josh climbed wearily into his hotel bed. Misery settled in around him as he pondered the evening's events. He tried to pray, but his thoughts raced away from him. He couldn't stop them. Couldn't control the feverish working of his mind. There had been no one else in the apartment. They had found dozens of boxes of ammunition and explosives, plus a small assortment of firearms. In that sense, it was a hugely successful operation. It would have taken several months, perhaps years of planning for a terrorist cell to accumulate that amount of explosive material. And now it was out of their vile hands. Add to that the tally of two terrorists killed, and you've got a very fortunate outcome.

But the enemy had scored as well. One police officer killed, another severely wounded. Two of the terrorists had fled the scene and promptly vanished. No information was found in the apartment to suggest Terry's whereabouts, and no live terrorists remained to question further. It was likely that Terry's captors already knew what had happened, and less likely that they would keep him alive for any length of time. In many respects it had been a botched raid. *No, not a raid*, Josh reminded himself. They had simply gone to question a possible acquaintance of one of the kidnappers. *And ran into the proverbial hornets' nest. You were caught off guard, Josh. Way off guard. How many mistakes are you going to make before it's over?* He felt depression crashing down on him in his weariness.

God, please be with Terry. Please help me get him back.

Chapter 26

Terry's eyes blinked slowly open and he took in his surroundings. He was lying in a soft bed made with white linens, looking up at a white ceiling. Slowly he raised himself to one elbow and surveyed the spacious room. The walls were painted a bright white, and free from any decoration. A massive wooden door occupied the center of the wall opposite the bed, framed beside and above by great square timbers. To his left hung the only window, arched and surrounded by a frame that matched the door's, but smaller. The window stood open, swung outward on metal hinges. A warm breeze carried the scent of flowers and the song of birds into the room. Against the other wall stood a rustic wooden table and chair, simple and unadorned. Upon the table, a blue ceramic pitcher and matching cup.

Terry sat up in wonder. He was still wearing the business casual clothes he had worn to work on Thursday. But they were wrinkled and dirty, and there was a tear in the left knee of his slacks. He reached down and rubbed his knee, feeling the pain. Just bruised. He looked at his wrists. They were almost raw at the back of his hands, red and oozing in places. Now they burned with pain, as if seeing the wounds made them real. Terry grimaced. *This can't be real.*

Memories began to return, slowly at first. He had been tied up, shoved to the floor. The floor of what? A vehicle? It had been dark. A cloth soaked in something had been clamped over his face. He shivered at the memory.

Another memory, a car had collided with his. He had almost made it home from work. There was a maroon pickup truck. A bald man with a goatee, and another with a scar on his cheek, grabbing him, threatening him, suffocating him.

Terry's mind suddenly cleared. *They've taken me!* "Oh, God, help me," he breathed. But who were they? Terrorists? Yes, it had to be terrorists. He had given the FBI a clear description of the suicide bomber, and now the terrorists had decided to shut him up. Terry's heart beat faster as his mind began to work. He needed to get out of here, get to a phone and call Josh. He climbed out of the bed, and noticed that his shoes were still on his feet. He took a step toward the door and froze at the sudden sound of voices outside the window.

"Are you sure you should have brought him here?" The male voice sounded youthful and eager.

"Yes, yes." A second man sounded older than the first, maybe middle aged, and spoke with a calm and gentle quality. "But he won't stay for long, not more than a few minutes I should guess."

The voices drew near the room, and Terry's nerves nearly came undone. They were going to move him again, and that meant that they would likely try to drug him again. *God, what should I do? Please–*

"Really?" the youthful voice continued the conversation. "What are you going to tell him?"

"I'm not sure," answered the elder. "Hopefully something he needs to hear."

Terry's mind stalled. He had been ready to fling himself at the door and fight his way through whoever opened it. But the voices did not sound like terrorists. Their very tones seemed to carry with them a feeling of peace.

A knock sounded at the door. Why would his captors knock? Terry hesitated, still wary. Another knock, and finally he spoke.

"What do you want?" It wasn't exactly a warm response, but he was more than a little on guard. The door swung silently inward and two men stepped through. They were dressed in simple white robes. The younger came first. He was tall and lean, with jet black hair that fell in waves to his shoulders. His eyes virtually shone a bright blue, and were filled with life and wonder. The older man came after, and closed the door behind them. Shorter than the younger, his black hair was also shoulder length, and streaked with gray.

Stepping forward, the elder's blue-gray eyes sparkled as he offered a kindly smile. "Hello, Terry."

"Why have you brought me here?" Terry tried to sound forceful.

The man surveyed him thoughtfully. His skin was bronze and smooth like the younger's, but with the addition of tiny lines around his eyes. He answered Terry's question with a question. "You prayed for help, didn't you?"

Terry felt a tinge of hope. "Did you rescue me, then?"

Sadness entered the man's eyes as he shook his head. "No, we have not rescued you from the terrorists."

"So they *are* terrorists! Why are they after me? I already told the FBI everything I saw! What more damage could I do to them?"

The young man looked suddenly nervous, and glanced sideways at the elder. The gray haired man studied Terry for a moment, holding his gaze. Then he turned and walked to the wooden chair by the table.

"Come, Terry. Sit down and rest."

Terry suddenly felt very tired. He thought about refusing the request, but found his resistance waning. He sat, glancing at the pitcher and cup.

"Terry," the elder's tone reminded him of his grandfather, "it was given to me to offer you encouragement at this moment in time, and to remind you of that which you already know." He took the pitcher, poured its contents into the cup and held it out. Terry took the cup, and observed that the contents were clear like water. There was a pause and the two men watched him, obviously waiting for him to drink.

"Water?" he asked.

"Yes. Living water, from the eternal Source." The elder nodded for him to drink.

Raising the ceramic cup to his lips, he took a sip. Water. But such water he had never tasted! Pure, clear, cold. Just a hint of sweetness, but not enough to seem flavored. Terry closed his eyes and swallowed. The effect was immediate. His thoughts became focused, his senses sharpened. He opened his eyes wide with surprise, and the younger man grinned. Terry drank deeply then, finishing the contents of the cup. He sat back in the chair and inhaled, noticing that the pain in his knee and wrists had lessened, and his nerves were considerably calmer. He felt a sense of serenity wash over him, and his soul was quieted. *I wish I could always be this composed.*

"You can learn to be so," the elder said. Terry wondered how this man knew his thoughts. "The Word teaches us to be still, and in that stillness our soul knows that he is God, and that he is near. Remember this moment when you are under assault, and make your soul be still. Then you will be able to receive what you need."

"Having a bottle of this water handy would help too," said Terry.

The older man chuckled. "This pitcher is here to show you the effect of living water. What do you know about living water, Terry?"

Terry thought. "Jesus taught that living water would flow from within us, like a river."

"Exactly," the man nodded approvingly. "Be still. Know that God is near. Draw from his living water within you."

As Terry leaned back in the chair, his eyes closed. He again felt very sleepy. The elder sighed.

"I'm afraid your time here has already come to an end, Terry. I wish we had more of it." He paused, as if hearing something that no one else had ears to hear. "Remember, Terry, that men and women are at times called to take part in the Lord's suffering. It is not for the sake of punishment."

Terry opened his eyes slightly, fighting sleep for another moment. "What suffering?"

"The suffering that leads to salvation. Not just your own, but also that of many others. Those who remain faithful through suffering receive the greatest treasure."

"Great treasure," Terry mumbled, his eyes shutting again.

"Yes, the pearl of great price. Entrance into God's kingdom. This is the path you have desired to walk, Terry, from a young age. No matter how dark it gets, God will walk with you on this journey into his very heart."

"His kingdom." Sleep now overcame him.

"Quiet your soul, Terry, and do not fear."

◆

He was waking now, but let his eyes remain closed. His brain functioned slowly, like wading knee-deep in mud. He was sitting in a chair. The wooden chair in the white room. The pain in his knee and wrists was again more pronounced. His head was also aching. He would have to take another drink in a minute.

Without warning, Terry felt a hand slap the left side of his face, hard enough to get his attention.

"I said wake up!" a harsh voice commanded.

Terry opened his eyes, and was bewildered at the sight. He was not in the white room at all. Instead, he was sitting in a wooden chair in the middle of a cement room, looking up at the towering figure of the bald man. Terry blinked and looked around. The room was dimly lit by a single light bulb overhead and a small window near the support beams at the ceiling. He realized that he was most likely in the basement of a house. Through the little window he could see daylight. But what day was it? His head throbbed and he rubbed his eyes. He remembered being taken. On Thursday. He remembered waking up in a dark vehicle and being drugged back to unconsciousness. How many times had that happened?

Most clearly he remembered the dream of the white room. God had spoken to him in that dream, warned him of suffering leading to salvation and treasure. His stomach felt suddenly sick, either from the thought of suffering or the drugs he had been given, or both.

"That's better," his captor grunted. He stepped back to the only door in the room, revealing a small card table behind him. In front of the table stood a tall, thin man with his arms crossed, eyes studying Terry intently.

"Al-Masri!" Terry exclaimed. "You brought me all the way to France? What day is this?" It didn't seem possible. How long had they kept him unconscious?

Al-Masri's eyebrows went up when Terry mentioned France. He was clearly interested in the fact that Terry knew of his whereabouts. He let his arms drop to his side and slowly advanced toward the chair. Terry's arms were free, and he was not restrained in any way. He thought about standing up, but his entire body felt lethargic. He doubted that he would be any less vulnerable on his feet.

Al-Masri stopped three feet from him, looking down on him. A faint smile raised the corners of his mouth. Then his leg moved. That's all Terry's dulled senses registered; the commencement of motion. The impact to the left side of his face was a shock, an explosion in his ear. His body went rigid, and he threw his arms out as the room tipped. Too late. The other side of his face hit the cement floor as the chair clattered down next to him. He cried out in pain. His ears rang and bright lights danced in his vision.

Then the chair was slammed back into place, and Terry was roughly forced into it. He raised shaking hands to shield his face but al-Masri didn't strike again. Instead he turned and paced slowly back to the table.

"That was for speaking without permission." He turned again to face Terry. "You are my prisoner. I will ask the questions, and you will answer immediately and truthfully. Is that clear?"

"Yes." He answered immediately.

Al-Masri narrowed his eyes. "And you will address me as 'Mr. al-Masri.'"

"Yes, Mr. al-Masri." Again his reply was immediate. *You're acting like a scared little boy*, Terry thought with a stab of anger. *Don't let him own you.*

"Good boy." Al-Masri smiled coldly, as if reading Terry's thoughts. After a short pause he asked, "How did you know that I came back to France?"

Terry hesitated, trying to think. How much should he tell a terrorist?

"No, no, Terrence," al-Masri shook his head and wagged a bony index finger at him, "answer immediately and truthfully, or suffer the consequences."

"The FBI told me." Terry thought of the elder in the white room. *Be still, my soul. Quiet down. God, help me.* His thinking began to sharpen. *Be careful, Terry. Don't tell this man what he wants to know. God, what does he want to know?*

Al-Masri was speaking again, eyebrows raised.

"The FBI? You are still talking with them, then?"

"Yes." Terry saw no reason to hesitate on the simple questions.

"Why?"

"Because a week after I talked to them about the terrorist bombing in Louisville, someone tried to kill me."

"That was just an attempted robbery at a gas station, wasn't it?" al-Masri asked.

"And how would *you* know about that?" Terry's tone was accusing. "I never reported it until days later, and you disappeared long before then."

Al-Masri's mouth twitched and his dark eyes flashed. Terry had scored a blow. Not the same as a kick to the side of the head, but it would do for now. *Come on, you devil. Ask your questions. Let's see who learns more about who.*

Al-Masri instantly regained his calm demeanor. "So," he said slowly, "you think you're smart, do you, Terrence?" Terry responded with a silent glare. "You think that you can outsmart me with words? Is that what you think?" He let out a low, menacing laugh and approached the chair. Terry prepared himself. This time he would be ready.

"I don't think you will." Al-Masri stared at Terry for a full ten seconds, and then his arm moved.

Terry saw it this time and lunged sideways. But his muscles were still heavy, and his opponent moved much faster than he had ever seen a man move. Al-Masri's hand caught Terry's right cheek just below his eye, and he flew back over the wooden chair. His legs up-ended and he reached back desperately, searching for the concrete floor with his hands. The back of his head found it first, and blackness again fell over him like a curtain.

Chapter 27

Josh stared at the laptop screen on his temporary desk at the Louisville Metro Police Department headquarters building. It was 10:30 a.m., Saturday, and the computer screen displayed his report of the previous night's events. He sighed heavily as he proofed what he had written for the third time. It was complete in every detail, including one that he had until now kept to himself. This report told the truth that he, Josh Kepler, had been working in cooperation with the Louisville police as an FBI agent, when in fact he had been suspended by the FBI two weeks earlier. The report laid out all of his actions and the information he had gathered while working as a rogue agent.

Rogue agent. How did I get myself into this?

He had been wrong to do it, hadn't he? And what had he accomplished? His illegal actions – noble though they may have been – had achieved little. He had failed to decipher the duffle bag clue in time. Of the three key people in the investigation, the CFO was dead, his killer had escaped, and Terry had been taken in broad daylight. It was likely that he was dead already. Josh thought of Terry's family, and felt a lump in his throat. He wanted to cry. Instead, he slammed his fist on the desktop, rattling a half-empty coffee mug. Two officers sitting at desks nearby looked up for a moment, and then went back to their work.

Josh had not anticipated that the news about the previous night's gun battle would spread so fast. The national media had immediately pounced on the story, perhaps due to the lack of any bombings during the last week. The media – and the public – were starving for information, anything to indicate whether the lessening of violence indicated an increase in safety.

The incident had gained urgent attention from multiple law enforcement agencies. Before the evening ended the ATF had decided to get involved in the case. So had the FBI – officially now – and the Department of Homeland Security. Seeley had made an attempt to handle the case himself and cover for Josh, but once the DHS joined in the fray it became impossible to hide the fact that Josh was a suspended agent. The Louisville police chief had gone ballistic. So had the DHS. They demanded that Josh be at police headquarters this morning and write a full report while waiting for the arrival of the DHS chief now overseeing the FBI's counter-terrorism arm.

Josh would be thrust aside, no doubt, put out of the way. Perhaps it was for the best. At least now there would be a dozen agents on the case, looking for Terry. The report that Josh had written would give them a head start on their investigation. Maybe that was the roll he had been called to play. Sacrifice his career, and possibly spend some time behind bars, so that others would have a leg up once they figured out the case was worth investigating. The thought did not make him feel any better. He saved his report and sent it to the printer, gloomily wishing for this day to be over.

"Agent Kepler."

Josh looked up and blinked. A man approached, dressed in the all-black pants and long-sleeved shirt worn by agents of the Department of Homeland Security. A black baseball cap crowned his head, with the white letters "DHS" above the bill. To his surprise, Josh recognized the man. Agent Matthew Larsen had been an FBI special agent in Chicago, up for promotion to unit chief. Josh had worked with him on a case last year, and they had got along well. The DHS must have seen fit to recruit some of the FBI's finest to be their field agents.

Josh stood and shook the man's hand. "Hello, Matt."

They sat down, facing each other across the desk, and Josh waited for the DHS chief to begin.

"Josh, I don't have to tell you, you're in big trouble here."

Josh smiled. "Yeah, I've gathered that much." His voice was calm. Knowing that the case would now be fully investigated, he was resigned to his fate, whatever that might be. "No one was taking this case seriously, Matt, and Seeley didn't have available agents to put on it."

Larsen glowered. "Don't talk to me about Seeley. Someone else is dealing with him, and he may be in worse trouble than you."

"Look, Seeley tried to get my suspension lifted. There was no clear reason for suspending me in the first place, and no reason to shuffle me off to the side indefinitely. But your guys weren't responding."

"I'm not going to argue with you about it. There are procedures that have to be followed. Seeley knew that better than most."

Josh leaned forward. "Seeley didn't do anything wrong. I chose to pursue the case myself. Seeley couldn't have stopped me. That's the way I put it in my report."

"Seeley should have turned you in!" Larsen's eyes flashed his anger, but he continued in a lower tone. "He knowingly let you continue, and it'll be the end of his career."

Josh decided to change the subject. "So, what about me? Are you going to arrest me now?"

Larsen leaned back in his chair. He looked at Josh for several seconds, as if pondering the question for the first time.

"No," he finally said, "I'm not going to arrest you, Josh. I don't think having you behind bars will do society any good."

Josh had not even realized that he was holding his breath, and he now let it out audibly with a sense of relief. "Thanks. I appreciate that."

"Well, don't thank me yet." He paused, and Josh knew what was coming next. "I'm afraid I can't save your job, as much as I might want to. I'm going to have to call in some favors to keep you out of prison, and that's all I'll be able to manage. The higher-ups in the DHS don't think much of the FBI these days." He shifted in his seat. "There probably won't be any severance pay. Just so you know."

Josh slumped in his chair, feeling the weight of his situation. He had given almost nineteen years of his life to the FBI, and now it was suddenly being taken away from him. Not that he didn't own a part in it. He had known he was taking a serious risk over the last two weeks. But he was sure he had been right to do so. Almost sure. He looked at the DHS chief.

"So, am I free to go now?"

"Is your report finished?"

"On the printer."

"Okay, then. I need to take your gun, and get a number where we can reach you if we have questions. Then you can go back home." The man looked into Josh's eyes for a moment. "I'm sorry, Josh." Josh smiled faintly and reached for his handgun. He kept his next thought to himself. *I don't think I'll be going home quite yet.*

♦

Jennifer sat on the sofa in her living room and said a prayer as she dialed the phone. Mitch was struggling to deal with Terry's kidnapping, and she was worried about him. He had stayed home from work on Friday, and had refused her offer to get together for dinner. Jennifer understood, for she had felt the guilt as well. They could have made Terry go home after lunch on Thursday. They could have driven him home after work. But they didn't.

She knew, however, that God was directly involved in the lives of men and women, and that he had his plans. He was never surprised, never taken off guard. One way or another, his plans for Terry would come to pass as he desired. And since he was good, Jennifer concluded that his plans would also be ultimately good. The knowledge comforted her.

"Hello?" Mitch sounded tired.

"Hi, it's me. How are you?"

"Tired, not getting much sleep."

"I know what you mean." Jennifer longed to comfort him. She had come to care deeply for him. She decided to go out on a limb. "I've been praying for you."

"Huh?" A pause. "Oh."

Her heart sank a little at the lukewarm response. Jennifer knew that Mitch didn't believe in God, didn't want to believe. He had only experienced religion as a child, and now rejected its validity in every day life. She doubted he had ever experienced God himself. His kindness. His peace. His acceptance. Not like she so recently had.

She continued further out the limb. "I pray for you every day. I ask God to show you that he is in control of what is happening. That he is working it out." She paused. "You shouldn't blame yourself, Mitch."

"Whatever." There was a lack of emotion in his voice, and Jennifer couldn't find words to continue the conversation. Suddenly Mitch spoke in a more forceful tone.

"If God exists, and if he's so great, why does he allow terrorists to blow up churches? Why does he let them kidnap his followers? Why does he let the bad guys exist at all? Tell me that, Jennifer."

"I don't know, Mitch. He knows the big picture, not me."

"Don't you see how ludicrous it is? The idea of an all-powerful good God that allows evil to exist? And not just exist, but actually flourish. Right out in the open, spreading pain and misery to good people around the world. That makes no sense, Jennifer."

He was becoming more animated now, and Jennifer resolved to offer a calm response. "I don't think it's ludicrous. If God forced everyone to be good, we'd be nothing more than robots. What kind of life would that be?"

Mitch scoffed. "At least he would be truly good. Looking at the world today, there isn't much evidence of a good God up there."

"God is more than good, Mitch. It's not simply a good versus evil thing, God versus Satan. That's what religion focuses on; good and evil, saved or sinner, clean or dirty. If that's all there was to it, then yes! God would simply destroy evil. But God is much more than that, much deeper." Jennifer found herself surprised at the words which tumbled out, and the passion and conviction with which she spoke them. "God is kind, Mitch. He is the kindest person you will ever meet. God is a forgiving person, more so than anyone I have ever known. And God is love. He loves me for who I am, not for the good things I try to do. And the best way to experience the kindness, forgiveness and love that someone has to offer you is to be in a relationship with them. Right? Like us, right?"

Mitch didn't respond, and she quickly continued. "And a relationship doesn't just happen by chance, does it? One person cannot make another person have a relationship with them. Relationship is a mutual decision. It has to be a mutual decision. If it's not, if it's forced in any way, then you have something other than kindness, love and forgiveness. Something other than God. *That* is why God allows good and evil to exist, Mitch. Because the whole thing has to be a choice."

She took a breath and waited for Mitch to respond. "It still doesn't make sense to me," he said flatly.

Jennifer felt a pang of sorrow in her heart. "All I know is that God chose to reach out to me, to offer me kindness. I chose to respond to him, to believe in him, to trust him. And now he's real to me, and means more to me than my life."

She hoped his silence meant that he was considering her words.

"Mitch?"

"What?"

"You should come to the Givens' tomorrow morning for our church gathering. We're going to pray together for Terry. Pam and Roger are going to make lunch for everyone afterwards, and–"

"No," Mitch interrupted, sounding irritated. "I'm not going to a prayer meeting, Jennifer. That's for people who can't cope." His voice softened. "You should come over here tomorrow instead. I really need someone to help me get my mind off all this."

Jennifer felt a lump forming in her throat. Her heart was coming apart. He was asking her for help. He needed her. But she recognized that he was also trying to manipulate her, forcing her to make a choice. She took a deep breath, and told herself to be strong. "I have to go to the Givens tomorrow to pray. Why don't I come over tomorrow evening, and we can have dinner?"

"Why do you have to go? Who's making you?"

"No one is making me, Mitch. I want to. It's who I am now."

"Well I'm not going that way, Jennifer." His voice was irritated again, bordering on anger. "You will have to choose God without me."

"Maybe so." Her voice wavered.

"Do you understand what I'm saying? You are making a choice here."

"Yes." She was sinking now, despair washing over her.

"Fine." The word rang with finality, and the phone clicked. Mitch was gone.

Jennifer pressed the "Off" button on the cordless phone and let it drop to the floor, reeling in the shock and agony of what had just happened.

"Oh, God."

It was a short prayer, but it was all she could manage before she buried her face in the couch and cried.

♦

The black curtain of darkness pulled away, and light burst upon Terry's eyes. His head felt like it had been bashed with a club. The pain hammered against his skull with every beat of his heart. Terry closed his eyes against the sudden brightness. He tried to clear his scrambled thoughts and remember the details of where he was. His hands were secured tightly behind him, and he could still feel the burning in his wrists. He listened. There was no sound, except the soft blowing of air from a heater somewhere in another room. His neck, back and shoulders ached with stiffness. A musty smell filled his nostrils, and the air was cool and damp. He shivered.

Terry opened his eyes again, squinting momentarily as light stabbed painfully into his head. He was sitting in the wooden chair in the middle of the cement floor, and suddenly realized that his feet were also bound to the chair. He was unable to move more than his head. The card table sat about fifteen feet in front of him, near the wall. To his right was the only door to the room, closed. The single light bulb shone over his head, and sunlight still filtered through the small window at the top of the wall to his left.

He came to the same conclusion as before; he was being held in a rather large room in a basement. He wondered where the door led. How many other rooms were there? If he got a chance, he would go through that door and look for a staircase. The way out of the building would most likely be on the floor above.

Terry suddenly became aware of a different kind of pain. Thirst, and hunger. They assaulted him now like a cruel enemy. How long had he been held captive? He tried to remember. He could recall brief moments of consciousness while they were transporting him. He had obviously been drugged, and the images were twisted and confused. They must have let him use a restroom somewhere along the way. An image of a crowded bar flashed in his mind, but the details escaped him.

It would have taken at least two or three days to smuggle him to France. His stomach was telling him that it had been that long since he had eaten. His body felt weak, and his mind reeled. *How could they have kidnapped me across the Atlantic Ocean?* The thought was staggering, and terrifying. Even if he had the chance to escape, where would he go? He didn't know anything about France.

He had to get some answers from al-Masri. Maybe he could bargain with him. He would agree to answer one of al-Masri's questions, as long as al-Masri answered one of his. The idea immediately struck him as stupid. Al-Masri wasn't the bargaining type, and could not be trusted to answer any question truthfully.

Terry's soul began to sink under the combined weight of fear and despair. He felt like he might do anything for a drink of cool water, of living water. He encouraged his soul to be still, to listen for God.

He prayed. He waited.

Chapter 28

Josh left police headquarters and realized that he now had nothing to do and nowhere to go. For an hour he drove aimlessly around town, contemplating whether he should return home to Indianapolis. He finally decided against it.

Josh stopped at a Taco Bell for lunch, and called Roger Givens on his cell. He told Roger that he had been fired by the FBI and quickly recounted the details. When he finished, he apologized for not being completely honest about his involvement. He wanted to ask if he could stay in touch, to keep up with how the investigation was going, but he half expected that the man would scream at him for conducting an illegal investigation of his best friend's kidnapping.

Instead of screaming, Roger invited Josh to come to his house on Sunday morning for a time of prayer for Terry. Josh gratefully accepted. He liked this group of friends very much, admiring their calm faith and strong unity. Their relationship with God and each other seemed to be the foundation of their daily lives, to an extent that Josh had not witnessed in other Christians. Being around them had actually been a source of strength for him during this difficult time.

He ate his tacos slowly to use up some time, and then returned to the hotel, where he tried unsuccessfully to catch up on his sleep. Lying on the bed, staring up at the ceiling, he wondered if he might go insane before the day ended.

God, I can't just lay here and do nothing.

As if in answer, his cell phone rang, startling him in the quiet room. He glanced at the clock by the bed. 3:08 p.m. Looking at the phone's display, the caller was identified as "UNKNOWN."

"Hello, this is Josh."

"Agent Kepler, this is Randal Neumeier from Kellor Computing's Internal Auditing Department. You gave me your number when you were here investigating Mr. Parker's death."

"Yes, Mr. Neumeier, I remember. What can I do for you?" The man obviously had not heard that Josh was no longer employed by the FBI.

"Ever since the CFO's murder and Mr. al-Masri's disappearance, we've been scrutinizing the books to see if we could come up with anything suspicious."

"You've found something?"

"Yes, sir, we have. There were two multi-million dollar deals that Mr. al-Masri crafted in the last quarter with a Saudi company. Those deals alone brought enough profit to keep Kellor from missing its earnings by a penny or three."

"You mean the revised earnings, which were already adjusted down by ten cents?" Josh had done his homework on Kellor Computing Group in the last few weeks.

"Yes, that's correct. Kellor was going to miss even the adjusted earnings forecast, until al-Masri's deals resulted in sales of nearly forty million dollars this quarter."

"Wow, that is a lot of money rolling in conveniently at the eleventh hour, isn't it?"

"Not really. Not in our business of selling high-tech computer hardware, software and services. The amount of money is not what made these deals unusual."

"Okay, then, let's skip to the punch line, Mr. Neumeier. What have you discovered?"

"These deals were unusual for a couple of reasons. First, the amount of money that was paid up front was unusually large. A full fifty percent, even before we shipped anything to them. And second, the items purchased seemed unusual. There was no rhyme or reason to them. It was a hodge-podge of stuff, some of it completely unrelated."

He paused, and when Josh offered no response, he continued.

"After scrutinizing all the numbers, Agent Kepler, we found that there is money unaccounted for."

"So that's the punch line, then. How much money?"

"A million dollars from the first deal, and a million and a half from the second."

"You're sure?"

"Absolutely. We had to look through records from several different departments. It wasn't obvious at first, but we are certain. The money came in from the deals, and shortly thereafter several bogus internal transactions were made by the Finance Department."

"Do you have any idea where the money went, or exactly who took it?"

"There's no way to know where it went. But one thing is for sure. That much money could not have disappeared without Parker's knowledge, especially since he was watching the company's financials so closely."

"Could he have done it alone?"

"Possibly, if people simply carried out his instructions without question. We are still investigating to find out who else might have known."

"Okay, thanks for the information, Mr. Neumeier. I assume you have told the local authorities there?"

"Yes, they know."

"Good. If anything else comes to light please let me know."

"I certainly will."

As he ended the call, Josh felt a momentary pang of guilt. It really wasn't his job to know this information anymore. He brushed the feeling aside, telling himself that he was now acting as a private investigator working on behalf of Terry Whitman's family. Besides, he would share any information with Larsen's boys at the DHS. He punched a number on his cell phone. No sense in waiting.

"This is Agent Larsen."

"Matt, it's Josh."

"Oh." Larsen's voice was guarded. "What can I do for you, Josh?"

"I just got a call from one of the Kellor bean counters I talked to in Panama City after Parker's death."

"Josh, you know that you can't be talking to witnesses on this case any more!" Larsen sounded irritated. He was lecturing. "You should have told them that you are off the case, and given them my number. Did you do that?"

"No," Josh said flatly. He had not anticipated such a strong negative response.

"No," Larsen repeated. "No, of course not. You let them think you were still an FBI agent, and listened to everything they had to say."

Josh raised his voice now. "I made sure he told the authorities there too. I assume you have an agent in Panama City to look into things there?"

"Of course I have an agent in Panama City!"

"Then he probably already knows. I just thought I'd give you a heads-up, Matt."

"We don't need any help from you, Josh! Do you understand me? The Whitman case is in our capable hands now, not yours. I suggest you find something else to do with your life. Starting today, Josh."

"What do you mean by that?"

"If you keep snooping around DHS cases, I'll reconsider having you brought up on charges of illegally operating as an FBI agent." Larsen paused to let the statement sink in. "*Now* do you understand what I mean?"

"Perfectly."

Josh hung up before Larsen could respond. Infuriated, he pounded his fist on the night stand and shouted to the empty room.

"Arrogant fool!" Hurriedly he dialed another number into his cell phone. After two rings the phone clicked in his ear.

"Federal Bureau of Investigations, Indianapolis," a man answered. "May I help you?"

"Agent Seeley, please."

"May I ask who is calling?"

"This is Agent—" Josh stopped himself. "Uh, Josh Kepler."

"One moment please."

The phone went silent and Josh paced the floor. Surely his unit chief would be receptive to hearing new information from him. When the phone again clicked to life, it was an unexpected voice that greeted him.

"Hey buddy." His partner of the last two years.

"Dickerson! It's good to hear your voice. Are you back in action yet?"

"Are you kidding?" Dickerson sounded annoyed. "I just came in to see if I could speed up the process a bit. These DHS guys are in no hurry to help an FBI agent, though."

"Where's Seeley? I need to talk to him."

"Seeley's been suspended, Josh, pending some investigation."

Josh winced, and fought back the urge to curse Larsen's DHS. "That didn't take long," he said bitterly.

"Do you know what's going on? What exactly is this investigation about?"

Josh sat down on the bed. Didn't Dickerson know? He rubbed his temple and stared at the floor. "You do know that I've been fired, right?"

"Yeah," his partner answered softly, "sorry."

"It's alright."

"But no one is telling us why. It's like these DHS guys are looking for a reason to get rid of all of us! They probably want to get rid of the FBI altogether."

"I doubt they'll be able to pull that off." Josh sighed. "Just keep your head down and get your job back, Dickerson. Okay?"

"He's gonna resign, Josh."

"Who?" Josh asked. And then it hit him like a slap in the face. "Not Seeley!"

"I talked to him this morning." Dickerson lowered his voice, "He said he's too close to retirement to let them drag him through this. They'll probably give him an early out, and let him keep his pension."

Josh felt like he was going to cry. "Okay, I've got to go. Thanks for the info, buddy."

"Are you going to be alright?"

"Yeah," Josh answered, even though he didn't feel alright. "I'll talk to you later."

"Okay, take care of yourself."

Josh set the phone on the nightstand and fell back on the bed. *God, is this all my fault?*

♦

Terry smiled. His situation had not changed in the last hour. He still sat alone in the basement, hands and legs bound. His wrists continued to burn under the tight chords, and the pain in his head had settled into a constant throb. He still had no reason to believe that he would live through the day.

But something *had* changed. Terry had been praying for most of an hour, talking to God, quieting his soul to listen for a response. And God had responded, with five words. His voice was at the same time small and unfathomable, and audible only to a quiet spirit.

I won't leave you, Terry.

In Terry's experience, God didn't often use a lot of words. In this case, there was no need. Along with those few words, God had given him much. Comfort. Assurance. Peace. He was *not* alone. Would never be alone. The God who had created him was on his side. If it wasn't his time to die, then al-Masri couldn't kill him. And if it was his time to depart this world, God would be there to lead him home. The situation had suddenly become very simple.

Terry laughed as he thought of his earlier dream. "Living

waters!" he said out loud. He began to worship, singing softly at first.

You are God, you are holy
You are God above all the earth
You set me free, to serve you only
You are God, the only God in all the earth

Terry raised his voice now, not caring who might hear him.

You are Lord, you are worthy
You're my Lord, deserving of praise
You set me free, I'll serve you only
You are God, the only God in all the earth

As if on cue, the door opened, and al-Masri entered, looking annoyed. Terry looked into the eyes of his captor, and then looked up to the ceiling and finished his hymn.

You've set me free, I'll serve you only
You are God, most holy God in all the earth

He let the last note linger, half expecting to get a boot in the face again. Al-Masri simply closed the door and turned to face him with a look of amusement. He was holding a small notepad and pen in one hand.

"Very nice, Terrence. Let's see if your misguided faith will give you the strength to stay conscious a little longer this time." He left the pen and paper on the table, withdrew from under his shirt a knife with an eight inch blade, and walked around behind him. Terry swallowed as his heart beat faster.

Al-Masri grabbed his wrists and sliced through the rope easily. Terry's hands were free. He grimaced at the sight of his bloody wrists, and began moving his hands to regain feeling.

Al-Masri returned to the table. "Now then," he said, as he

retrieved the pen and pad of paper, "I want you to write down the name, address, and phone number of everyone that you spoke to about the duffle bag. I am especially interested in knowing who in the FBI, the CIA, and the DHS you have spoken to, and exactly what you talked about." Terry blinked back at him, prompting a glare from al-Masri. "Names on the paper," he directed as he handed the pen and notepad to him.

Terry had decided that he was not going to give al-Masri anything that would help his cause. He held the pen and paper calmly in his lap.

"Could you please tell me exactly where I am first?"

Al-Masri shifted his weight, and Terry realized too late what was coming. His hands were still in his lap when al-Masri's foot impacted his mouth. He grunted as his head snapped back, and the chair tipped. Al-Masri immediately spun into a roundhouse kick as Terry instinctively jerked forward to keep the chair upright. The second blow landed with much more force, on the side of Terry's face. Pen and paper flew from his hands as he and the chair crashed again to the concrete floor.

"Get up!" al-Masri shouted, withdrawing the knife again. "Get up or I'll end this right now!"

With his feet still bound to the chair, Terry awkwardly returned to a sitting position. Al-Masri looked at him with a hateful gaze, and struck again, hitting him in the face. Terry's fists came up, and instantly the knife was at his throat.

"Hands down!" growled al-Masri. Terry had no choice but to comply. Another fist to the face, harder this time. The chair tipped back again, but al-Masri brought the front legs firmly back to the floor with his foot. Terry's head rolled forward with the motion, and al-Masri struck a savage blow to his left eye. Pain stabbed like ice cold daggers into his head, and he clenched his eyes shut tight. From the darkness came yet another fierce punch to his face. Terry raised his arms in an attempt to shield himself, not opening his eyes.

"Stop! Please!" he pleaded.

The next impact came like a baseball bat to his stomach, and lifted him out of his seat. Breath fled his lungs as he and the chair crashed to the floor yet again. His momentum caused him to tumble over and land face down with the chair on top of him. Still clenching his eyes shut, he gasped for air and wondered if al-Masri was going to kill him after all. He braced himself for the next blow, but for the moment, it didn't come.

    Terry felt sick to his stomach, and tasted blood in his mouth.

God, make him stop.

Chapter 29

Angela felt it deep within. Much deeper than the shifting surface thoughts of the mind. Deeper still than the pull of the heart's emotions. From within the domain of her spirit it sprang. A prompting to pray. Quietly at first, all but lost in the shallow waters of her being.

With mop in hand, she was helping Pam clean the kitchen. The women had chatted about various topics: children, home schooling, funny movies they had seen. Anything to keep Angela's mind occupied. But the quiet urge had steadily intensified, and now she abruptly stopped talking.

"What's wrong?" asked Pam. Angela leaned the mop against the wall and looked at her friend.

"We have to pray for Terry. Right now."

Pam didn't give Angela a questioning look, as others might have done. She simply set her rag on the counter and started toward the hallway. "Let's go into the spare bedroom."

Angela followed Pam into the room and closed the door behind them. Pam sat on the edge of the bed and looked up at her. "Do you want to start?"

Angela closed her eyes for a moment and tried to gather her thoughts. There was only one thing that she wanted to ask of God: that he bring her husband home to her, safe and unharmed. It might be a selfish request, but she didn't care. She would be honest with God.

Her voice choking with emotion, Angela began to pray.

♦

Al-Masri looked down on his prisoner, and loathing filled his heart. The man lay awkwardly on his stomach with one arm under him, wheezing heavily. The wooden chair, still bound to his legs, rested on top of him. *Allah would be more than pleased to see this unbeliever broken and bleeding.* Al-Masri contemplated killing him now, without wasting any more time.

For him, *jihad* – the holy war – was life. He had made it his focus, given it his complete dedication. Allah had directed him to become its skilled practitioner. It was his identity. There were other great leaders in the war, to be sure, but none yet had realized what he was now accomplishing; bringing *jihad* to the heartland of Allah's most arrogant enemy. Not just a single day of coordinated attacks, like 9/11 had been, but a protracted holy war, waged by a small army of Allah's most faithful. It had taken years of painstaking preparation. Lesser warriors had tried and failed. Al-Masri had persevered, guided by a brilliant mind, and driven by a passionate desire to see Allah's followers rise to their rightful place of prominence in the earth.

Whitman was stirring, moving his head to look up at him. Al-Masri gripped the handle of the blade, longing to cut him open, to spill his blood for the glory of Allah. He had killed countless hundreds before, but the pleasure derived from sending another infidel to hell never waned. Especially when his victim was a man like Terrence Whitman; a proud citizen of earth's Great Satan, and an unashamed follower of western Christianity. The vilest of Allah's enemies.

Reluctantly, al-Masri shoved the knife into its sheath on his belt. Patience and discipline were his allies. They had allowed him to carefully advance toward this moment, where he now stood on the threshold of his greatest battle. There was no need to abandon discipline for a moment of passion. This infidel had information that would be of service. Primarily, who was pursuing him, and how much they actually knew.

He dragged Whitman and his chair roughly to their upright position, and retrieved the pad of paper and pen from where they had landed.

"Names, Terrence," he said as he thrust the pen and paper into his lap. "I am growing impatient." The man looked up at him for a moment, dazed. He was going into a state of shock, his mouth bloody, and his left eye nearly swelled shut already. Al-Masri held his gaze with an icy stare, knowing that the man's resistance was failing. Whitman finally looked down and began to write.

"Good, Terrence," he said approvingly. He returned to the card table to watch from a comfortable distance. "And while you are thinking of names, I'll just ask you some questions, alright?" Whitman looked at him briefly, and then wrote another name on the paper. Al-Masri smiled and leaned against the card table.

"First of all, where does the FBI think I am?"

Whitman answered without looking up from his list of names. "They know you took a flight to France."

"Yes, but where in France do they think I am?"

"I don't know."

"Okay," al-Masri responded thoughtfully, "I'll accept that for now. And why exactly are they searching for me?"

A short pause, then, "You killed Parker."

Whitman still didn't look up from his paper, and Al-Masri pondered the response. He knew that he was a suspect, most likely the primary suspect, in Parker's murder. But certainly they didn't have proof. He hadn't left any proof.

"That answer was not entirely truthful, Terrence," he said with an intentional air of amusement. "They may consider me a suspect, but they don't know who murdered Mr. Parker." Whitman paused in the middle of writing another name, shrugged his shoulders, then continued to write in silence. *Not up to debating me this time, are you, Terrence?*

"What else?" al-Masri asked. Whitman had stopped writing, but did not respond. "What else does the FBI suspect me of?"

Whitman looked up at him with an empty expression. "You mean, something worse than murdering our CFO?"

Al-Masri scrutinized his captive. Was this man playing with him? If so, there was nothing in his face to indicate it. Was there truly nothing else to know about the FBI investigation? He took a step forward.

"I was specifically wondering about the duffle bag, Terrence. The one that you saw, both in Parker's office and on the shoulder of a suicide bomber." He studied Whitman's face like a hawk, intent on spotting any reaction. What he saw was bewilderment.

"You've asked me about that before. I did tell the FBI about it, but they didn't feel that it meant anything, since you can buy a duffle bag in any of our company stores and on the website."

"Did you tell them that the bag was sold in our stores, or did they just assume that?"

"I told them."

Al-Masri took a step closer and pressed the issue further. "Were they going to follow up on that?" Whitman again looked confused, and al-Masri impatiently restated his question. "Were they going to check with any of the company stores, to follow up on any recent purchases of that duffle bag?"

Whitman shook his head. "No, I don't think so."

Al-Masri felt relief growing within him. *Could I really be this fortunate? Do they not even suspect?* He knew that if they considered him a potential terrorist sympathizer, the FBI and DHS would pursue him relentlessly. He allowed a grin to spread on his face.

"Good!" he declared as he snatched the pad of paper from Whitman's lap. He read the names scrawled on the page.

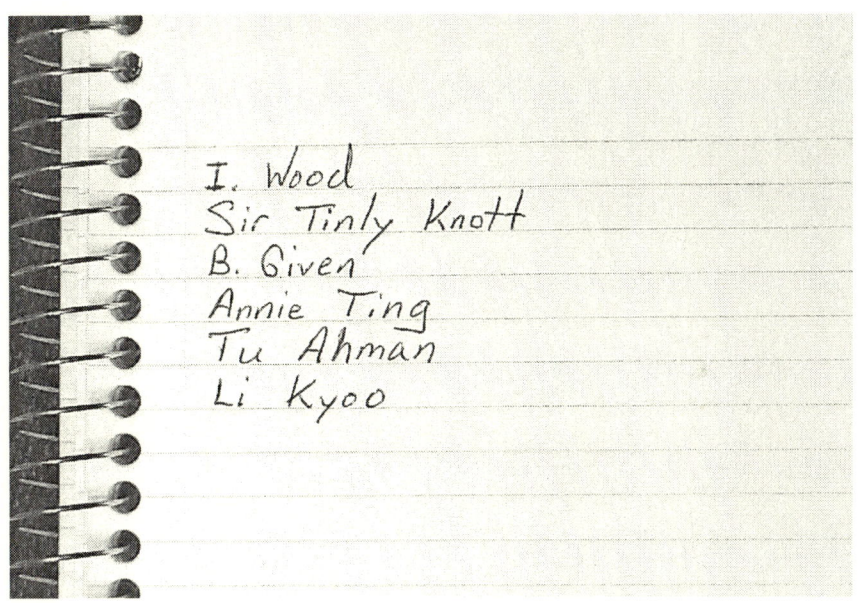

The names looked nonsensical. It took a moment for the meaning of the writing to form in al-Masri's brain. Not a list of names, but a single sentence. A statement of defiance. He felt his face grow hot with anger, and he unsheathed his knife once again. Whitman wasn't in shock after all! On the contrary, the man's brain was functioning quite well under pressure. He was playing games now, treating al-Masri like one might treat a common uneducated thief.

Knife in hand and feet rooted to the floor, his eyes bore down on Terrence, who returned his fiery gaze with the now familiar blank stare. Al-Masri felt himself holding his breath, trembling. How he wanted to end this pitiful, arrogant life! Every cell in his body screamed for action – to bring justice, exact vengeance, spill enemy blood. For a brief moment, he visualized himself plunging the knife into Whitman's neck, causing the blank look to twist with terror and pain.

Al-masri let his breath out, and eased his grip on the knife. He couldn't do it. Not yet. Not now. He looked again at Whitman's list of phony names, and let his eyes fall on the one that mattered. *Ahman*. The Saudi billionaire who had helped to plan and finance so much of al-Masri's *jihad*. What were the odds that the FBI had actually traced the money to its true source? At least a thousand to one. And if Whitman knew, would he really be smart enough to pull a stunt like this? To let on that he knew, without admitting to it outright? Certainly Terrence wasn't that smart.

No. Whitman's clever message simply ended with the phrase "...to a man like you." The appearance of the name "Ahman" was coincidence.

Al-Masri began to pace as he continued to stare at the notepad.

It had to be coincidence.

But what if it wasn't? It seemed just as improbable that Terrence would by pure chance write the name "Ahman" on this piece of paper. Al-Masri could not allow himself to believe it. He had to assume the worst. Discipline and brilliance had always demanded that he plan for the worst case scenario. In this instance, the worst case was that Whitman's infuriating note was in fact stating that even if he were tortured, he would not "give anything to Ahman," like al-Masri had done. Terrence – and therefore the FBI – knew the identity of his greatest financial and planning resource.

The revelation caused his mind to click back into gear, and al-Masri fully understood his next course of action. He must learn everything that Whitman knew. He would pull the information out of him piece by bloody piece if need be. There wasn't much time, however, and it was now clear that it would take more than violence to break him. Without a word al-Masri strode from the room and closed the door behind him.

◆

Terry blinked at the door in wonder, trying to comprehend what had just happened. Al-Masri had left the room in a hurry, and Terry's hands were still untied. He immediately reached for the ropes which bound his legs to the chair, and began to work them loose.

The effort was futile, for at that moment the door opened, and the large man with the goatee stepped into the room. He closed the door and stood in front of it, arms folded across his chest. He looked at Terry and grinned wickedly. "Don't bother with those ropes."

Terry sighed and straightened up in the chair. His head throbbed behind his closed left eye, and his face felt swollen and painful. Even though his throat was parched and he was dizzy with hunger, he decided not to beg for any favors just yet. Instead, he forced himself to think. He had expected a severe reaction to his act of noncompliance with the names, and at first al-Masri had undeniably looked furious. But the look quickly gave way to a stunned silence, as if his captor had been shocked speechless. Terry's stunt had obviously caught al-Masri completely off-guard, and he had no idea why.

He prayed that al-Masri would stay away from the basement room for a long time. At least long enough for Josh and the FBI to rescue him.

◆

Josh took a sip of hot coffee, allowing it to warm him from the inside. "This is good coffee, Mrs. Alovar." She smiled and sat down next to her husband across the small kitchen table. Josh surveyed the undersized apartment, noting that the layout was the same as the apartment directly below. His mind flashed back to the previous night's gun battle, and he closed his eyes in an attempt to erase the image from his mind. He took another swallow of coffee.

From his hotel room, Josh had contacted Manuel Santos, director of the community center at the Heartland Apartments. He had introduced himself as a former FBI agent who was now working as a private investigator and looking into the kidnapping of Terry Whitman. Mr. Santos had agreed to arrange a meeting with the Alovars. Josh hoped that this family, having lived directly above the apartment that had housed the terrorists, would be able to provide him with some small clue to help locate Terry.

"Mr. and Mrs. Alovar," he began, "do you know why I am here today?"

Mr. Alovar answered. "Sí, señor. To ask about the men downstairs."

"That's right. Do either of you know the names of anyone who visited downstairs?"

"Señor Hendawi lived there. But they don' talk much, and don' make a lot of noise. I don' know any other names."

"You never overheard any interesting conversation? Never saw anything unusual?"

Mr. Alovar thought for a moment. "Sometimes they bring boxes inside from their cars. Like they storing things there."

"Did they ever leave with these boxes?"

"Sí, sometimes."

"But you never heard them talk about what was in the boxes?"

"No, señor."

"What about your son?" Josh hoped they wouldn't think he was asking too much. "Could he have heard or seen anything?"

Mrs. Alovar gave her husband a concerned look, but he stood up and called toward the living room in Spanish. "Marcos! Ven aquí."

The boy appeared in the doorway, and his father directed him to sit at the table. "Señor Kepler quiere hablar contigo."

Marcos peered at Josh with large brown eyes, studying him for a moment. Then he moved to sit down in the chair. "Okay."

Josh smiled. "Hi Marcos, I'm Josh."

"Hi."

"How old are you, Marcos?"

"Twelve."

"I thought so," Josh said with a smile. "I have a daughter that's just one year older than you." Marcos smiled politely, showing minimal interest. Josh decided to dispense with the small talk. "Did you ever hear the people downstairs talking about anything interesting?"

The boy looked at his father, who nodded for him to answer. He turned back to Josh. "I don't know. Like what?"

"Well," Josh thought out loud, "during the last couple weeks, did they ever mention any names? Or did they talk about what they were doing, or planning to do?"

"I heard some men yelling downstairs a few days ago. I was coming up the stairs after school. They were arguing about someone."

Josh nodded. "That sounds interesting. Do you remember what day that was?"

Marcos looked down at the table for a second. "Wednesday."

"Excellent," Josh smiled. "You have a very good memory, Marcos." The boy smiled a little more sincerely this time. "Who was arguing?"

"A man was yelling at Mr. Hendawi. I don't know his name."

"And do you remember who they were arguing about?"

"Yes. Someone called Ibrahim."

Josh felt his pulse quicken. *Could they have meant James Ibrahim al-Masri?* He had discovered the middle name while investigating al-Masri's disappearance. "Just Ibrahim?" he asked. "They didn't say a last name, or any other name?"

"No, just Ibrahim. Mr. Hendawi said something to the man that I couldn't hear, and then the man yelled, 'You better get things in order, or Ibrahim will pay you a visit.' Then Mr. Hendawi said that Ibrahim never stayed in the country long enough to visit, and the other man said that this time he would. He said that Ibrahim was coming to Indiana to manage things himself. That's all I heard because they started talking quietly after that."

Marcos stopped. Josh leaned back in the chair and set down his coffee, his heart now creating an audible thumping in his ears. *Ibrahim never stays in the country very long.* It had to be al-Masri! His gut was telling him that al-Masri had not left the country, and that he was playing a pivotal role in more than Terry's kidnapping. His head was telling him that he couldn't be sure. He leaned forward and looked again at Marcos.

"Did they say where in Indiana?"

"No, they just said Indiana."

Josh sighed. "Think very carefully, Marcos. When the man was yelling, did it sound like he meant that Ibrahim would be right across the river, in Clarksville or New Albany? Or further away, maybe up in Indianapolis?"

Marcos hesitated. He looked at his mother, who put her hand reassuringly on his shoulder. Then he looked back at Josh with a nervous expression. "I don't know – they didn't say how far away."

Josh smiled at the boy. "That's okay, Marcos. You have helped me a great deal today."

After confirming that the Alovars did not have any additional information, Josh thanked them for their hospitality and left. He was able to speak with another neighbor in the building who offered no information at all. Realizing it was past dinner time, Josh decided to drive back to the hotel and eat there. He thought about making another attempt to share his new lead with Larsen and the DHS, but quickly decided against it. He would instead call Dickerson. Or Seeley. They could alert the FBI in Indianapolis to be on the lookout for a man in Indiana named Ibrahim, a terrorist possibly also known as James Ibrahim al-Masri.

As he drove, Josh fought against the sense of futility that was beginning to gnaw at him. Even if al-Masri was in Indiana, and even if Terry was with him, there was seemingly no way on earth to find them. He knew that for Terry, time was running out – if it had not run out already. There had to be other leads to follow.

There had to be!

He just couldn't think of any at the moment.

Chapter 30

Terry watched al-Masri as he stooped over the card table and wrote something on the notepad, and he wondered what would come next. For the moment it seemed that his captor had changed his tactics of interrogation. In more than ten minutes of questioning, Terry had not been struck once. For this he was grateful, since his head and face still ached from the earlier beatings. His left eye remained swollen shut and the throbbing pain behind it was becoming nearly unbearable.

Al-Masri's questions focused again on Terry's knowledge of the FBI investigations into Parker's murder and the terrorist bombing at the toy store. And the duffle bag. Always the duffle bag. Terry had not given complete answers to most of the questions and had repeatedly refused to give names. Once he went so far as to defiantly ask, "What duffle bag?" At several points al-Masri had become agitated. But instead of resorting to violence, he had simply walked to the table and penned something on the notepad.

Terry focused his working eye on the items which al-Masri had brought into the room with him. A clear pitcher of water, an empty glass, and a plate with a sandwich on it, cut into halves. He had set them on the table where they remained until now. The inside of Terry's mouth felt like a dry washcloth and he found it increasingly hard to swallow. His entire being was desperate for a drink of water. His heart beat for it and his mind stubbornly resisted thoughts of anything but the pitcher and the glass. Had the man with the goatee not bound his legs tightly to the chair again, Terry might have attempted a lunge for the table.

Al-Masri had not offered him a drink, of course. He was waiting for Terry to ask. To beg. To bring himself willingly under his kidnapper's control.

He closed his eye, and tried to imagine the living water of his vision. He could not allow himself to be broken. He didn't understand why the duffle bag was so important to al-Masri, but it was. He would never give al-Masri the names of those who knew about it. He would not endanger the lives of his friends. He prayed silently for strength. For living water.

Al-Masri set the pen down on the table. Terry opened his good eye and saw that he was being scrutinized with a dark stare. The narrow face was hard, the jaw line sharp, and the eyes like black pools of hate. He wondered what evil schemes were being planned behind those eyes, and pondered again the many questions he had about this man. Terry had no doubt that al-Masri was a murderer. Apparently a leader of some sort, judging from the way the man with the goatee acted toward him. But leader of what? How large of a following did he have? And what was his connection to terrorism? A sympathizer only? A money launderer? As Terry continued to look back at him, he couldn't help but fear that al-Masri was something far worse than simply a cold-blooded murderer.

Finally, al-Masri looked away and took hold of the pitcher and glass. He poured himself a drink and set the pitcher down. Without looking at Terry, he took several swallows of the water, and then bit into half of the sandwich. Terry lowered his eyes to stare at the floor. The dislike he felt for his captor boiled suddenly to the surface. He tried in vain to swallow, and almost choked as his tongue stuck to the roof of his mouth. He clenched his jaw and fought the urge to scream. The glass of water and sack-lunch sandwich were suddenly pushing him to lose control.

Al-Masri noticed.

"A little more cooperation from you, Terrence, and I'd have them bring you some lunch." He took another bite of the sandwich. "It's not much. Peanut butter, bread and water. But I imagine it would taste alright."

A peanut butter sandwich? He had hated peanut butter since he was a boy, and the irony of that fact now washed over him. Terry laughed bitterly and looked al-Masri in the eye. "You think you can purchase what I know for a peanut butter sandwich?" He laughed louder, a hoarse laugh from his parched throat. "I *hate* peanut butter, al-Masri! Ham and cheese might have got you somewhere, but you can keep your peanut butter."

Al-Masri's jaw clenched and his face grew red. He set down the sandwich and snatched the notepad from the table. Terry stopped laughing. Al-Masri crossed the floor in three long strides and thrust the notepad in front of Terry's face, causing him to flinch.

"My list," al-Masri said through clenched teeth. "Certainly not as clever as yours, Whitman, but you might find it interesting."

Terry looked at the notepad and saw a list of names. His heart stopped.

Terrence Whitman
Angela Whitman
Nicholas Whitman
Anthony Whitman
Briana Whitman
Daniel Whitman
Becky Whitman

They were the names of his family, including his parents who were now retired in Montana. Terry looked again into the face of his captor, as a new dread descended upon his heart. Al-Masri smiled cruelly.

"How is that for a list?"

Terry didn't answer.

"These are the names of the people that I will kill if you don't decide to cooperate with me."

Terry's heart pounded in his ears and he felt a desperation that seemed to crush his chest and constrain his lungs from drawing breath. He tried to keep his thoughts from racing in panic, as al-Masri continued.

"I didn't want it to come to this, Terrence. But time is short, and you have brought us to this point. I am now going to ask you a question, and you are going to give me a truthful and complete answer. If you choose not to do that, then you will be sentencing your family to death." Al-Masri straightened and withdrew the notepad from before Terry's eyes. "And I can assure you that their deaths will be anything but quick and painless."

Terry hated the man standing over him. He wanted to grab him and beat him senseless, but the stabbing pain in his eye reminded him that it would be wasted effort. He thought of Angela and the children, and a hot rage engulfed him. How could this man threaten to take their innocent lives? Al-Masri was a personification of evil, and did not deserve to breathe. But none of this mattered. Terry was powerless to oppose this man. He waited for the next question.

"I want to know," al-Masri spoke slowly and deliberately, "what the FBI knows about Ahman. Every detail."

Terry blinked. His insides turned and he felt suddenly sick to his stomach. He had no idea what al-Masri was talking about. *Who is Ahman?*

"You have three seconds to start talking, Whitman!"

"I don't know anything ... I don't even know who that is!"

"You've lost your chance to play stupid with me!" Al-Masri pointed at him with the notepad. "You wrote his name on your list! Did you think you would rattle me into delaying my plans?" His voice rose to a shout. "You severely misjudge me! I'm going forward unless you can tell me something that warrants a different course!"

Terry remembered his fictitious list of names. *Tu Ahman.* It had seemed like a clever way to offer some passive resistance at the time, but now he realized his terrible mistake. There really was a man named

Ahman! Terry could not bear the thought of his family being brutalized by these men. He was desperate now to cooperate.

"I just made up that list! You've got to believe me!"

Al-Masri tossed the notepad on the floor at his feet. "Unfortunately for your family, I don't." He turned to walk toward the door.

Terry suddenly forgot about living water. He forgot about opposing evil men. He thought only of saving his own family. "Wait! I'll tell you about Ahman! I'll tell you whatever you want to know!" Al-Masri stopped and turned to face him. "I can tell you who knows about the duffle bag too," he added.

Al-Masri smiled. "What do they know about Ahman?"

"They know that he is involved with you somehow, but not the details."

"How did they get his name?"

"I don't know. Agent Kepler asked me if I had ever heard anyone mention the name Ahman at the office. I told him no."

Al-Masri walked toward him. "There has to be more than that. They must have been speculating about him. Tell me what they were thinking!"

Terry closed his eyes and willed himself to think faster. He had to make this lie believable. The pain in his head beat like a drum, and his mind stalled.

"Speak!" Al-Masri slapped him in the face and Terry jolted in the chair.

"They thought he was helping you!"

"With what?"

"Killing people!" He was simply blurting the first thought that came into his head now, like a crazed man shooting at a bulls-eye in the dark. But al-Masri's eyebrows went up at his answer.

"How did they link him to me? What clue do they have?"

"They found..." he stopped. *Found what?*

"Tell me now! Was it the letter?" Al-Masri's face was intent. "Certainly *they* weren't the ones who intercepted it!"

"Yes!" Terry nearly shouted now. "Yes, they found a letter!"

Al-Masri bent down and placed his hands on Terry's shoulders, eyes burning with intensity. "The one Ahman swore he sent me from Libya! The FBI has it? Are you certain?"

"Yes, yes! They mentioned a letter from a man in Libya named Ahman. But they didn't tell me what was in it. I swear!"

Terry's heart was pounding in his ears, as the pain pounded in his head. He felt suddenly dizzy and disoriented. Al-Masri's eyes cooled into a smirk, and he stood slowly upright. "You're still lying to me, Terrence."

"No!" Terry shook his head, as al-Masri turned again toward the door. "I'm not!"

"Ahman doesn't live in Libya, and there was no letter. Which is really too bad for your family, Whitman."

Terry's stomach again tightened as he realized he had been caught. His hands began to shake, and he choked back a sob of despair.

"So sad for your family," al-Masri repeated.

Terry threw his head back and screamed in frustration. A rasping wail of emotion. His torturer paused at the door, but did not look back. Terry shouted, "You won't be able to harm my family, al-Masri! The FBI will be protecting them now! You won't even get close to them!" It was a sudden thought that gave Terry a measure of comfort as he expressed it.

Al-Masri opened the door and spoke to someone out of view. "I need the syringe." The man with the goatee stepped into the doorway and handed a needle to al-Masri. The two men then approached Terry.

Al-Masri chuckled. "You have no idea who I am, Terrence, or what I am capable of. I have coordinated *jihad* in ways that none have equaled." His steel eyes glinted down at Terry. "Riyahd, for example. May 12, 2003. In three separate car bombings I sent twenty-five infidels to their deaths on that day, and wounded two hundred more. Four days later in Casablanca, five bombings within twenty minutes killed forty-one."

He paused and his eyes looked past Terry, in thought. "Madrid.

March 11, 2004. Three simultaneous train station bombings added two hundred to hell's count. And now in your own country I have shown myself to be possibly the greatest warrior that Allah has ever smiled upon." He looked back into Terry's eyes and his face glowed with pride. "I think I can manage the six Whitmans that will be left on my list after today."

Terry felt suddenly numb. His limbs tingled and a ringing grew in his ears. The man with the goatee grabbed him from behind, holding his arms in an iron grip. Al-Masri brought the needle to Terry's neck.

"This needle is poison, Terrence. You will join your infidel brothers in hell in a matter of minutes. Fortunately for you, I don't have time to draw this out any longer."

Terry found that there was no will in him to resist. As the needle pressed into his neck, he silently asked God to forgive him, and to save his family. He began to weep, and then blackness pressed in to swallow consciousness.

♦

Al-Masri closed the door behind him, and walked toward the stairs. Following close behind, Jared broke the silence.

"Why don't you just kill him and be done with it?"

"Because he's still not telling me what he knows." He felt irritation at being questioned.

"It can't be anything important. I mean, he's just a regular guy, right?"

Al-Masri whirled around with an icy stare. Though Jared easily possessed a hundred pound weight advantage, he took a step back. He knew his place. Without a word, al-Masri turned and proceeded up the stairs.

"Well," Jared offered in a conciliatory tone, "I imagine he'll be more cooperative when he wakes up with those drugs in him."

Chapter 31

Saturday night, 11:50 p.m.

Jennifer lay in her bed and stared up at the ceiling. Her eyes would not stay closed. Her thoughts would not rest, replaying her phone conversation with Mitch for what must have been the thousandth time. It always ended with a desperate urge to run to the phone and dial his number. In her head she listened to herself apologizing and agreeing to meet him tomorrow.

She closed her eyes and sighed heavily. For what must have been the thousandth time she tried to pray.

God, please help me.

Again the prayer faltered. What could she say to this God who had so recently entered her life? She was ashamed of her conflicting desires; longing to know God and build relationships with others who knew him, but nearly as willing to put him aside to pursue the man she loved. *What must God think of my divided heart?*

Jennifer quickly pushed the question away. Instead she thought of Terry and Angela, and decided that she could pray for them. She prayed that Angela would gain courage and comfort from those around her, and from God. She prayed for the children to be safe and happy with their grandparents. And she pled in earnest for Terry's life. She asked for his safe return. She begged God to give some sign that he was still alive, and to show them what to do next.

When she was finished, Jennifer was sure that she had made the right choice to spend the next morning at the Givens.

Then, she slept.

Or did she?

Jennifer felt suddenly disoriented. *It's okay,* she thought. *Just go on down the stairs.*

She continued down the narrow wooden staircase toward the hallway below, and shivered in the cool air. It was not until her foot hit the floor that Jennifer realized with a shock that she had no idea where she was.

This isn't right! I was just in bed! She stifled the urge to cry out in alarm. Wherever she was, it was quiet. Probably still night. No sense in waking up whoever might be in the house. She would simply go back up the stairs and find her way out.

She turned, but something bright caught her eye. At the end of the little hallway stood an elderly man, clothed in white. Jennifer's mouth dropped open, but not in fear. Seeing this man was like beholding peace. He was tall. His gray streaked hair fell shoulder length, and there were the faintest hint of lines around his blue-gray eyes. *Maybe not so elderly.* He winked at her as he put his hand on the knob of the door on the right, opened it, and stepped through.

Jennifer's pulse surged. Where was this place? She knew she shouldn't be here, but there was now only one impulse that drove her. She had to follow that man. Reaching the end of the hall, she looked through the open door, and the sight filled her at once with hope and apprehension. A lone wooden chair faced her direction from the middle of the room. In it sat Terry, his face badly bruised and swollen. He appeared to be sleeping. The man in white placed his hand on Terry's forehead, and spoke something softly to him.

Jennifer wanted to run to her friend, but her feet remained rooted to the floor as she watched in wonder the scene before her. *Am I dreaming? Is this real?* As if in response to her thoughts, the man turned to look at her. He gave a kind smile and another wink, and then knelt down near Terry's feet. Jennifer suddenly noticed the ropes binding Terry's legs to the chair. The man tugged them lightly, and they loosened, settling to the floor. He then rose and again spoke something quietly into Terry's ear. Jennifer wished she could hear what he was saying. Who was this man? An angel? A prophet? Jennifer thought that his face was the kindest face she had ever beheld.

She blinked, realizing that he was looking at her again. She held his gaze for a moment, and felt peace wash over her like a warm breeze. Her knees went unexpectedly weak. And then he was gone. She didn't see him disappear, exactly, but suddenly realized that he wasn't in the room any longer. It was as if she lost her train of thought for a moment, and he slipped away.

Jennifer looked at Terry, and knew that he needed to wake up. The man had loosened his ropes, and he would now be able to walk. She could lead him up the stairs to freedom.

"Terry," she spoke quietly, not wanting to alert anyone in the house. "Terry, wake up." He did not move.

"Terry." She spoke louder and in earnest. His eyelids fluttered this time, but nothing more. Jennifer started toward him, but stopped abruptly when she heard voices from the top of the stairs. She couldn't make out what they were saying, but they sounded agitated.

Jennifer hurried to Terry's side and knelt down by the chair. From up close, the bruises looked even worse than she had first thought. Her heart ached for him, and she wished that she could let him sleep. But the voices from upstairs were growing louder now, almost to the point of shouting. She leaned close to Terry's ear and spoke as loudly as she dared.

"Terry!"

Jennifer's eyes snapped open and she bolted upright in bed. Her bed. Her room. The sound of her own voice had awakened her from the dream.

Terry!

No, it wasn't a dream! It was too real. The musty smell of the basement lingered, and she shivered even though her room was warm. Her mind halted on one thought. God had shown her that Terry was still alive, and that he would now be able to escape his captors!

Joyous hope overwhelmed her, and she both laughed and cried. *Thank you, Jesus!* She suddenly thought of Angela. "I have to tell her!" she exclaimed out loud. Jennifer looked at the clock by her bed. *2:30 a.m.* It was the middle of the night. The realization challenged her excitement. *Was I just dreaming, God? It was so real.* She inhaled through her nose, and smelled only her own room. She strained her ears for any sound, but heard only the silence of night.

She lay back on her pillow. Maybe she should try to get a few more hours of sleep. She could tell Angela about her dream in the morning. *Was it just a dream?* No, it had been more than a dream. She was sure of it.

◆

Terry opened his eyes with a start. The sights and sounds of consciousness flooded his brain once again, and this time everything was sharp. For the moment, his mind was clear of the shock, hunger, fear, and drugs. His eye was still closed and hurting, but the pain wasn't as bad as before.

In an instant Terry took in the room and realized that he was alone. The elder was gone. He had been here, in Terry's dreams, and had given him another draught of the living water. Then he had loosened the ropes. *The ropes!* Terry stared in wonder at his feet, and the slack rope that lay around them. He was free. He had dreamed of someone else as well, urging him to wake up. He could not remember who, but at the moment he was more interested in the arguing voices coming from another part of the house.

He stood up, went to the closed door and pressed his ear against it. The voices were not close, but loud enough for Terry to hear much of what was being said.

"That was over twenty-four hours ago!" Al-Masri sounded on the verge of losing control. "Where have you been?"

Terry could not make out the answer, but he could hear al-Masri's response.

"It took you that long to steal a car and get up here? I thought you were competent! You should have called me on the cell."

A pause for the response.

"I know I said not to use it! But this was an emergency!"

Another voice spoke up. "It wasn't our fault. We don't know how they found us."

"You were careless!" roared al-Masri. "Otherwise they wouldn't have found you! Do you realize the setback this has caused us? I should cut both your throats!"

Terry's hand was on the door, and he slowly turned the knob. He prayed that his guard would be occupied with the argument. The door opened a crack. When nothing happened, Terry pushed the door enough to cautiously peer into the hallway beyond.

Empty.

Al-Masri continued his rant. "Monday is the day we are supposed to strike. Three cities, three schools. I have focused my entire life toward this moment!"

Terry stepped quietly into the hallway. Just as he had expected, there were stairs leading upward at the other end. The hallway was dark, but light came from somewhere upstairs, along with the voices.

"And now, you come to me at two-thirty on Sunday morning and tell me you've lost half of our explosives!"

Terry stopped at the foot of the stairs, aghast. They were planning to blow up schools! He gingerly placed his weight on the first step. It didn't creak. His heart raced, and he prayed for favor. This moment was his chance to escape, while his captors were occupied with their dilemma. He crept up the stairs, step by cautious step, easing his weight onto each one to avoid making any audible noise.

The voices were quieter now, as Terry neared the top step. The room beyond was mostly dark, but he could make out a small kitchen table and chairs through the open staircase door. Light filtered dimly from another room in the house. Terry paused and surveyed the kitchen. It was small and the table and chairs were the only furniture besides the normal kitchen appliances and cabinets. A dark, heavy coat was draped over the back of the nearest chair. To his right, a phone sat on the counter, next to a door with a small window leading out into the night. *And freedom.* Terry fought the urge to bolt wildly for the door. He had to think! Where would he run? It was the middle of the night, and he was in a country that he knew almost nothing about. Above all else, he must not alert his captors to his departure. What if the door's hinges were squeaky? What if it wouldn't open?

Al-Masri was still speaking to the others. "It's settled then. This afternoon you two will take half of what's left in the van, drive to our second target, and proceed as planned. We will stay here and be ready on Monday morning. Two cities, two schools. The infidel children in Louisville will have to live a while longer."

Terry held his breath in disbelief. He wasn't in France! Hope ignited. He would be able to run to the next house and get help! He had to stop these men! He stepped into the kitchen and silently lifted the coat from the chair. He would put it on when he was outside and out of earshot. As he turned toward the door, another man spoke from the other room.

"Well now that it's settled, I'm going to look for something to eat. I'm starving!"

Terry cursed under his breath as panic overtook him. He grabbed the doorknob and noisily jerked it open. A screen door with a glass window met him on the other side, and a surprised voice behind him yelled, "What's that?" Terry punched the handle of the screen door and jumped, clearing all four steps to the ground. He stumbled, recovered, and flung the coat over his arms as he ran. Then his legs were pumping as hard as he had ever made them, and he willed himself to not look back. He was crossing a small field toward a caliginous line of trees. A thin layer of snow crunched beneath his feet, and large flakes fell from the sky. The night was starless, but the clouds gave off a very faint glow, perhaps the reflection of distant city lights. He glanced to his left. A looming hill with shadowy trees scattered randomly on its slopes. To his right, a downward slope and a black strip of road leading away from the house.

From behind Terry heard shouting. "I thought you said he was drugged!"

"He *is* drugged!" Al-Masri's voice. "Shut up and go after him!"

Terry heard footfalls on the steps. He reached the tree line just as al-Masri called out a final chilling order to his men. "Don't bother bringing back the body!" Terry plunged into the woods between two large trees. Darkness instantly fell on him as pine branches closed overhead. He slowed down, but not enough. An unseen branch whipped his face in the blackness and his foot caught on something rigid. He threw out his arms as he fell, crashing to the cold hard ground. He let out a groan, and noticed for the first time that something of substantial weight was in the pocket of the coat he had taken.

Voices laughed behind him, and footsteps slowed. "He's not going much farther, from the sound of it."

Terry reached into the pocket and felt cold steel. The barrel of a gun. He carefully felt for the handle and the trigger, and then held it in his hand in the darkness. His mind began to swim. He had only fired a gun a few times in his life, on a shooting range with his uncle in Wyoming. Terry knew how to pull the trigger, but what if the safety was on? What if it wasn't loaded?

He scrambled around on his knees and peered back toward the house. A rather large tree trunk stood nearly in front of him, and a dozen feet beyond it the trees gave way. Terry could make out the house with the porch light now on, and al-Masri and the man with the goatee standing at the back door. Two dark shapes approached the edge of the wood. He carefully aimed the gun at the chest of the larger man.

Dear God, if this isn't your will then let this gun be empty, and find another way to rescue me.

The explosion caused Terry to jump, and he gasped as he observed the man crumple to the ground without uttering a sound. *Oh God!! Forgive me!* The second man screamed a profanity, and extended his arm in Terry's direction as he dropped to one knee. Terry dove for the tree trunk as multiple gunshots rang into the cold night air. Bullets whistled around him, and a few smacked sharply into the tree. Then silence.

Terry lifted his face from the dirt and peered around the base of the tree. The man in the field was crouching on his feet now, looking intently into the dark woods. The two others were cautiously descending the steps with weapons in their hands. Terry prayed that the shadowy figure would return to the house. Instead, he took a step toward the woods. Terry stayed prone to the ground and aimed again, this time at the man's feet.

Two explosions in succession caused Terry's ears to ring. The man jumped up and ran full speed back toward the house. Al-Masri and the other man sent a volley of bullets into the woods again. Their aim was wrong, and Terry realized that they couldn't see him in the dark. He felt a new wave of anger crash upon him, and almost without thinking, he aimed across the field at the man who had threatened to murder his family.

Two more explosions sent all three terrorists scampering up the steps like startled animals. A third shot caught the man with the goatee in the arm and Terry heard him cry out as al-Masri flung the screen door open. The men fled into the house, and a fourth bullet shattered the door's window as it slammed closed. Then silence.

Terry lowered his head to the ground and relaxed his grip on the pistol. He was shaking, and his breath came in short gasps. He had missed, and Al-Masri was still alive. *God help me*, he prayed.

He looked up at the house, silent now, and suddenly wondered how many children would be at the targeted schools on Monday morning when the terrorists arrived with their explosives. The thought calmed his nerves, and gave him reason to act. He had to get to the authorities and stop al-Masri's plans. They would come after him, of course. They might be trying to sneak up on him already, coming around from another direction. He turned quickly away from the house, and staying on all fours, he began to crawl through the woods as fast as he was able in the dark. Feeling ahead for obstacles, Terry asked God to steer him in the right direction.

♦

Jennifer's eyes would not remain closed. She longed for sleep, but only because sleep would speed the coming of day. Her mind rebelled, replaying the images of her vision yet again: the peaceful man winking at her, calming her, loosening Terry's ropes. All doubt as to the reality of the vision had left her, and Jennifer was certain that Terry was alive. In danger, but on the verge of escaping his kidnappers.

I have to tell Angela! This can't wait until morning. She will want to be praying for him.

Jennifer sat up and reached for the lamp on the nightstand. She took the address book from the drawer and looked up Angela's cell phone number. A few seconds later she heard a sleepy hello on the other end of the line.

"Angela, this is Jennifer." She tried to keep her voice calm. "I'm so sorry to bother you in the middle of the night."

"That's okay, Jennifer. What's the matter? Are you okay?"

"Well—," there was no easy way to lead up to it. "I'm pretty sure I just saw a vision of where Terry is being held."

"*What?*"

Jennifer recounted the details of her experience with a rush of words, and then recounted it all a second time after Angela asked her to slow down. When she finally stopped, there was an uncomfortable silence on the phone.

"I'm sorry," Jennifer suddenly blurted, "you probably think I'm being silly."

"No," Angela answered, "I don't think that." Her voice quivered and Jennifer heard a little sniffle. "I'm so glad you called, Jennifer. We need to pray hard for Terry now. That's why God showed you what he did. I'm going to call some other close friends to ask them to pray as well."

"Okay, I will be praying from now until I see you later this morning."

"You can come over early if you want. I'll be awake now."

"Alright, I'll see you in a few hours."

She said goodbye and hung up the phone. Kneeling by her bed, Jennifer folded her hands and prayed again for her friend.

Chapter 32

Terry clawed forward through the darkness. The going was painfully slow, and after only a few minutes his fingers grew numb with cold. He stopped and thrust his hands into the coat pockets. As expected, his right hand felt the cold steel of the gun, but he was surprised to find that his left hand also grabbed something familiar—a cell phone! With a wild rush of hope, Terry took it out and pressed a button, lighting up the phone's tiny display. The dim glow forced darkness to retreat, revealing the nearby trees around him.

He looked at the phone. The date and time told him that it was 2:50 a.m. on Sunday morning, and a tell-tale "No Signal" message indicated that the phone was out of range of a cellular tower. Hope fading, he entered Angela's number, praying for a miracle. A few seconds of the phone's silence informed him of what he already knew. A phone call was not possible.

He had to act quickly to find help, or at least get within range of a cell tower. Holding the phone out in front of him, it gave off just enough light to allow him to jog through the trees at a comfortable pace. The business-casual shoes he wore were not particularly conducive to running, but they would do. He pressed on through the dark woods, listening intently for any sound of pursuit. The minutes ticked by.

Terry was glad that he had taken up jogging for exercise. He knew he could be miles away within an hour. He checked the phone often to keep track of time. Ten minutes. Fifteen minutes. Twenty. Each time he looked, the words "No Signal" looked back at him from the phone's display, a defiant message deepening his despair. Though the terrain was mostly wooded, there were small clearings and fields to cross. He always steered toward a faint glow on the horizon, assuming it to be a city of some size.

Presently his legs began to weaken, and his breathing became labored. Terry looked again at the phone. He had only been running for thirty minutes, but in his debilitated physical state this cross-country run was grueling. Coming to an open spot at the top of a small ridge, he stopped and sucked the cold air into his lungs. Snow continued to fall and a stiff icy breeze cut at his face. He tried to think of a better course of action than running and hoping, but there was no other course. He had to find shelter, people, or a cellular signal. None of these would find him in this clearing. He asked God for strength and willed his legs to continue.

The landscape now became more open as woods gave way to rolling hills. Terry stumbled often, his leaden feet catching on an unseen rock or low bush. He prayed that he would not break an ankle in a hole. Just when his mind seemed completely numb with exhaustion, he crested a hill and blinked at the sight before him.

A gentle slope led down to the dark looming shadow of a building. It appeared to be a barn, standing silent in the night. Terry stopped and tried to listen over his heavy breathing. There were no other sounds of life that he could hear.

He shuffled his feet cautiously down the hill and came directly to the large double doors of the barn. They stood partially open, and the inside was black and still. From up close, the wooden doors appeared aged and worn. He pushed his way inside, too tired to care about trespassing. The dim light of the cell phone did not illuminate to the back of the barn, but Terry immediately noticed a pile of hay in the corner nearby. Bone-weary and disheartened, he sank down into the hay and tried to pull some of it over him for extra warmth. The instant he was settled, sleep overtook him.

◆

Al-Masri stared into the back of the van, his mood sullen. There were only four boxes of explosives, timers, and other assorted essentials for the mission in Decatur. It was less than half of what he had planned for. His bold *jihad* called next for three elementary schools to be destroyed by blasts large enough to rock the surrounding communities. The shock of such devastation would result in a closing of the nation's schools for an extended period of time. The farther-reaching effects would accomplish the true goal.

He had already succeeded in making people afraid to go out Christmas shopping. Retail sales for the season were at a record low. Now the churches were virtually empty on Sundays too, and the masses were fearful to leave their homes unless absolutely necessary. With the completion of the next phase, the education system would grind to a halt, and parents would be forced to miss weeks of work. The great U.S. economy – envy of the modern world – would very likely come crashing down like a house of cards. The stock market had already taken a perilous plunge over the past weeks, teetering on the brink of total collapse.

All of this had been al-Masri's doing.

But now he faced the first bump in what had been a remarkably smooth road. Now there would only be two schools to blow up, and the explosions would not be nearly as terrifying to behold. The effect of the attacks would still be considerable, if his teams executed properly, but not as devastating as al-Masri had hoped for. Not as perfect as he had painstakingly prepared for.

He actually contemplated delaying his plans in order to acquire more explosives. Any delay, however, would be too risky. The elimination of the Louisville cell had been evidence enough that the FBI could turn up a deadly lead at any time. And now that Whitman had escaped, it would be impossible to remain in this area of the country any longer. Al-Masri fumed as he thought of the man who had caused him so much trouble. He should have killed him. It had been a blunder to keep him alive, fretting about what the FBI might know. If he ever got the chance, al-Masri would not hesitate to rectify this mistake.

Locking the van's doors, he pondered Whitman's escape. Nothing about it made sense. He knew that Terrence should be too drugged to think straight. Yet he had escaped, and shot one of his men dead in the process. His aim had been far too accurate to dismiss as blind luck. Perhaps he was resistant to the drugs. Perhaps the drugs had been diluted by the supplier. Whatever the reason, Whitman was gone and apparently thinking clearly. They had searched the woods for forty-five minutes, circling around from behind, and found nothing. While it would take some time before Terrence could reach help, al-Masri was now determined to be gone before daylight.

He shook himself out of his thoughts, and walked quickly back to the house. In the kitchen, Jared looked up from a chair, his right arm wrapped in a bloody bandage above the elbow. "Are we all packed?"

"Mostly. Are the others resting?"

"Yes," Jared answered, "they were pretty beat. I told them to try to get an hour of sleep."

"And what about you?" Al-Masri looked hard at his soldier, one of the few U.S. native-born citizens that had joined Allah's cause over the years. "How is your arm?"

Jared snorted loudly. "Oh, I've had worse. Bullet just grazed me."

"It cut through the muscle. It's going to hinder your effectiveness."

Jared stood slowly to his full height, and his face grew hard. "No, sir. It won't." He flexed a muscular left arm. "I can shoot plenty straight with a machine gun in my left hand. Especially when most of the targets will be screaming children."

Al-Masri studied the man before him, and finally nodded in agreement. The truth was, he needed Jared. Their cell count was now just four. The other three would carry out the attacks on the schools, and he alone would live to activate the remaining cells for the last phase of the *jihad*.

Jared returned to his seat and shivered.

"Why don't you get your coat?" al-Masri asked. An icy glare reminded him that it had been Jared's coat that Whitman had stolen. He shook his head. "Serves you right, leaving your gun—." Al-Masri stopped and stared.

"What?" Jared demanded.

"Did you have anything else in your coat pockets, Jared?"

"Huh?" Jared thought for a moment, before his face went pale. "My cell phone!"

Al-Masri's eyes grew wide, and heat spread across his face. "You stupid..." he couldn't think of a term that was derogatory enough. "He's probably called the police!" Jared looked petrified as al-Masri strode to the counter and snatched up his own cell. "There's one way to find out," he mumbled as he dialed the stolen phone's number.

◆

Terry's arms were heavy as he tried to push through thick tree branches in the dead of night. He knew al-Masri was close now, pursuing him like a tireless bloodhound. His heart beat faster, even as his progress slowed. The branches pushed against him, and there was no light. He shielded his eyes with one arm and tried to force his way forward, leaning into the pine needles. *How can trees grow so close?* he thought desperately.

Suddenly Terry heard the sound of twigs snapping behind him. Al-Masri was almost upon him! He lurched forward, but this time the branches did not give way. They sprang back, throwing him to the ground. He heard al-Masri's cold laugh.

The terrorist's voice was close, but Terry was blind in the surrounding darkness. He screamed out in terror, "SOMEBODY HELP ME!!" The suffocating blackness pressed in on him, and silence was the only answer. Then he heard a sound, like bells across a great distance.

Not bells, but a muffled ringing that repeated. Not far away, but very close. It was the cell phone in his pocket!

Terry rolled over and tried to sit up, but the branches made it difficult. He groped in his pocket and found the phone.

"Hehhhmmph." He meant to say hello, but the word came out muddled.

"Hello?" Al-Masri's voice reached him through the night, soft and chilling like an arctic breeze. "Terrence, is that you?"

Terry tried to stand, but his legs were unsteady and the branches still encroached on him. He managed to get to his knees and gather his voice.

"I know you're here, al-Masri!" he shouted. "I heard you coming!"

"You did? Terrence, where are you?"

"You know I'm here! You know where the thick trees are!" Terry peered wide-eyed into the dark. "SHOW YOURSELF, MURDERER!"

There was a pause, and Terry brushed the hay out of his hair. *Hay??*

"You're in the thick trees, Terrence?" Al-Masri now spoke slowly, patronizing. Terry reached down and felt more dry straw all around.

"No," he mumbled into the phone, "they aren't pine trees. It's hay."

"I see, Terrence," al-Masri continued to patronize. "It's thick *hay*, then?"

"No!" Disoriented, Terry jumped to his feet, stumbled, and fell back to his knees. The floor was hard, made of wood. The distinct feeling of wood beneath him caused his mind to race back toward reality. *I'm in a barn! I must have been having a nightmare when the cell phone rang and woke me.*

"Terrence, are you still with me?"

"Stop confusing me." Terry took a deep breath and let it out. "Just go away al-Masri."

He hung up the phone and stared at the display. It was 3:55 a.m., and to his astonishment, the "No Signal" message was gone. He had forgotten to look one last time before falling into the pile of straw. The display was also indicating that the phone's battery was all but spent.

With shaking fingers, Terry pressed the numbers of Angela's phone. After only one ring, he heard a sound like beautiful music.

"Hello?"

He choked back a sob of emotion and took a deep breath to steady himself.

"Angela, it's me."

"Oh, thank God! Terry, where—"

"Angela, listen to me!" His voice was firm, and she stopped mid-sentence. "I can't talk now. I don't know where I am, exactly, but I have to talk to Agent Kepler right now. Please get me his cell phone number."

◆

"What was that all about?" asked Jared with interest. Al-Masri smiled across the table at his long-time disciple.

"Apparently I was right after all." He chuckled. "The drugs still seem to be in his system, and working quite well."

Jared looked doubtful. "How can you be sure?"

"He didn't know if he was in the woods or a hay field! And he thought I was there with him. Said he heard me coming." Al-Masri laughed now, out of relief.

Jared grinned and laughed along. "Well, I guess he's pretty messed up then!"

"Yes, and he's still miles from any help." Al-Masri sighed and closed his eyes, allowing himself to relax. He should have learned by now to trust that Allah's ways would prevail over the ungodly. After a moment, he stood and looked at Jared. "We both could use a little sleep before we leave." Jared remained in his chair, but looked hopeful.

"Are you sure?"

"Yes," al-Masri nodded. "Even if Whitman chanced upon

another human being in the next two hours, he would never be able to lead them to us in his state of mind. We should sleep for three hours. After that, we go."

Chapter 33

Terry peered at the cell phone display as he entered the number Angela had given to him. He tried to commit the number to memory, and begged God for enough battery power to complete the call. Three rings, and a groggy voice spoke on the other end.

"Hello?"

Terry was not entirely sure that the voice belonged to Josh. "Agent Kepler, is that you?"

"Yes!" came the instant reply. "Terry, where are you?"

Terry spoke quickly, his words tumbling out in a frenzy. "I'm in an old empty barn in the middle of nowhere, and I'm calling you on a cell phone that I stole from them, and it's about to go dead, so listen fast. Al-Masri is behind all of it. Do you hear me, Josh? He's the one running the show for the terrorist cells here in the states, and he's not in France. They are planning to blow up some schools tomorrow, one in some other city and one near here, wherever *here* is. They were going to blow one up in Louisville too, but something happened that messed up their plans, and they lost half their explosives in the process."

Josh interrupted. "Okay, hold on, Terry! You've got to tell me where al-Masri is hiding. An address, or a street name or something."

"Uhm…" Terry thought franticly. "They are in a little country house, and there was a van parked in the driveway I think. Maybe gray."

"Terry, you've got to give me more than that. Help me find you. Did they mention the name of a street or a town, or even the state they are in?"

"I don't know! I barely got away alive, and it was dark! I didn't see a house number, and they didn't say anything. They only mentioned Louisville by name."

"But they are not in Louisville?"

"No. There are two cities where schools will be attacked. One near here, and another one somewhere within a day's drive."

"That could be anywhere." Josh's frustration was obvious. "Okay, Terry, listen to me. Are you on foot?"

"Yes."

"Did you see any landmarks in your area that might give us a clue?"

"No, not really. There were a lot of woods, mostly pine trees. After a couple miles the trees thinned out a little, and the landscape is small hills with some rocky terrain. Nothing that stands out."

"Can you see the stars from where you are?"

Terry stepped out of the barn. The snow had stopped but the sky remained dark with clouds. "No. It was snowing pretty good, and it's still cloudy. There is a glow in the sky, probably from a city in the distance, but I can't even tell you what direction that would be. I finally ran far enough to get a signal on this stupid phone."

There was a pause, and Terry knew Josh was trying to think of any other piece of information that might help define his location. He looked around, though he didn't know what he was looking for.

Suddenly Josh shouted into the phone. "Terry, the cell phone! What is it's number?"

Of course! It would at least tell them the area code. Terry looked at the phone and quickly navigated the menus. Luckily it was not very different from others he had owned, and he was able to find the number and read it out to Josh.

"That area code is Indianapolis!" Josh exclaimed. "Terry, listen to me! I can be up there in less than two hours. You've got to call me back with a street name, or something else that will help me find you when I get there. Understand?"

"Yes, I'll try."

"Don't just try, Terry! Indy is a huge area, and we won't find you *or* al-Masri without some better directions. A lot of lives depend on what we do in the next two hours, Terry."

"Okay, I understand. Josh, there's one more thing. Al-Masri mentioned another name. Someone that is involved with them somehow. Someone named *Ahman*. I don't know if that's a first name or a last name, but al-Masri seemed to be very upset when he thought that the FBI had found out about him."

Terry paused, and there was no response.

"Josh? Did you get that?"

The only answer was the icy breeze gusting through the barn door. Terry looked at the phone in his hand, and noticed the display was blank, the battery spent. He had just lost his only link to help. It didn't matter. He had escaped, and Josh was coming.

♦

Jennifer listened on the phone as Angela repeated the amazing news, "Did you hear me, Jennifer? Terry escaped! Just like you said he would!"

"Yes, I heard you. Now slow down and tell me everything. What did he say?"

"He couldn't say much. I couldn't believe I was hearing his voice again! I am so relieved, Jennifer!"

"Yes," Jennifer tried to be patient, "but what did he *say*? Where is he, Angela?"

"Well, he didn't know for sure. He said he was in the middle of nowhere, in a barn, and that the cell phone he was using was almost dead, so he couldn't talk. He needed to get Josh's number and call him right away."

"And Josh called you too?"

"Yes, Josh called me right after he spoke to Terry. Can you believe it, Jennifer? Your dream was *real*! Isn't that incredible?"

Jennifer laughed. "Yes, I can't believe that God showed me that! I wonder why he wanted *me* to see it?"

"God loves to get people involved in what he's doing. He knew that you would call me, and that we would start praying for Terry."

"And we sure did! I was praying so hard, Angela." Jennifer felt joy bubbling within her, like a spring of clear water. "But tell me what Josh said."

"Oh yes, Josh... Well, Josh talked to Terry for only a few minutes before the phone went dead. Terry told him he had escaped, and that the vice president from your company is the one who kidnapped him."

"You mean al-Masri," interrupted Jennifer.

"Yes, that's him. Al-Masri is some kind of terrorist cell leader, and he is planning to blow up some schools tomorrow, but Terry didn't know where."

"He didn't have any idea where he was?"

"No, but the number of the cell phone that Terry had taken was an Indianapolis area code, so Josh is going to drive up there."

"Now?" Jennifer felt worried again. "But what if that's not where Terry is? How will Josh know where to find him?"

"Well, Terry is looking for a road or a house or something. And then he will find a phone and call Josh back. If he *is* near Indianapolis, then Josh will be half-way there by the time Terry calls."

"Maybe he is still near Louisville," Jennifer hoped out loud.

"No, Terry heard them mention Louisville, and he was certain that they were no longer around here."

"Well, we have to keep praying then, that Terry will find help soon."

"And that he finds a phone. I'm going to call some others to tell them the news and have them keep praying."

"Okay. Thank you so much for calling, Angela. I'll talk to you soon."

Jennifer hung up the phone, her mind spinning. Terry was alive! And for the moment, out of harm's way. She would continue to pray for his safe return, and that al-Masri would be stopped. But first she decided to call Mitch and tell him the good news. He would want to know.

Mitch sounded less than fully conscious when he answered the phone, but was quickly roused when Jennifer told him of Terry's escape. When she finished by saying that Josh was leaving right away to go look for Terry in Indianapolis, Mitch couldn't contain himself.

"WHAT? He's driving up there now? I'm going with him!"

"Mitch," Jennifer responded, "don't be silly."

But Mitch had already hung up. She tried to call him back, and heard only a busy signal. *God, don't let him do something stupid.*

◆

"Absolutely not," said Josh. "This is an official FBI case, Mitch." He winced as soon as he said it.

"From what I understand," challenged Mitch, "you are no longer with the FBI. Which means I have as much right as you do to go looking for Terry."

Josh didn't have time for an argument. "Fine. Good luck then."

"Please, Josh, don't hang up!" Desperation colored his voice. "You can't go after him by yourself anyways! What if you run into those terrorists?"

"What if I do?" Josh responded evenly. "I've been specially trained to deal with just that kind of a situation, Mitch. You have not. These men are killers."

"I've got some training too, Josh! My *357* and I can take care of ourselves just fine."

Josh closed his eyes to think, suddenly reminded that he was unarmed after turning over his weapon at the station. Of course he would pick up another gun at his home in Indy, but what if Terry called first?

Mitch continued, "I can hit the bulls-eye of a target ten times out of ten, and I seriously doubt that al-Masri can outrun a bullet. I'm not lying when I say that I could be of use to you, Josh."

Josh sighed. A voice inside was telling him to go along with the events that were unfolding. This group of friends around Terry was something special. Angela had not even sounded surprised by Terry's phone call, and had briefly recounted the details of Jennifer's vision. There had been a dozen people praying for Terry's escape this very night. It occurred to Josh that Terry belonged to a cell of his own – a network of allies united in opposition to the forces that had come against them – and Mitch was a part of that network.

"Josh," Mitch broke the silence, "are you still there?"

"Yeah, I'm here." He smiled to himself. "Mitch, do you have any other guns besides your *357*? Mine's been confiscated."

"You'd better believe it! Will a shotgun do?"

◆

From the top of a small hill, Terry peered forlornly across the little valley toward the dull glow in the clouds on the horizon. There had to be a city of some size in that direction, but how far? He looked over the dark terrain below him in all directions, searching in vain for signs of life. All was dark, quiet and cold in the early morning hours. He turned and looked back down the hill in the direction he had come. The old barn below him remained the only sign that humanity had ever known these hills. Beyond it, Terry studied the upward slope and sparse trees which led back toward the terrorist hideout.

Which direction should he go to find safety and a phone? He remembered the last words Josh had spoken to him before the cell's battery went dead. *Don't just try, Terry... A lot of lives depend on what we do in the next two hours.* He knew that Josh was right. Unless al-Masri was stopped, he was going to blow up two schools in the next twenty-four hours. It would be impossible to stop him if nobody knew where the terrorists were.

I know where al-Masri is.

The thought clicked in his mind, like a light switching on. He quickly suppressed it. He had to find a house! He could borrow a phone, and the owners could tell Josh where they were. But in which direction should he set out from here?

Terry stomped his foot on the ground in frustration. "Come on, God," he mumbled, "give me a sign or something. Which way to the nearest phone?" He closed his eyes, cleared his mind, and tried to listen. Instead of hearing the voice of God, another thought clicked.

I know where a phone is. He could see it in his mind, on the kitchen counter by the back door through which he had fled.

He opened his eyes and looked back past the barn again. Towards the house. Towards terror. A dread began to settle upon him, and several thoughts now poured into his mind at once. The terrorists' house might be the only one for miles around, which would make sense. The realization that he was the only one who knew how to get there was quickly followed by the thought that he was the only one who could do *anything* to stop al-Masri.

An idea that had been nagging at the back of his brain now burst forth with clarity. *I have to try to stop him myself.*

Shaking his head, Terry attempted to resist the conclusion that had worked its way into his mind. He could not go back. It would be the worst decision of his life. He would be killed, and al-Masri would blow up the schools anyway.

"What good would that do?" he shouted to the clouds. "I'd be dead! And for nothing!" The wind whipping past his ears was the only answer.

He again felt the gun in the coat pocket, and the image of the terrorist crumpling to the ground replayed in his mind. Maybe he could shoot more of them. Maybe he could kill al-Masri. Who else could?

No one.

The thought resounded in Terry's brain, like a gavel announcing a death sentence. He shivered and closed his eyes, wavering. Fear and dread waged war against the desire to be brave. Then he remembered the words of the elder in his dreams.

Sometimes it takes great suffering to bring about salvation. Those who remain faithful receive the greatest treasure...entrance into God's kingdom.

Opening his eyes, Terry asked God for help, and then started back at a quick jog. His struggle against fear was over. His struggle against terror was not.

Chapter 34

Terry jogged through the cold early morning hours, now without a light to aid him. When the trees grew thick he took time to work his way around them, always bearing to his left. He had seen the road leading straight away from the house in that direction, and thought that he would do best to find that road and follow it to the house. He might be lucky enough to find a sign or another house.

He came to one wooded area that seemed too large to circumvent, so he plunged into the trees and crawled on all fours, feeling his way forward with his hands. After many long minutes Terry began to perceive the shadows of the trees again. Soon he was making his way on foot, and came presently to an area of sparser trees. He realized with some relief that the clouds were dissipating in the breeze, and stars were beginning to shine brightly down.

Terry made his way around or through more patches of trees, driven onward by the conviction that this was the course he had been given to follow. His conversation with God was constant now. He said prayers for his family, for Josh, for his friends, for the children in the schools. Prayers against the evils of terror, against al-Masri and his cells, against the plans of the spiritual enemies of God. He also added the simple request that God would allow him to live through another day. He didn't know which of his prayers would be answered favorably, but he had learned long ago that conversation with God was important regardless of the outcome.

When Terry finally came to a road, he stopped only for a moment to catch his breath. He was certain that it had taken more than an hour to get this far, but it was impossible to know for sure. He could see no road sign in either direction, so he turned to his right and began to jog along the road, presuming the house to be less than a mile away. Terry returned to his prayers as he ran, only mildly aware of the increasing pain in his head and side.

♦

Josh kept one hand on the steering wheel as he reached to answer his cell phone.

"This is Kepler."

"We found the owner."

Josh recognized Dickerson's voice. "The owner of the cell phone Terry used?" He glanced toward the passenger's seat and noticed Mitch's eyes widen with interest.

"Yes. His name is Jared Cabrera, and he lives right here in a downtown apartment."

"I knew it!" Josh exclaimed as he steered the car toward an off-ramp. "Did you pick him up yet?"

"Negative." There was disappointment in Dickerson's voice. "We knocked on the door and got no answer, so we let ourselves in."

"The door was open?"

"That's not what I said, Kepler. Now are you gonna let me finish?"

"Yes, but say it fast. Terry could call at any moment."

"All right, all right. I was saying it plenty fast 'til you interrupted me." Josh clenched his jaw and forced himself to remain quiet. His ex-partner let the silence linger and finally resumed with, "Now, where was I?"

Josh came to an abrupt stop at a red light. "The apartment!!" He wondered why Dickerson always insisted on pushing his buttons at times like this.

"Oh, yeah, the apartment! That's right. No one's been in there for at least a couple weeks. We've got someone watching it, but don't hold your breath."

"Did you check for prints?"

"Yes, and it appears that only Cabrera has been in there."

Josh sighed as the light turned green, allowing him to proceed through the suburbs of Indianapolis. "Who is this guy anyways?"

"Well, we haven't had time to get all the details, but he's an interesting fellow from the looks of it. Age twenty-seven, born in New York City to a single mother on crack. He was placed in foster care of course, and it appears he landed in a different home every time he got into trouble."

"What kind of trouble?"

"In and out of juvenile detention on three different occasions, between the ages of fourteen and sixteen. When he turned eighteen, Jared decided he was truly all grown up, and proved it with an armed robbery."

"And time in prison," concluded Josh.

"Not as much as he should have done. New York has that silly 'youthful offender' status for criminals under nineteen years old, so instead of getting the minimum of five years, our boy Jared served a mere three."

"Anything since then?" Josh asked, not wanting to hear a discourse on under-age criminal sentencing.

"That's where it gets interesting. His prison records indicate that Jared became a member of a Muslim religious group at the prison, after which he was never written up for bad behavior. Shortly after he got out, he moved to Indianapolis and took a job on the production line at one of the automobile plants here. And that's the end of the story. No criminal activity for the past five years."

"Except for the part where he became a terrorist, you mean," Josh said.

"Yeah, except for that."

"And you found nothing in the apartment indicating where he might have gone?"

"Nothing."

"So we are still at square one."

"That's about it. We'll try to contact his employer later today, but it's Sunday. Unfortunately we've got nothing unless your hostage calls in again."

"Thanks, partner. I'll let you know when he does."

Josh ended the call, feeling as if a new weight had been placed on his shoulders. He wondered what he would do if Terry wasn't in Indy after all, but quickly pushed the doubt from his mind. *Come on, Terry. All you have to do is find a phone and make one more call.*

◆

Terry peered at the road sign, grateful that the clouds had dispersed and the moon now shone down from low on the horizon. He could just make out the designation of "Highway 167" for the road he was following, while "Briar Creek Way" split off in another direction. He committed the names to memory, and at the same time reminded himself of Josh's cell phone number. He thought of the phone by the back door of al-Masri's house, and wondered if the door would be locked. How would he get inside? How many seconds would it take him to make the call and tell Josh the address? How long would it take Josh to get there?

With no answers to satisfy him, Terry cleared the questions from his mind and set out once more along Highway 167, presumably toward the house. He knew he must be close now. As he crested a small hill his suspicions were confirmed. By the moon's light he could see that the road veered to the right and down the hill, where it curved back to the left and ascended a long gentle slope of scattered trees. Two-thirds of the way up the slope Terry could make out a house on the right side of the road. Two vehicles sat in the driveway on the near side, and there was a small open field behind the house, bordered by a wall of thick trees.

His heart nearly stopped at the sight, but Terry forced his feet to keep their stride down the hill. Then he slowed to a walk, listening carefully for any sound. The wind rustled through the trees. Nothing more. The house was dark; the porch lights were off, and no light shown from the windows. Terry crossed to the opposite side of the road and stopped behind a good-sized tree, only a stone's throw from the house.

He rested for a time, allowing his breathing to slow, and formulated his next actions in his mind. He then proceeded quickly and quietly toward the mailbox at the front of the driveway. After he noted the number, Terry crouched low and ducked behind the first vehicle, an SUV. Staying out of view from the house, he knelt by the front tire and fumbled for the air valve. After a few seconds he found it, and the air began to softly hiss out of the tire.

Minutes passed. It seemed like hours, and Terry begged God to keep the terrorists inside. Finally the tire sank to a level of flatness that would prevent the vehicle from being driven any distance. He moved silently to the van, keeping the vehicles between him and the house, and began the process a second time. More minutes passed. As the van's tire slowly sank, Terry's apprehension rose. He wondered if al-Masri was awake in the house. He wondered if the van was already loaded with explosives. He flinched at every imagined sound in the night.

He had intended to flatten two tires on the van, but by the time he finished with the first, his fear of being caught had grown too strong. He turned away from the house and sprinted a hundred yards down the slope. Remembering his plan, he angled to his left, heading for the dense trees. He was leaving footprints in the snow of course. Al-Masri would see them.

Presently, Terry was forced to slow his pace to a walk. Surrounded by trees, the moon provided scarcely enough light to make his way. He followed a wide arc through the woods, circling behind the house and around to the other side. When he was certain he had gone far enough, he made a final turn – his best guess at a straight line back to the clearing. In a matter of minutes his guess was proved correct. He stepped out from the trees and looked across the small field to the house. From where he stood, the driveway was now on the far side, and he could just make out the front half of the van in the moonlight.

Satisfied, Terry crouched back into the shadows and knelt to the ground behind a large tree where he could watch the house unseen. It had taken him at least ten minutes to make his way to this spot from the driveway, maybe more. If they followed him it would take them as long. Al-Masri would follow. Terry was counting on it.

♦

Angela listened as Pam, Roger, and Jennifer took turns praying. She had called Jennifer to suggest that she come over and pray with them, and Jennifer had readily agreed. It was still early – 6:20 in the morning – but they all knew this was a critical day for many reasons. Although Terry had escaped, he still had not been found. It was likely that the terrorists were looking for him as well, and Angela would not rest until he was safe.

There was also the matter of the plot to blow up the elementary schools. Josh had said that the FBI in Indianapolis was considering several options, including shutting down all schools in the city. But since there were targets in two different cities, and no proof that Indy was one of them, the decision was on hold for the moment. The only sure way to stop the attacks would be to find al-Masri today. Thus, finding Terry quickly was the key to saving many innocent lives.

So Angela and her friends intended to pray until Terry was found. She had seen to it that many people were praying. Several more would be joining them at the Givens' house later in the morning. She took comfort in the knowledge that so many were banding together to resist the enemy through prayer. A passage from the Bible ran through her mind. *Two people are better than one... One person can be overpowered by an enemy, but two can resist, and a triple-braided rope is not easily broken.*

Her thoughts were suddenly interrupted by her cell phone

ringing. She answered it immediately. "Hello?"

"Angela, this is Josh. Mitch and I have made it to my house in Indy, but Terry hasn't called yet." Angela's heart sank, and she tried to steady her emotions as Josh continued, "I was wondering if there was any chance that you had heard from him there."

"No," she answered quietly, "he hasn't called here either." She looked at the others, and saw the disappointment in their eyes.

Josh sighed. "Alright, I'll check back with the authorities here, and we'll try to figure out our next move."

Angela felt desperate for more news. "Is anyone else looking for him yet, Josh?"

"Yes, the FBI and the local police have some choppers in the air now, but it's a needle-and-haystack scenario at this point. There's a chance he's not even in this part of the country. We're just guessing."

"No," she answered emphatically. "I don't believe that. You are close, Josh. I know it."

"To be honest, I'm not so sure Angela."

Tears suddenly fogged her vision, and Angela's voice filled with emotion as she answered. "Just pray, Josh. Ask God where Terry is. He will show you." Josh remained silent, so she pressed the issue with a question. "Why would God allow the enemy to win when Terry is in a position to stop their plan?"

Josh sighed again. "That's a good question. Okay, Angela, of course I'll keep praying."

She smiled through her tears. "Don't stop until you find him, Josh."

◆

Josh hung up the phone and sat down in silence at his kitchen table, inwardly asking God for direction. He tried to quiet his thoughts and listen with his spirit. It was difficult. His mind was hard at work, trying to grasp some straw that he had until now overlooked. He realized that the effort was futile. Only God knew where Terry was, and why he had not been able to call. *So what's your plan, God?*

There was an idea, growing somewhere beneath the surface of his conscious thought. It was more of a feeling or a knowing, rather than thought. He had at first decided to remain here in favor of driving around with no clue where to search. Now he perceived the beginnings of a restlessness beyond his obvious frustrations. Waiting wasn't the right choice.

Mitch emerged from a hall bathroom and walked into the kitchen, stopping in the doorway and looking exhausted. "Well, we've got your car loaded with all your guns and gear. What now?"

Josh smiled. During their conversation on the road from Louisville, he had gathered that Mitch did not share the Whitmans' faith in God. He had not pressed the issue then.

"Do you believe in God, Mitch?"

Mitch looked surprised by the question. "I'm an agnostic."

Josh chuckled. "So, if I have my religious definitions right, that simply means that you don't know if you believe in God."

"Yeah, that's sort of right." Mitch gave a tired smile. "I believe that even if a god did exist, we wouldn't be able to know about it or understand it. Religion is just humanity's way of coping with life. It really doesn't prove the existence of a god."

"Well then!" Josh smiled broadly as he rose from his chair. "I guess that means I'm praying for both of us!" He reached for his laptop computer case on the counter, and turned for the door.

"Where are we going?"

Josh walked down the two steps into the garage, where his car was waiting. "I'm not sure," he answered over his shoulder, "I've just got a feeling."

"What? Is that how the FBI makes crucial decisions these days?"

"No, it's not," Josh laughed at the quip. "But I'm not with the FBI anymore, remember?" He climbed into the driver's seat and closed the door. When Mitch was settled into the seat next to him, Josh looked him in the eye. "It *is* how people who know they believe in God make decisions sometimes." He grinned. "If you've got a brilliant agnostic idea of what we should do next, I'm all ears."

Mitch shook his head. "Anything is better than sitting around here."

Josh pressed the garage door opener and started the car. Mitch looked away and grumbled just loud enough for him to hear, "It seems I'm surrounded by you people lately."

Chapter 35

Terry shifted his weight to keep his legs from falling asleep. How long had he been sitting here, waiting and watching? Light was just beginning to be perceptible on the horizon, but a shadowy darkness lingered defiantly around him. Hands thrust into the coat's pockets, he still shivered in the cold. He wondered how many bullets remained in the gun. He wouldn't have known how to check in the daylight, let alone here in the dark. It would have to remain a last resort, for defensive use only.

Terry looked again at the house, and noticed with a shock that the kitchen light had been turned on. Light now streamed out the window onto the back steps. His senses went on full alert, and he looked for any sign of movement.

Nothing.

He held his breath until he had to let it out. Abruptly the back porch light came on, and a man emerged carrying a bag of some kind. Al-Masri. He quickly went to the van, unlocked the door, and deposited the bag into the driver's seat.

Terry removed the hand gun and aimed across the clearing. What if he could shoot al-Masri from here, and end the whole thing? He quickly decided against it. His hand was anything but steady, trembling from the cold and fatigue. Even if by a miracle he killed al-Masri, the sound would bring the rest of them. If he missed, the sound would bring all of them. Too many chances for a bad ending. Reluctantly he returned the gun to its pocket.

Al-Masri went back inside, and momentarily emerged again, with a box this time. He carried it around to the other side of the van, opened the side door, and deposited it in the vehicle. Terry was impatient. *Come on, al-Masri. Look at the tires!*

Al-Masri did not immediately emerge from behind the van, and Terry found himself holding his breath again. Then he saw the terrorist leader walk slowly around the van, studying the ground. He looked in the direction that Terry had run, and then he made his way back up the porch steps. With a last look past the van, he pulled open the door and quickly disappeared inside.

Yes! You've got a problem, al-Masri, and you better go track it down. He heard shouting from within the house, in a language that he did not recognize. More lights illuminated inside, and shadows appeared in windows. He couldn't tell for sure how many terrorists there were. He had only seen two others besides al-Masri and the man he shot. He hoped there weren't more.

Suddenly the lights went off, the back door flew open, and three men emerged into the cold wearing dark coats and hats. He couldn't make out faces this time, but was certain that the one in the lead was al-Masri. He was carrying something in his hand, most likely a gun. The other two carried weapons that were large enough to spot in the faint light, and he assumed these were machine guns or assault rifles of some type. The men ran off away from the house, following Terry's trail in the snow. He watched them go until their shadows were lost among the trees.

His heart thumped in his chest, as if it would burst. He studied the house, now dark, and listened intently for any sound from inside. There was no noise, no movement. Now was the time to carry out his plan. He couldn't wait a second longer.

Pleading to God for safety, he gritted his teeth and set off full-speed for the back door. Half-way there he removed the gun and held it ready. He looked to his left. No sign of the three terrorists in the shadows. Then he was bounding up the steps, stopping, crouching, and trying to still his breathing.

As quietly as he could manage, he opened the door and let himself in. The phone was on the counter where he remembered it, and he immediately scooped it up and dialed. To his great relief he heard a click after only one ring, and a voice that he recognized.

"Hello, this is Josh."

"It's me," Terry whispered closely into the phone. "Their house is nineteen sixty-eight, Highway one sixty-seven. First house on the right, after the intersection with Briar Creek Way. Did you get that?"

"Yes, Terry, one nine six eight, Highway one six seven, after Briar Creek Way. And where are *you*?"

"I'm here too. I'll try to hide in the woods until you get here. Hurry!" Terry quietly returned the phone to its cradle. There was still no sound from within the house. He was going to make it! He put his hand on the door when he suddenly heard voices from outside. He looked frantically out the window, and to his horror saw the three shadows returning from the same way they had gone. They hadn't followed his footprints far enough! If he went out the back now, they would see him for certain.

Terry backed quickly away and turned to run for the front door. He could still make it if he hurried. He could get across the street and –

Something moved on his right as he came into the next room. Startled, Terry cried out as a hand shoved him from the darkness and knocked him off-balance. He tried to correct his stride and crashed into an unseen chair. He fell hard to the floor, and the gun in his hand unexpectedly fired. Ears ringing and mind reeling, he rolled to his feet and tried to get his bearings. As he spun toward his attacker, Terry heard the sound of an object being swung very fast through the air. He flinched, pulled the trigger one more time, and remembered no more.

◆

Al-Masri charged through the back door, followed closely by the others. Lights came on in the living room.

"Jared?"

"In here," came the unsteady voice.

Al-Masri rounded the corner and gaped at the scene before him. Jared was steadying himself against the wall with one hand, and in the other he clutched an aluminum baseball bat. A rocking chair was overturned, and next to it lay Terrence Whitman, motionless. Al-Masri could not believe his eyes.

He looked at Jared. "We heard the shots." He noticed that the bandages on Jared's arm had turned red, and he hoped the blood was solely due to the earlier wound. "Are you okay?"

"Yeah, just a little spooked," replied Jared. "But we've got trouble." Al-Masri braced himself for the news as Jared continued. "I was still lying down in the bedroom when I heard weird sounds from the kitchen. I grabbed the bat and when I came down the hall, I heard him whispering on the phone."

"What did he say?"

"I could only make out his last word, right before he hung up."

"*And?*"

Jared looked grave. "He said, 'Hurry.'"

Al-Masri stood silent as his thoughts raced to grasp the situation. *This can't have happened!* Whitman had completely outmaneuvered him. The escape had been baffling in its own right, but *this*? To come back to the house and use the phone to call for help.... It was unfathomable!

Al-Masri looked at the unconscious form, noticing blood where the bat had struck. As he stared, a storm of rage churned in his soul, and he wanted nothing in this world more than to end this man's hateful life. But once again he would be deprived, for Allah's sake.

One of the others interrupted his thoughts. "We have to do something!"

The man was within reach, and his eyes bulged as al-Masri slapped him hard in the face. "Shut up and listen to me! You two get out there and change those tires! You will leave as soon as the spares are on."

The two men immediately obeyed. Al-Masri looked at Jared and spoke quickly.

"It's time for me to leave. I'll use the other vehicle. It is imperative that I find and activate the additional cells to continue the *jihad*."

Jared nodded in agreement and al-Masri walked to the bedroom to retrieve a suitcase. He gave instructions over his shoulder. "Try to get out of here before they come, and carry out our plans for the glory of Allah. Use Whitman as a hostage if they get here first."

He returned to the living room with his belongings and stopped at the front door to look back. "If you get away, kill Terrence then. If you don't get away, kill him before you die. That is my one request of you, Jared."

Jared grinned. "No problem, Ibrahim."

Al-Masri smiled back, and felt proud of the man who had become his student and a faithful servant of Allah. He gave Jared a last nod, and stepped into the cold outside air.

◆

"Josh, turn left here!" Mitch yelled.

Josh saw the road now, coming up too fast. "Hold on, Seeley," he said into his cell phone, and then immediately dropped the phone into his lap and shouted, "Hold on, Mitch!" Gripping the steering wheel with both hands, he braked and turned. The tires squealed as the car slid dangerously around the corner and started to fish-tail. Josh expertly brought the vehicle under control and accelerated down the two lane road.

Mitch looked at the map again. "Okay, this is 167. We stay on this for about five more miles."

Josh picked up his phone again. "Seeley, are you still there?"

"Yes, I'm grabbing my coat now."

"Okay, Dickerson is going to get some agents out here, but you live the closest. We're less than five minutes away. How fast can you be here?"

"Fifteen minutes."

"Alright, we'll try to keep them occupied and in the house until we get some backup."

"Hey, Kepler," Seeley asked, "how did you just happen to be driving around out there before seven in the morning?"

Josh grinned, "Prayer and a hunch, chief. Just like I always tell you."

Josh heard a sigh on the other end of the line, and then, "I'm heading out the door, Kepler. See you in a few."

He put the phone down and glanced at Mitch. "Well, you said you could be of help if we ran into terrorists. I hope you're still up to it."

Mitch looked straight ahead. "Can't you drive any faster?"

◆

The sensation was like walking down a long dark hallway toward a far-off light. Or swimming up from deep water in anticipation of breaking the surface. For a long time no sound came to Terry's ears, and light was non-existent. When he finally did notice sounds, they were strange, far away and muted. More time passed, and then there were voices, and popping sounds, and a dull sense of pain. The world floated aimlessly for several moments, just beyond reach. And then....

A tidal wave of volume rushed in upon him – shouting, cursing, and loud bursts of gunfire. Terry's eyes snapped open and in an instant he took in the room – small, with no furniture and bare walls. There was one fairly large shot-out window in the wall to his right, and a closed door on the wall facing him. He was lying on his back on a hard wood floor with his head propped against the wall behind him. Near his feet, between him and the window lay the motionless form of a dark-skinned man. A pool of blood had formed around him.

Another man stood at the window, holding a small machine gun in his left hand and firing it in quick bursts. He was looking away out the window, but Terry could see the side of his face, and recognized him instantly – the large man with the goatee. His right arm was wrapped in blood-stained bandages, and the man held it carefully against his side. Sweat ran down his neck and darkened his blue t-shirt.

The right side of Terry's head throbbed and the side of his face was wet. He wiped his head lightly and grimaced at the sight of blood. He remembered the dark room, being knocked to the floor.

Another burst from the machine gun made him jump, and the man yelled defiantly, "Didn't you hear me? I said to stay put! I swear that this hostage is still alive, but if you don't back off he won't stay that way!" The man watched intently out the window. Terry didn't dare move. He silently asked God for help, and tried to focus his thoughts.

An unfamiliar voice from outside responded. "We don't want anyone else to get killed, Jared. The only way to guarantee that is for you to put down your weapons and come out."

"NO!" The man was enraged. "The only way is for YOU to drive out of here, leaving me one vehicle with the keys still in it!"

"We can't do that, Jared. Let's talk about some other options."

"NO OTHER OPTIONS! You have sixty seconds to get in your cars and drive off, or my hostage dies!!" There was no response from outside.

"Did you hear me?" the man yelled.

"Yes, we heard you. Okay, we're going to give you some room, alright? Just calm down. We're going to work with you."

Jared continued to gaze intently out the window. Terry heard a car door slam, and engines starting. *God, should I run now?*

At that moment, the man jumped back as an object flew through the window and clattered heavily across the floor. It was a short black metal tube with holes in the sides. *A grenade!* Terry instinctively covered his ears, clamped his eyes shut and turned away. A deafening blast shook the room. He felt heat from the blinding flash, and heard Jared's reaction.

"AAARRRGGH!"

Terry opened his eyes to see the terrorist take two shaky steps toward the door when it suddenly burst wide open, revealing a familiar face. *Josh!* In an instant the machine gun fired. Josh cried out and disappeared from view.

Then Terry's legs were under him, propelling him forward with all their remaining strength. Jared was still firing his gun when Terry lowered his shoulder and crashed into him. Taken completely unaware, the larger man lurched sideways and his wounded arm smashed into the wall under his full weight. The machine gun went silent as Jared gasped in agony, his face twisted with pain.

Terry let out a vociferous shout, like a warrior on the field of battle, and his fist hammered into the side of the man's face. He delivered three savage blows before the hulking man shoved him away with such violence that he was lifted from his feet and thrown to the opposite wall. He slid to the floor, stunned.

Jared looked down at him with loathing, blood gushing from an ugly cut near his eye. He swept his gun toward Terry, but his body suddenly convulsed as a gunshot sounded from the doorway, followed by another, and another. Terry watched, unable to move, as the terrorist's eyes rolled back, and blood flowed from a gaping hole in the side of his face.

Aghast at the sight, Terry didn't notice Jared's hand clench as he fell. He did, however, feel the hot stabbing pain tear through his legs and stomach, as the machine gun rang out for the last time. Terry's eyes grew wide with disbelief, and his lungs unloosed a groan of agony.

For a moment all was silent. Then pounding footsteps in the house, and the negotiator's voice from outside was near the door.

"Target is neutralized! Secure the area! We have an agent down in here!" A man stooped over him then, wearing a cap with "FBI" blazoned on the front. The lines around his eyes and gray streaks in his hair reminded Terry of the Elder, though he knew this was not a dream.

"The hostage is down too," the man called out with authority, "get the medic in here!"

There were more footsteps at the door, and then to his astonishment Terry heard Mitch call out, "Josh! You've been shot!"

"I'm not that bad," Josh responded, "go see about Terry."

Terry's mind swam, and he fought to stay conscious as Mitch knelt down on the floor next to him. "We finally found you," his friend said with a worried smile. Terry wanted to speak, to ask him what he was doing here, but the words wouldn't come. Breathing was difficult, and he felt increasingly dizzy.

Mitch put a hand gently on his arm and looked into his face. "You hold on, Terry," he said emphatically. "You are going to be just fine, alright?" Terry nodded and his eyes started to close.

"God, don't let him go yet!"

Terry forced his eyes open. Mitch was looking up at the ceiling. "If you are really there... if you listen to people when they talk to you... then please, God, don't let his life end like this. Please..."

"Sir, if you could please step aside, we'll take care of him from here."

Terry was aware of someone else kneeling beside him now, checking his pulse and looking over his bleeding body. Mitch was saying something to him, but the words jumbled as the room grew dark. He felt numb, weightless, very sleepy. And safe. At last, he was safe.

Chapter 36

When Terry awoke, he wondered for a moment if he would find himself in heaven. The acute sense of pain throughout his body, however, told him otherwise. He opened his eyes and realized that he was lying in a hospital room with an IV in his arm and various monitor wires taped to his body. He looked to his right, and his heart melted at the sight of Angela sitting in a chair. She noticed his movement and came to his side with a smile and tears spilling down her cheeks.

"Hi there." She put her hand in his, "welcome back."

"You look beautiful," Terry answered. "Where are we?"

"A hospital room in Indianapolis. The doctor thought you would wake up any time now. Are you in a lot of pain?"

"My legs, my stomach, my head, my eye. It pretty much all hurts."

"Let me call the nurse. She said she could give you something."

"Wait," Terry said. "How bad am I?"

Angela smiled. "They are pretty sure you are going to be alright, but it will take some time. You have a fractured skull and some swelling in your brain, but it doesn't look terribly serious at this point. They brought you in yesterday morning, and you were in surgery for over three hours to remove bullets from your legs and abdomen, and to repair your stomach. You lost a lot of blood." She wiped another tear from her face and swallowed back a sob. "Oh, Terry. Why did they do this to you?"

Terry squeezed her hand reassuringly. "Don't worry, sweetie. I'm back for good this time. They won't be able to hurt me any more."

Angela leaned down and kissed him lightly on the lips. For a brief moment, Terry thought again that he might actually be in heaven.

"I'll get the nurse," she said. He watched her go, and thanked God for allowing him to see his wife again.

No sooner had the door closed behind her, than it opened again and Josh entered the room, riding in a wheel chair and wearing a hospital gown of his own. His face was covered ear-to-ear with a beaming smile.

"Hey, Terry! You're finally awake!" He stopped next to Terry's bed and carefully shook his hand. "It sure is good to see you sitting there, alive and grinning."

"Well I think I felt a lot better when I was asleep. So what's your condition?"

"Oh, it's nothing. They took two bullets out of my thigh. I should be out of here tomorrow I'd guess, though my wife, Mary, is a wreck."

Terry started to laugh, but stopped short because of the pain. "I'd think she would be used to being married to an FBI agent by now."

"I had never been shot before, in eighteen years of service."

"Wow, that was quite a record to mess up."

"Yeah," Josh chuckled, "but I wasn't working for the FBI anymore, so that record is still good, in a manner of speaking. But this doesn't bode well for me, Terry. My first adventure as a normal citizen, and I get shot for the first time!" He laughed again, but Terry was frowning.

"What do you mean, you're not working for the FBI anymore? How long was I out anyways?"

"Well, you were kidnapped on Thursday, and it's Monday afternoon. A lot can happen in four days you know!" Josh suddenly looked serious. "It's a long story, Terry. I will tell it to you soon enough.

Let's just say that I've put my FBI days behind me." He sighed heavily. "I just wish I could've got one more crack at tying up the loose ends."

"What do you mean by that?"

Josh looked Terry in the eye. "Al-Masri got away, Terry. He wasn't in the house when we stormed it, and presumably had left before we got there."

"*What?* He was there when I called you. I saw him!" Terry felt overwhelmed by the news, and sat for a long moment in disbelief.

Josh broke the silence. "I was hoping you might have a clue as to where he disappeared to. Agents found some fresh tracks from an off-road vehicle not too far from the house."

"I don't know what happened. I was knocked out right after I called you, and woke up right before the grenade went off in that room." Terry shook his head. "He threatened to kill my family, Josh."

Josh thought for a moment. "I'll let the FBI know. But I wouldn't be too worried about it. We are pretty sure we've eliminated all the members of his cell here. I'd bet that he isn't going to stick around. He's not the type to go after someone for personal revenge. Al-Masri will look to establish a cell somewhere else, to continue the cause. The DHS and FBI will keep him on the run."

"I hope you are right." Terry looked down, still trying to grapple with the news of al-Masri's escape. A sudden flood of images played through his mind in rapid succession. The beatings that he was powerless to stop. His panicked escape to the woods. Killing the terrorist in the field. Feelings of pure hatred for his torturer.

"You alright, Terry?"

Terry looked at Josh and shook his head. "I don't know if I am alright." He paused and Josh waited for him to continue. "I can remember a lesson I taught to my children from the Bible just a week ago. Jesus taught us to love our enemies." He laughed bitterly and looked away. "But when it was my turn, I decided to kill one of them."

Josh leaned back in his wheelchair and sighed. "Terry, I am going to tell you the same thing I told a police captain in Louisville the other day. This is war. It's a violent and bloody war, and you got dragged right into the center of it. Even in the Bible, God's armies killed many of their enemies."

Terry looked at Josh again. "But I didn't feel any love for them, Josh. Not in that moment. Even now, when I think of al-Masri –" his voice trailed off.

"None of us are perfect, Terry. Not this side of heaven anyways. In this situation you did exactly what you had to do. You did exactly what a few hundred school children *needed* you to do. God knows your heart, and he will forgive you for any lines you may have crossed there. Keep that in mind as you think through things, okay?"

"Okay." Terry was thankful for the words of encouragement. Maybe Josh was right. Maybe he could not have done anything differently. It would take a while for his mind to work its way through the maze of emotions.

"Well, I have a question for you," Josh said in a lighter tone. "Mary and I are talking about moving down to Louisville, and I was wondering if you could tell me some good neighborhoods to look for a house."

Terry's mood brightened at the news. "Really?"

"Sure. Now that I'm out of the Bureau, it would be nice to start the next chapter of my life elsewhere." Josh shrugged. "You all seem like pretty nice people, so why not?"

"Why not?" Terry repeated, and then remembered something. "Hey! What the heck was Mitch doing here yesterday when you rescued me?"

Josh laughed. "He is very persuasive! He talked me into bringing him along to look for you, and it turned out that I actually needed the help. Your friend is quite a shot with a hand gun. We kept three terrorists pinned down in that house for at least ten minutes until more help arrived."

"Really?" Terry couldn't believe his ears. "You and Mitch? With no backup?"

"Yes sir, he held down the front of the house, and I watched the back. It was quite a feat for a couple of civilians!" Josh laughed again, and the sound made Terry forget about al-Masri for the time being. The door opened, and in walked Angela with a nurse, who busied herself adding something to the IV and checking his vital signs.

"I had to call Roger and Pam," Angela said, "to tell them you were awake. They are going to make the drive up here tomorrow to see you. And my parents will also be here tomorrow with the kids. Your parents will be here tonight."

Josh wheeled his chair toward the door. "Sounds like you'll have quite the crowd here to help you start your recovery. You should be out of here in no time."

"They told me we might get to leave on Friday," said Angela, "but that will depend on how things go. Monday is more likely."

"Christmas eve," Josh commented. "Well, I'm going to see to it that they don't keep me past tomorrow. I have to attend my unit chief's retirement party on Wednesday. But I'll have Mary drive me in each day to visit while you're here."

Josh stopped in the doorway and looked back. "Oh, I almost forgot. Be prepared for my old partner, Agent Dickerson, to stop by tomorrow to ask some questions. He'll most likely be playing second fiddle to some DHS guy now." Josh shook his head in disgust. "If you feel like it, tell them you are too tired to talk and you'll call them back when you feel more up to it. They'll each give you a business card. Then wait a couple hours, and call Dickerson directly with your information." Josh laughed heartily. "That would make his day, and mine!"

Terry tried to laugh, but the pain stopped him again. "Why don't I just tell you what little I know, and you can relay the message?"

Josh wheeled out the door and without looking back answered over his shoulder, "I'm retired from that business, remember? I'd rather talk to you about normal stuff from now on, Terry."

Terry looked at Angela and smiled. He then called out, "See you later, Josh."

◆

Eight days later, Christmas Day

Terry sat in the comfortable rocking chair in his living room, and looked around at the faces of his friends and family. His parents were settled comfortably on the sofa, along with Roger and Pam. Jennifer sat in the other rocking chair, sipping a cup of hot coffee. Dave and Sheri Lydon, who had been of great encouragement during the last three weeks, were also present. Angela sat in a chair next to him with her hand on his arm. The children could be heard laughing and playing in the basement.

They had just finished a time of prayer together, after reading from the Bible the story of Jesus' birth. Terry pondered the age-old story of hope and a new beginning for the world. This Christmas he was himself filled with hope, and gratefulness for the new beginning he had been given. God had delivered him from evil, and his faith was stronger on this side of the experience. As he listened to the casual conversation in the room, Terry was nearly overwhelmed with joy.

"Are you alright, Terry?" Angela asked. The room quieted as everyone looked in his direction.

"I'm just happy to be here with all of you."

"I think," Roger said, "that this little group is going to grow over the next few months."

"That's for sure," agreed Pam. "How many people were at our house for worship and prayer on Sunday?"

"Oh," Roger thought, "I guess ten adults, and I don't even know how many children."

"Ten!" Terry repeated. "And we weren't even back from Indy yet. Who all was there?"

"Well, Dave and Sheri told some people from their church about our gatherings, and two families decided to come – the Hatches and the Johnsons. And Jennifer brought another single lady from work."

"You know Judy," said Jennifer. "She's on my team."

"Yes," answered Terry. "Does she not go to church on Sundays?"

"No, but just like me, she has been thinking about spiritual things a lot during the events of the last few weeks, so when I invited her, she was eager to come."

"After all the attacks on churches," said Sheri, "the families we invited are still nervous about being in a church building on Sunday. They really enjoyed the informal time of prayer and talking about God. I'm pretty sure they will be hanging out with us in the future."

"That's great," Terry said. "We may as well have a weekly church meeting in our homes now, at least until the regular churches get back to normal." He paused, noticing Jennifer's sudden look of melancholy.

"Thinking about Mitch?" he asked her.

"Yes. I wish he had agreed to come today. He didn't want any part of a prayer meeting, said he hasn't seen anything to convince him that God exists."

"Everyone has to make their own choice to trust God." Terry smiled knowingly. "But I think Mitch is closer today than he was a couple of weeks ago."

"We can hope," Jennifer said.

"And," Terry continued, "it looks like Josh Kepler and his family will be moving down here to hang out with us too."

"Oh, that's wonderful!" exclaimed Sheri.

Terry nodded. "Roger, did you know that Josh has already got a job here, as the head of security for the Heartland Community Apartments?"

"Yes," Roger laughed, "he actually called to tell me himself. He wanted to know if I'd be willing to facilitate a weekly Bible study for the community there. I told him that he could probably get several of us to help."

"I'd be up for that." Terry looked into Angela's eyes. "I won't be spending so many hours on my career from now on, so I'm sure our entire family will be able to help out together." Angela smiled and leaned over to put her head on his shoulder.

The others readily agreed to help Roger with a Bible study in the low-income community. Terry listened as the friends talked about ways to serve people in the area, and there was no shortage of suggested ideas for doing good. He marveled at the upbeat nature of the conversation, and smiling to himself, he thanked God for this group of people – a close-knit fellowship, eager to demonstrate heaven's grace to one another and to a world plagued by evil.

This was the way life was meant to be lived.